STEVEN MOORE

THE OAK ISLAND ENIGMA

BOOKS

Vinci Books

vinci-books.com

Published by Vinci Books Ltd in 2025

1

Copyright © Steven Moore 2022

The author has asserted their moral right to be identified as the author of this work in accordance with the Copyright, Designs and Patents Act 1988. This work is a work of fiction. Names, characters, places and incidents are the product of the author's imagination or are used fictitiously. Any resemblance to actual persons, living or dead, places and incidents is entirely coincidental.

All rights reserved. No part of this publication may be copied, reproduced, distributed, stored in any retrieval system, or transmitted in any form or by any means, including photocopying, recording, or other electronic or mechanical methods, nor used as a source for any form of machine learning including AI datasets, without the prior written permission of the publisher.

The publisher and the author have made every effort to obtain permissions for any third party material used in this book and to comply with copyright law. Any queries in this respect should be brought to the attention of the publisher and any omissions will be corrected in future editions.

A CIP catalogue record for this book is available from the British Library.

Paperback ISBN: 9781036706852

The EU GPSR authorised representative is Logos Europe, 9 rue Nicolas Poussion, 17000 La Rochelle, France contact@logoseurope.eu

Printed and bound in Great Britain by Clays Ltd, Elcograf S.p.A.

By Steven Moore

The Hiram Kane Archaeological Thriller Series

The Condor Prophecy
The Tiger Temple
The Feathered Serpent
The Samurai Code
Of Curses and Kings
The Shadow of Kailash
The Oak Island Enigma
Killing Koreana

You must discover this treasure, as it's the key to making sense of all your life experiences and knowledge."

– Professor John O'nians

Prologue

Off the coast of Nova Scotia, Canada

November 27th, 1814

Captain Wesley gazed out across the surface of the foreboding ocean surrounding his ship as evening crept towards night. The bruised sky was darkening rapidly and very soon all would be black. The ship was the *HMS Fantome*. Wesley loved the *Fantome*, and it had been his life's honour to have captained her for the British Navy on numerous voyages up and down the eastern seaboard between the Chesapeake and Canada. It had been rewarding, important work. Yet, he considered this sailing, *HMS Fantome's* final voyage, by far and away the most important of them all. Wesley knew it might result in his death, and the deaths of his small, dedicated crew. Yet if it came to that, it would have been a worthy sacrifice and one that would be a fitting end to half a century of loyal service to The Crown.

The captain sighed. It was almost time.

"It is done, Cap'n," said First Mate Chisholm, trotting up to him on the bridge. "The hull is loaded with so much gun powder she'll be blown all the way back to Washington." The young first mate leaned over, panting from exertion.

The captain smiled. He loved the kid, as loyal a mate as he'd ever known, though he knew that loyalty was as much to The Crown as it was to him. It was a loyalty they shared. He hadn't had children of his own. The ocean was Captain Wesley's mistress and had been since he'd first boarded a fishing boat out of Penzance in 1763. He'd never married, and his only legal union was to the Navy, a bond that would never be broken.

He and the kid had been through a lot together since the boy had first joined their ranks in ought-six. He only hoped the kid survived. Once this was all over, he'd have a hell of a story to tell. Which of course he never would. Their mission was of the utmost secrecy, and of such national importance—international importance—that to mention it beyond this wheelhouse even once was tantamount to signing one's own death warrant. It would be to the gallows for them both. For them all.

"Good work, son," the captain stated. "Now go, and load the rowing boat with enough supplies to last two weeks. That should see us around the coast to Clam Harbour."

"And if it isn't?" The kid's eyes widened, and the captain saw in them a mix of pride and fear.

"It will be, lad, don't worry. But if it isn't, then we'll succumb knowing we've done our duty, and that is always enough. Now go on, son, get to the boat."

The first mate saluted, then bustled off below decks to prepare the supplies.

The captain sighed. This was only the first part of the mission. He knew he would need an unlikely amount of luck and good fortune to complete the second leg. Though a God-fearing Christian, Captain Wesley wasn't naturally a praying man. He'd seen storms toss ships around as if they were driftwood and knew Mother Nature was far more powerful than any revered human deity. Nevertheless, despite himself, the captain had indeed prayed, for his success could not depend upon good luck and fair seas alone.

He let his eyes drift once more at the flotilla of other ships that formed their convoy. He knew that on board those boats, the other captains would be having similar conversations with their crew and first mates. The *HMS Fantome* was one of only six ships on the mission. They had all been loaded with unimaginable riches looted from the Whitehouse several weeks earlier in a daring raid that had seen the Whitehouse destroyed, but not before the soldiers had stripped it of everything of value. Treasures from the colonies in South and Central America, including Aztec and Incan gold, and artefacts from the Mayan civilisation, once procured by the Conquistadors several centuries earlier then later claimed by the Americans. Jewels. Silver. Paintings of the Founding Fathers, Presidents and other noblemen and dignitaries. Now it belonged to The Crown.

But only Captain Wesley alone knew that the treasure wasn't the most important cargo aboard the *Fantome* and the other ships. He subconsciously placed his hand to his breast, feeling the small scroll tucked into his jacket, a scroll that contained secrets so important that they would need to be kept secret for a thousand years, lest the world descended into chaos and outright war between the New World and the Old.

With a final glance around the wheelhouse, the Captain stared out at the horizon, now fading as the storm descended, just as he knew it would. There he stood, and saluted, more proud in that moment than he ever had been in decades of servitude. Then he stepped down from behind the wheel of *HMS Fantome* for the very last time as a distant flash of lightning and a roar of thunder in the heavens above heralded in a new era.

Captain Wesley and first mate John Chisholm rowed swiftly and silently away from the *Fantome* on a dark surface that was chopping up as the wind grew beneath a burgeoning storm. The shadowy bulks of five other rowing boats traced their arcing route away from the flotilla, and when they were a hundred yards away, they drifted to a stop and waited. Only one smaller boat had remained, bobbing within a musket shot of the ships. Corporal Miles Smythe, the best marksmen in their ranks, stood aboard, musket in hand.

Captain Wesley couldn't see the young shooter but knew he was there by the faint glow of the oil lantern sitting beside Smythe on the bench. He also knew Smythe wouldn't fail them, even though the surface was beginning to rise and fall in blossoming swells.

Lightning continued to flash in the distance, but the thunder rumbled ever closer. It was a fitting scene for what was about to occur, but no accident. They had waited days for the storm to come, and it was finally here. *Perfect.*

The flash of a distant musket glowed momentarily, but the captain heard no retort. A second flash followed, then a third, then the oil lamp began moving slowly to the north as Smythe rowed the boat closer to the three remaining ships.

Suddenly a massive, concussive boom echoed across the surface, immediately followed by another and a third as the *Fantome* and two of her sister ships exploded in a mass of flames and splintering timbers. The booms were so loud Captain Wesley felt them in his chest, and again, his hand unwittingly moved to his breast, checking for the twentieth time in the last hour that the scroll was where it should be. Where it had to be.

He felt only a little sadness that the *Fantome* would soon be nestling in broken pieces on the shallow floor of the North Atlantic Ocean, alongside the other destroyed vessels. It was his solemn duty, and what needed to happen.

Within just twenty minutes, Captain Wesley and his fellow captains from His Majesty King George the Third's Royal Navy had successfully scuttled an entire fleet of ships. Just days ago, they had been filled with more treasure than had even been assembled in one place in modern history. That treasure was now somewhere else, somewhere even Captain Wesley himself was not privy to. That didn't matter. The tangible treasure was not his concern.

He had a more important duty now: transport the scroll to England and personally place it in King George's waiting hands.

When he awoke, it was to the sound and feel of sledgehammers pounding hard against his skull. The beat, he didn't recognise. Tommy Ramone? Nah, more like John Bonham. The pain was too familiar. Dhum! Dhum! Dhum! And annoying, like Phil fucking Collins.

Bile rose north towards the junction between his guts and his throat. It stung, and tasted like acidic shit. That, too, was familiar. He swallowed it down. His eyes watered. The pain rattled his brain. The throbs radiated, each one like a tourniquet on his mind, easing off like a receding wave, then crashing back down like a big one at Mavericks.

Drowning. *Am I drowning?* If he was, it was deliberate. Wasn't it?

Hiram Kane had seen enough. The deaths, so many of them. Worse than death was the dying. Dying was noisy. Death was silent. It was death he craved... silent death... Sometimes. Not often. Not yet!

In his more cognisant moments, Kane mused that in some ways he'd always had a bit of a death wish. That's what others had been telling him for years, anyway, and it made sense the more he thought about it. The more he reminisced. Is that what he'd call it? Reminiscing? *No, idiot!* At the very least, it was commiserating. With himself? Ruminating? Whining? Self-pitying? *That's a lot of gerunds, Kane,* he thought, ruminating some more.

"Too much fucking thinking mate," he heard himself say as he rolled over and puked on the floor. *Floor?*

Kane glanced around. He was indeed on the floor, the evidence proven by his rat's eye view. But whose floor? Where?

Instincts caused him to spin over, eyes suddenly wide and scanning left and right, searching for his killer...

Something jabbed him in the ribs. It felt like a stone dagger. That's what it felt like. The truth was a little less exciting. His phone. A few moments later, after both the bile and the fear had subsided, he took stock of his situation.

Alive? Yes.
Feel like death? Also yes.
In any immediate danger? Hmm... probably not.
Injured? Hmm... that will need further investigation.

With a hearty, fully fledged groan, Kane hauled himself up onto his haunches and dared a long, thorough look around. Ignoring the storm in his belly and the clash of imaginary titans in his skull, Kane worked out that he was in a dark corner of some quiet, apparently abandoned warehouse.

Hungover like a bastard.

Why? Why am I so wasted? What am I doing here? Where the hell is here?

Something metToullac clattered in the darkness and Kane spun, expecting the worst. He saw nothing, despite the hairs on his neck getting short-lived boners.

"What the fuck?" Kane muttered into the void. No one answered. *Why am I so edgy?*

Kane stood up wearily. With the palms of his hands, he undertook a swift evaluation of his physical state. He concluded that, while he was in one piece physically, mentally he was in several.

His eyes scanned the gloomy interior of the huge building again. The hint of natural light from a distant window beckoned him over. He looked down for any personal belongings. *Nope. Nothing here of mine.* He checked his pockets. *Wallet? Yep. Phone?* Also yep, but with no relief, as no one ever called. He also had zero expectation anyone would. No one. *Not even...*

He couldn't even say her name. Could barely stand to think it.

How have I let it get so bad?

Career? Relationships?

Life in general?

One minute I'm a famous explorer, working an important job for the British Museum, continuing the proud family name and... the next minute I'm nothing. No one. How? Why?

And then, Hiram Kane wept. The haunting sound of his powerful sobs echoed back at him from the dark, damp and featureless walls of an unknown building in an unknown town in an unknown country on an unknown continent.

"Jesus, where the fuck am I?" he muttered as he cuffed tears from his eyes.

That's when the shooting started.

Chapter One

Rabbit Island, Cambodia

A Week Earlier

It was supposed to have been a new start. A change of pace. A great opportunity. A chance to do something good and positive. Something less dangerous.

Kane almost laughed. Almost. In truth, it wasn't remotely funny.

Things had begun so well. It was with great pride that he'd taken his position as leader of the Artefact Repatriation Committee at the British Museum in London. In his role, he only had one job to do: oversee the safe return of the Rosetta Stone to Egypt.

Just one job. And he had cocked it up.

Despite the fact that Kane, according to official records, had done nothing wrong, and ignoring the reality that multiple external forces had conspired against Kane and his ARC team, he had embraced the failures as his own. He had been in charge. The complex operation had been his responsibility.

Kane had been recommended for the job by his grandfather, Hiram Kane Snr. He had humbly accepted the important responsibility, despite his own misgivings that he wasn't qualified and nowhere near up to the task. Higher-ups at the British Museum, as well as his grandfather, had convinced him he was perfect for the role, based on his experiences, his leadership skills, and above all, his world-renowned reputation of unrivalled integrity.

"Ha... how'd that work out for you? Idiot!"

"I'm sorry, sir?"

Kane glanced up as the barman approached.

"It's... sorry, it's nothing," Kane said, embarrassed. He hadn't realised he'd spoken aloud.

Kane looked around. A few other drinkers were scattered along the quiet bar. The afternoon had been long and winding, and of course lubricated. Kane had hardly moved from his seat at the far end of the long bartop, other than for an occasional visit to the loo. His flip flops lay empty in the sand beneath his bamboo stool. The palm trees above him swayed serenely in the gentle breeze, the fronds whispering an unknown tune. Modest waves gurgled onto a white-sand beach a dozen yards behind him.

It was an hour shy of sunset. Kane considered getting something to eat, something to line the stomach before commencing the evening session of sorrow drowning and misery seeking. He glanced at a waitress taking out plates of food to a handful of customers sitting on beach chairs. Nothing looked good. Nothing had for ages. He'd probably skip dinner again.

"A French 75, please," Kane heard someone say a

couple of yards down the bar. The words were English. The accent was French. Kane didn't bother to look up.

"Of course sir, an excellent choice. Celebrating?"

"Actually, oui, I am celebrating. So, I would like to get one for my friend here too, if you don't mind?"

"Certainly sir. Two French 75s, coming right up."

Kane knew the man couldn't be talking about him. Kane knew nobody on the island, and he didn't have any friends, at least not within several thousand miles. He glanced to his right. Standing two barstools along from Kane was a small yet well-put-together man. His colourful shirt was tight to his toned, tanned body. His winning smile was bright. His sunglasses were expensive.

"I hope you'll join me for a cocktail?" the new man said, his French accent barely noticeable.

Kane's weary eyes studied the man. Life had made him more cynical in recent years and he couldn't help being suspicious.

"No," he said, a little stronger than he'd meant. "No, thank you. I'm fine with the beer. Enjoy your cocktail."

"Please, forgive the intrusion," the Frenchman said. "I just wanted to celebrate. I don't know anyone else here, and since you're sitting alone, I thought I'd offer you a drink. Please forgive me. I will leave you to your beer."

Kane nodded and looked away. He glanced left. The sun was minutes from retiring for the day, and the sky was on fire with reds and oranges and pinks, the kind of cracking tropical sunset he used to appreciate. Kane didn't smile. He hadn't spoken to another human for days, other than the rotating bar staff and sometimes the mirror. *What the hell!*

"What is it you're drinking?" Kane asked quietly,

turning to face this newcomer to his commandeered corner of the bar.

"Ah ha," the Frenchman replied, his champion smile widening plenty. "It's a French 75, a classy mix of gin, lemon juice and sugar. Of course, the most important ingredient is Champagne. It is the perfect cocktail for a celebration. And, my new and only friend, I plan to buy you many of them on this perfect celebratory night."

Chapter Two

The sun had long since set, dropping with surprising speed as it tended to do in the tropics. The only thing that had gone down quicker than the sun was the drinks Kane kept pouring down his gullet. Yes, it was thirsty work being a complete loser. *Perhaps not this thirsty*, Kane mused as he slugged the last of his sixth or seventh cocktail and signalled the barman for another.

"You like the French 75s very much," Francois said. "Almost as much as me."

"They are especially delicious in this climate," Kane agreed, slurring slightly. It wasn't just the cocktails. He'd only been drinking those since the Frenchman had started buying. It was more to do with the dozen beers he'd sped through in the afternoon. And the fact he'd skipped dinner. Again.

Kane rose unsteadily from his bamboo stool. "Back in a moment. Nature calls."

"I'll be here. There's a lot more merriment to be had,"

the Frenchmen stated, then added, "and when you return, I'll be ready with an exciting proposition for you."

Kane's ears pricked up. Exciting propositions made in southeast Asian bars came with all sorts of connotations, and usually a well-concealed manhood. He'd deal with that shortly. Not the manhood, obviously.

Now he just needed a piss.

Kane wambled—a combination of wandered and stumbled he'd coined for himself after recent experiences—down the beach towards the modest men's bathroom; basically a bamboo tiki hut with a hole in the ground. He thought about the other drinkers back in the bar. A few backpackers, drinking the cheapest things on offer; in this case, *Angkor* beer in a can. A few old-timers, European, perhaps in Cambodia for all the wrong reasons. He didn't want to think about that right now. Cambodia, along with many other southeast Asian destinations, had a gained justified and terrible reputation for sex trafficking and pedophilia in the eighties and nineties. Although the authorities had cracked down in recent years, Kane knew it still very much existed. He was on Rabbit Island. He knew that if he let that train of thought fester, he'd end up down a depressing rabbit hole—pun intended. He shook his head and focused on pissing in the hole and not on his bare feet.

Then there was the Frenchman. Well dressed. Plenty of cash. Clearly educated. And he'd sat next to Kane at the bar. Kane was unshaven. His hair had grown long. He hadn't washed his clothes in days. He probably stunk. So, why had this apparently classy Frenchman come to this humble, relatively unknown and totally random island off the south coast of Cambodia? This would usually set alarm bells ringing in Kane's mind.

Tonight, though, whether it was the cocktails, the

weather, the inactivity of the last few weeks—or, if he were being honest with himself, the total lack of action over those same weeks—Kane found himself intrigued.

"Proposition, huh?" he grumbled at a fly buzzing around the hole as he proceeded to piss on the sand next to it. At least it missed his feet. "I'll hear your proposition."

Kane shuffled back along the beach to the bar on the prettiest beach on Rabbit Island. A gentle breeze rustled his baggy clothes. The murmur of the sea as it lapped onto the island's shore from a million miles away promised everything, as it always did, and yet always delivered disappointment. He arched his neck and looked at the stars blanketing the vast empty blackness above, once again making Kane realise just how insignificant he was in the world. How small. Unimportant.

A drunk fucking loser.

"Fuck it," he mumbled to nobody. "Je suis tout ouïe, Français… I'm all ears."

Chapter Three

"You see, the problem is, Mr Kane... may I call you Hiram?" Kane nodded. "I am not allowed into the United States or Canada, Hiram. It is because of... certain dealings with my, um, friend, Omar Abdel-Rahman. I believe you know him?"

Francois sensed Kane was suddenly on high alert. Omar Abdel-Rahman was a criminal, Francois had learned, now deceased. Before his death, however, online news reports had suggested he was actually a good guy who'd been corrupted by financial greed and the more powerful drug of collecting the uncollectable. He watched as Kane nodded almost imperceptibly.

Francois took that as his cue to continue. "In fact, it was Omar who recommended I contact you. But this was many, many months ago, before... well, you know, even before Egypt." Francois looked away, and he sensed Kane couldn't tell if it was out of sadness or guilt.

Francois eyed Kane, appraising him. In Kane's eyes he saw questions: *What is your connection to Omar, and Egypt? Who the hell even are you?* It didn't matter, Francois knew, since it was all total bullshit. He'd never met the Egyptian. Never even heard of him until he'd selected Kane for the mission he was about to propose, and Google was everyone's friend when it came to procuring resources for one's important operations. The Frenchman turned back to Kane.

"It was with good reason Omar suggested I reach out to you. Your reputation... ahem... your former reputation, was unrivalled. The best modern-day explorer on the planet. The perfect man for the job."

"What job?"

"I will get to that in a moment. But I trusted Omar, so I did reach out. I tried to contact you many times. You are a hard man to track down."

Kane shrugged half-heartedly.

"You didn't receive my letters? I sent three hand-written letters and many emails, detailing everything about what I'm going to tell you now."

Kane offered another half shrug, and Francois sensed at least a little recognition.

"My fear now is that it is too late," Francois continued. "That is why I have made this special journey in person to find you here in Cambodia. It was too important not to."

"You got all the way here from... France?"

"Paris, oui," François confirmed.

"You came all the way here from Paris just to buy me cocktails on a Cambodian beach? Are you mad?"

Francois chuckled. He eyed Kane up and down, as if assessing the man's physical state. He looked about to say something, to confirm Kane's 'mad' assessment of him, but thought better of it. "No, Hiram, I'm not mad. I remain convinced this will not have been a wasted journey. The question is, though... who are you now, Hiram? Who is this man before me? Are you the famous explorer and philanthropist Hiram Kane, from the legendary Kane family, discoverers of Machu Picchu and Vilcabamba, and you, purveyor of many other great archaeological triumphs? Or are you a washed-up bum who doesn't see the need for shoes and clean clothes, and has forgotten what self-respect is?"

It was a gamble to be so forthright, but something told Francois it was the right approach. He glanced over Kane's shoulder, casually looking towards the line of palm trees that flanked the bar. He nodded imperceptibly, then turned back to Kane. The fact Kane hadn't punched him yet was a good sign, and he surged on. "I am only interested in offering this magnificent, once-in-a-lifetime opportunity to the better version of you." Francois eased himself off his barstool and took a few steps away, before turning back towards Kane, who now wore an expression that was somewhere between anger and shame.

Good, thought Francois... *that got his attention*.

"I intend on having a few more drinks this evening. However, after I leave later, I will be back here tomorrow morning at nine. I will wait only twenty minutes before I depart for Paris. I wonder, Hiram... not whether you will show up or not. I know you will. You will find it impossible not to after what I will tell you. I'll tease you with just two words. Then the only question will be... which one of you will arrive?"

With that, the mercurial Frenchman turned and made his way to the bar, pausing only to say "Oak Island" over his shoulder, smiling inwardly at how easy it was to land a big fish with a fake hook.

Chapter Four

Kane gazed into the darkness out over the still, silent ocean. *Washed up bum?* He glanced down at his linen shirt, where several different food stains made their presence known. He cuffed at a stray thread of dribble that had escaped the corner of his mouth, then at the stray tear that had escaped the corner of one eye. He hoped no one had seen that as he turned back to the bar.

Kane did recall receiving some letters from an unknown source. He'd never opened them. And he never read emails anymore. They never delivered good news.

The man's two words revolved in his mind. Oak Island. Any explorer worth his salt had heard the legends surrounding Oak Island. He sat up a little straighter in his chair.

Kane had to admit, he had been the one to locate the legendary lost city of Vilcabamba when hundreds before had failed, including his own grandfather. That meant nothing now, of course. Kane sometimes couldn't even find his flip flops in the morning, let alone setting out on another wild goose chase after lost treasure, which may or may not even exist.

Still… there was something about this one, about this legend, that appealed to a long-missing sense of adventure. Not long in terms of time… it was only a few months ago that he'd been involved in the repatriation of The Rosetta Stone to Egypt, and while almost the opposite of searching for something—he'd been tasked with returning it from London to Alexandria—it was an adventure nonetheless. That it had gone to shit was the reason he was here in Cambodia licking his considerable wounds and skulking about with his tail between his legs. But his tail couldn't remain there forever. It had to wag again at some point, didn't it? Perhaps this was it? Perhaps Francois, or whoever the hell he was, was presenting him with an opportunity too good to turn down. A chance at redemption? A chance to right some serious wrongs?

A chance to become whole again?

Francois returned to the table and placed another round of drinks in front of Kane. "Toilette," he said, grinning as he disappeared along the beach.

Kane didn't know anything about Francois. He had once thought himself a good judge of character, someone who could see through most people's bullshit and know who they really were, and what they truly wanted. He had at first got that right with Omar Abdul-Rahman, the architect of the robbery of the Rosetta Stone. Then that man had changed, and it turned out he was a good guy gone bad through his own greed and morality failures. How about Francois? He claimed to have known Omar. What did that say about the man? Was he a scoundrel, too? Were his intentions noble?

Does it even matter anymore?

Chapter Five

These were the questions Kane found himself mulling over as Francois returned from the bathroom, an expectant look on his handsome face.

"Have you given it any thought?" Francois asked as he retook his seat across from Kane. "I hope you have, and that it is something positive for both of us."

Kane nodded. "I have given it plenty of thought. Perhaps too much. Tell me, Francois... why should I trust you? Why me? Why now? And who the hell are you?"

"Good questions, Hiram, and you're right to ask. To answer your first question, as to why you should trust me... well that is simple. You have as much reason to trust me as I do to trust you. Let us be honest; you are not the man you once were, at least not publicly. After Egypt... well, let's just say that your reputation is somewhat in tatters, even if you were the victim of some unfortunate circumstances. I know you did nothing wrong, even if the record will forever say that it was on your watch the world's most famous artefact was stolen... and innocent people died. Yet, here I am, willing to trust you, when perhaps no one else would. It is, then, is it not, a fair trade of trust, as well as our respective skills? You are the treasure hunter and explorer. I am the financier of the mission. Thus, we are equal. No more, no less. Would that be fair?"

Kane's head tilted just enough to have been taken for an affirming nod. Francois continued. "As for the why you, and why now? Well, they too are easy to answer. For all the reasons previously stated, you are, quite simply, the best man for this particular job, present physical condition notwithstanding. The timing, too, seems right. I believe that soon, the world's treasure hunters are going to descend on Nova Scotia, especially Oak Island, now that those Canadian brothers have finally backed away and conceded defeat. That is why I reached out to you all those months ago, and why I have tracked you down now. Soon, I fear our window of opportunity will be lost... and perhaps shut forever. We must commence our search now, Hiram. There is no time to waste. So, what do you say? I will need your answer soon."

Kane looked away from Francois as the mercurial Frenchman leaned back in his chair. Kane was comfy here. No one here knew who he was, at least not until Francois had arrived out of the blue. The anonymity was refreshing. The accommodation was nice and peaceful. The drinks were cheap, not that money was really an issue.

Yet something was definitely missing. There was no spark anymore... only booze, and time. Time to dwell, and mope. To pine for things lost. Something had to give, and Kane knew what it was; his inability to say no to a new, probably dangerous mission.

He looked back at Francois, who sat across the table, patiently yet with eyes full of expectancy. Kane noticed the

Frenchman's eyebrows rise and his mouth twitch into a grin. It seemed to Kane as if Francois knew what was coming. As if he'd always known.

"I will go," Kane said. "And I will find your missing treasure, even if it means bad news for you. I accept."

"It will not be bad news," Francois stated decisively. "The treasure is there, of that I am certain. Anyway, I will bid you a *bon nuit, mon ami,* and I will see you in the morning." With that, Francois placed a huge bundle of local currency on the table and walked with purpose along the beach, Kane envying the man's sure-footedness, despite the amount of booze he'd consumed.

Kane eyed the cash. It was several times more than was needed to pay the bill. He briefly considered cToullang it a night, then almost laughed at the ridiculous notion and instead ordered three more French 75s. *One for now, and two for the road,* he thought as he cuffed at yet one more stray tear escaping tired eyes that had seen too much trauma but couldn't resist the risk of seeing more.

What they hadn't seen moments ago was Francois nodding at someone over his shoulder as Kane gazed across the sea towards the Cambodian mainland, hidden under complete darkness other than the faintest twinkle of distant lights.

Chapter Six

Kane groaned as he forced one eye open, then the other. After a moment of regret, during which his stomach roiled, and being near blinded by the dazzling sunlight that lanced through curtains he'd forgotten to close, he sat up and swung his legs over the side of the bed.

Why do you do it to yourself? he chided inwardly. Of course, there was no one there to listen to his complaining, but that was another story. Kane checked his watch, expecting mid-morning. He was relieved to find it was still only six thirty, just after dawn.

He sucked in a deep breath of the moist, warm air, then slowly stood up. After a quick stretch, Kane made his way to the modest bathroom and stepped under a cool shower, washing away both cobwebs and regrets alike. It was only temporary. These days, it always was. After downing two large glasses of chilled water, he shrugged on a vest and yanked on a pair of shorts and his running shoes, before stepping out of his wooden beach hut and striding with something like purpose down to the shore, where a low tide revealed a perfect stretch of firm golden sand along which to go for a swift run.

Sluggish at first, Kane soon got into his stride. Despite being miles off his top physical condition, he was still no slouch and his long strides powered him along the beach at a good clip. And it felt good, too. Not only to clear the mind, but because there was something waiting for him at the end of his run. Not another beer session for breakfast. No, not today. Yesterday evening his interest had been piqued by the random Frenchman... *Francois?* It had been months since Kane had been interested in anything other than wallowing in his own misery and self-pity. Today could be a turning point. Could be. Had to turn up first. But the intention was there. That was a start, at least.

After twenty minutes of running, followed by a refreshing dip in the passive ocean, Kane showered and dressed in his best clothes... a pair of tailored shorts, and a simple yet clean guayabera shirt he'd been saving for a special occasion. This wasn't what he'd had in mind, but nothing else special was happening so it was time to relieve the shirt of its coat hanger and slide it on for its maiden outing.

He checked the time. 8:15. Good. The bar, which by morning was a cafe, was only a five-minute walk. He'd be early, with plenty of time for breakfast and coffee before Francois turned up.

Kane was somewhat dismayed to arrive to find Francois already there. The Frenchman stood up to greet Kane.

"*Bon matin*, Hiram," he said cordially with something akin to a smug grin. "I knew *this* Hiram Kane would turn up," he said, seeming to appraise Kane's appearance, which Kane had to concede was vastly improved from the previous evening. "And early, too. A man after my own heart. Thank you for coming."

Kane nodded and accepted the extended hand. The two men shook firmly.

"I'm not sure what it is I've come for, exactly," Kane said, "but you're welcome. May I?" he asked, pointing to a seat.

"Please. Coffee?"

Kane considered ordering a Bloody Mary, then thought better of it and instead ordered coffee and a basket of pastries from the waiter who'd ambled over.

"It is my opinion that you won't regret coming this morning," Francois said confidently, his eyes fixed on Kane's.

Kane nodded, still lacking any idea of what this was really about. Yet, something about the man's countenance, and his knowledge of Kane and his recent history, chequered as it was, suggested he was serious about whatever it was he wanted to discuss.

"You've heard of the *Fantome*, I assume?" Francois asked casually. It wasn't really a question.

"If you mean the infamous British military vessel that allegedly sank off Canada about two-hundred years ago, then yes, I've heard of it. And?"

Kane watched as Francois took a deep breath. The Frenchman glanced casually about the cafe, devoid of any other customers this early. Once he seemed satisfied it was safe to talk, he leaned forward, almost conspiratorially, it seemed to Kane. "Then I can also assume you've heard of the legend of the Money Pit?"

Kane grinned. "You mean the curse of Oak Island? And the lost treasure that's never been found? Yes, I've heard of it. Load of crap if you ask me."

Francois leaned back in his chair, his gaze never leaving Kane's. Kane noticed the smug smile return. "Load of crap, eh?" Francois said warmly. "You really believe that?"

The truth was, no, Kane didn't really believe it was a load of crap. He recalled his grandfather talking of the mysterious Oak Island many years ago, and how he'd wished he'd had the chance to search for the infamous lost treasure himself. Kane had never really known whether his grandfather was serious or not, but then again, Kane Snr wasn't a man to joke about such things, at least not often. Kane had always wondered how much of the legend was true and how much was myth. He'd never considered mounting a search for it himself, so he supposed that suggested he didn't fully believe in the legend of The Money Pit.

Alright, let's hear it, Kane thought, nodding for Francois to begin whatever pitch he was poised to make.

The Frenchman didn't hesitate.

"Forgive me if you know a lot of what I'm going to tell you, but please, humour me." Kane nodded, to which Francois returned his own. "Almost two centuries after the mostly forgotten war between Britain and the newly formed United States, the so-called War of 1812, a new argument has risen between the relevant governments, all surrounding the truth about what really happened to a British warship that was allegedly wrecked off the Nova Scotia coastline. That ship was believed to be carrying an unimaginable hoard of priceless artefacts stolen from the White House in Washington after it had been destroyed by the British."

"Allegedly," Kane said.

Francois nodded, the hint of a grin creasing his brow. "Allegedly, oui." The Frenchman continued. "Recently, a team of American divers ignited the dispute after they discovered the wreck of what they believe to be the *HMS Fantome*, the British Navy ship leading a convoy of ships from the US capital to Halifax. I happen to believe them, that it is indeed the *Fantome*. History suggests that a battalion of British troops stormed the new capital and set fire to the White House. Nowadays, under current Nova Scotian law, anyone can explore such shipwrecks, as long as they hand over ten percent of anything they make on their discoveries. As such, if they pay their dues, they get to keep anything they find."

Francois paused, and Kane sensed he was appraising his reaction. In truth, Kane offered very little reaction outwardly. Internally, however, the first stirrings of excitement fluttered in his overworked kidneys. He remained silent for now, and Francois pressed on.

"So-called experts have always assumed that the *Fantome*, and other ships in that accursed convoy, lie wrecked beneath the lethal shallows outside the harbour in Halifax. What isn't in any historical doubt is that the ships went down during a terrible storm in late November, 1814, just weeks after the British burned the White House... allegedly. At that time, the most important British garrison in North America was in Halifax, so, to me it all makes perfect sense. No?"

This time Kane offered the hint of a nod. For Francois, it seemed enough. He cleared his throat. "What we also believe is that important historical documents have since been stolen from the archives in Nova Scotia... which seems very convenient, doesn't it? There are believed to be more relevant documents in the records of the Admiralty in London." Another brief pause. Then, he said, "Hiram, I am convinced that the *Fantome* is indeed wrecked outside of the harbour at Halifax, and—"

"—and you want me to go and find the lost treasure?" Kane finished.

At this, the Frenchman actually laughed. "No, you misunderstand me. Don't forget the Money Pit, Hiram. Of course, the Money Pit, and Oak Island, have been all over the television in recent years. And yet, despite the legend being two centuries old, and dozens and dozens of people have spent fortunes trying to find it, no one has yet found as much as a scrap of anything that could be labelled treasure."

"And you think I can?" Kane said, almost sarcastically. "You think I can find what all those dozens—hundreds of people—couldn't?"

Kane realised his face must have offered Francois an almost-comical expression, yet it was telling that Francois' own expression remained serious. For long moments, the two men stared at each other. Finally, Francois nodded.

"Yes, Hiram," he stated flatly, "I do. That is why I am here. After all, was it not you who discovered Vilcabamba, the lost city of the Incas, when no one else could?"

Chapter Seven

Before he left, Francois handed Kane a small valise. Kane took a cursory glance inside and found a credit card with his name on it, a business card with only the initials F.D., and several large bundles of cash. The money was in differing currencies, including Cambodian riels, and both U.S. and Canadian dollars. A quick scan suggested to Kane there was upwards of ten thousand dollars in the valise. There were also some envelopes. Kane held one out to Francois and shrugged.

"Copies of the letters I sent you, just to prove how serious I was, and still am."

Kane nodded and slipped the envelope back inside. The last thing he found was a one-way air ticket to Washington D.C. from Phnom Penh.

Hmm...

Until now, Francois hadn't mentioned anything about the U.S. capital. Kane had been there before. His work and travels had taken him to most of the world's big cities, and while he didn't especially love the east coast of the United States, at least compared to the spectacular west coast, he did enjoy visiting Washington D.C., with its grand architecture, world-class museums and, perhaps more interesting to Kane, an underlying current of mystery and intrigue stretching back to the nation's formative years.

Well, it looked as if he was heading back for the first time in over a decade. Although it had come as a surprise, Kane found it wasn't an unpleasant one.

The two men exchanged a farewell and Francois turned to leave, but before he did he paused and turned back to Kane.

"You don't want to fuck this one up, Hiram." His tone was flat, and his eyes had lost their sparkle.

Kane was taken aback. Gone was the GToullac charm. Instead, a cold seriousness had replaced it and it was the first vaguely unpleasant thing Francois had said since they'd met the previous evening.

"We will be keeping an eye on you," Francois added deadpan, still unsmiling as he eyed the valise containing the money and credit cards.

"We?"

"Oui." Francois nodded. "We. I have people working for me. As you have seen, I am investing heavily in you for this mission. I expect results."

Francois' gaze rose to meet Kane's and remained fixed there for a long uncomfortable moment, before his grin finally returned. "I am confident you will succeed in doing what I need you to do," he said, then he spun on his heels and disappeared.

That exchange with his—*what, benefactor?*—left Kane more than a little bemused. *Was that a threat?* He didn't think so. Then again, he didn't know the man and couldn't be sure. A stranger materialising out of the blue and flashing a small fortune around should have alerted Kane's innate warning system. But despite the apparent randomness of it all, it hadn't.

Sloppiness? Probably, Kane realised, but to his surprise, he found he no longer cared as he left the beach cafe.

That too *was* a genuine surprise, if not to Kane, then to the barman, who'd been happily serving the usually scruffy Englishman drinks all day, every day for the last two months or more. He had never caused the barman any trouble, despite how much booze he consumed on a daily basis. Far from it. The more Kane drank, he knew, the quieter and more reserved he became. Kane also knew that the most the barman had ever heard him speak was the previous evening, when his tongue had been loosened by a dozen French 75s and the chance of redemption, whatever that meant to him. Kane had appreciated the barman's wise choice not to ask too many questions during his near-permanent residency at the bar.

Kane had been intrigued when Francois had mentioned redemption, and on more than one occasion. It was the lure of finding that, Kane realised, that had whetted his whistle, much more than the discovery of a famous lost treasure. Although that certainly had its merits too.

So, as he strolled along the beach, Francois' package tucked securely under his arm, Kane analysed what had transpired over the last dozen or so hours. First he'd been approached in a bar by a stranger, who had apparently known about him for many months. A mutual acquaintance, Omar Abdel-Rahman—Kane couldn't call him a friend—had apparently encouraged Francois to seek Kane out for his mission, long before the events of Egypt. That was intriguing. The mission, according to Francois, was to find something no one else had managed in over two centuries... the lost bounty from the *HMS Fantome*, which most people believed had been hidden in the infamous Money Pit on Oak Island, Nova Scotia.

That treasure, allegedly worth millions of dollars, was to be used by Francois, a self-proclaimed philanthropist, to help thousands of less fortunate people around the world, if Kane found it, of which of course there was no guarantee, and in fact was very, very unlikely. How could he, when so many others had failed before? A year ago, he might have felt bold enough to say, *well I found Vilcabamba... a little treasure shouldn't be so hard.* That was then. He'd fallen so far from grace since then, and fallen so hard, that he'd never be confident about anything else ever again.

And there was the crux of the matter. The main reason he'd agreed to the gig. The one thing that had tempted him above all the other reasons, as noble as they were. Redemption. Over the last couple of boozy, sozzled and sloppy months, in which he'd given up on happiness, love, and of ever feeling anything like self-worth again, redemption seemed a million miles away.

Now, along had come Francois, the jaunty, quirky but apparently well-connected Frenchman, offering Kane the chance to redeem himself on a silver platter. Well, in a flute of French 75, anyway.

What does it all mean? How has all this happened?

Kane wasn't sure... in fact, he had no idea how this had transpired, other than the few tenuous tidbits Francois had told him.

Kane's instincts were to stay well clear of such endeavours, at least those not conjured up in his own former ambitious mind. And yet, he'd agreed, and it had only taken the simple offer at a chance of redemption. This to Kane was evidence of just how much he craved it deep down, despite his apparent desire to drink himself into an early, sandy grave here in Cambodia.

He glanced out across the calm waters surrounding Rabbit Island, and spotted the small ferry approaching half a mile off shore, transporting the next batch of tourists from the mainland. It was that moment Kane decided for sure.

This is it. It's time to leave the island.

Kane sprinted to his accommodation. He hustled about the once-fancy but now-messy suite and snagged up all his stray clothes. Two minutes later, he'd completed one final check under pillows and in drawers and, satisfied he hadn't forgotten anything in his rush, darted outside. He'd made it ten yards when he stopped sharply.

Jesus!

He ran back into the suite and strode to the safe, punched in the number and retrieved his wallet and his passport.

Almost, you idiot... almost.

Ten minutes later, Kane had returned to the bar and left his friend, the barman, a considerable chunk of Francois' cash. Then he'd boarded the modest ferry, which now chugged its way back to the mainland where it would dock at the pier in Kep City. From there, Kane would once again use Francois' money and check into a hotel for a night before taking a taxi the following day all the way to Phnom Penh International, some three hours' drive.

The layover in Kep would allow Kane the time to try and make sense of all that had occurred over the last thirty-six hours or so. Kane sensed he was missing something.

Something bigger, perhaps more ominous. Still, contrary to what usually happened, no internal alarm bells were causing him any undue anxiety, yet Kane knew better than most how often he had been wrong about such things before.

Chapter Eight

A couple of leisurely hours later, Kane had checked into a fancy resort by the beach in Kep City and, unable to resist the lure of the array of beach bars dotted about on the long stretch of glimmering golden sand, especially at the Frenchman's expense, Kane soon found himself sipping cocktails beneath the thatched roof of the nearest tiki bar. It wasn't yet eleven in the morning, but the sun was shining and Kane was on his third strawberry daiquiri. It wasn't his usual tipple, but today was not a usual day.

Despite his earlier reservations, Kane felt on the cusp of something. The pull of a new adventure. The chance at achieving something great. Successfully finding ancient treasures others hadn't been able to find? He didn't think so. In truth, it was for personal reasons that his guts had begun fluttering, the first time they'd done that in a while, at least in a good way. As he gazed out across the calm, shimmering surface of the ocean that lapped gently onto the shore a dozen yards away, Kane's thoughts turned to the Frenchman.

It was a genuine surprise when Francois had rocked up to the bar on Rabbit Island. The man was so sure of himself, a trait Kane admired, and something he'd strived to become better at throughout his adult life. A natural introvert, Kane usually preferred to let his actions do the talking. But it was because of that confident manner Kane had been convinced to join the mission.

The mission? That's one way to put it. Probably a wild goose chase if truth be told, Kane mused as he paid his tab and took a walk along the beach to the next watering hole.

It was now lunch time and this bar was much livelier than the last had been. Groups of tourists sat around on beanbags drinking beer and eating local delicacies, such as grilled tarantulas, silkworms and fried crickets. While Kane appreciated the temptation to experience local cuisine on his travels—*when in Rome and all that*—today he'd be giving those things a miss. Instead he'd focus on the drinks.

There were also the random older dudes, there in the bar for less scrupulous reasons, as well as couples and solo travellers in Cambodia for the beaches and the magnificent temple complexes to the north Kane had explored many times himself.

Also in the bar were a few scantily clad local women Kane assumed were working girls. Kane would never consider employing the services of such local attractions, and in fact, he found the business of organised prostitution abhorrent. However, he also knew that in poverty-stricken nations like Cambodia, young women were often left with little choice, and he pitied them. Kane knew if he lingered around long enough, one or more of the ladies would inevitably come to tempt him into doing business. Kane didn't mind that. He would politely decline, tell them the truth that he was in love with another woman, and offer to buy them a meal instead. Some accepted that kind of response, usually relieved, while others took it as a personal insult and stalked off, likely cursing in their native tongue.

The afternoon meandered into a lazy, sultry early evening. Kane had been reasonably restrained so far in terms of drinks. He wanted to remain alert, recToullang Francois' parting words. *We will be watching you.* Well, Kane had kept his eyes peeled for any sign of someone watching him from afar, but as yet he'd seen nobody he thought suspicious. Of course, it could literally be anyone, and not necessarily someone who looked like a bear in a tight suit, the kind of heavies you see in the movies. It could be one of the young tourists sprawled out on the beanbags. It could be the barman or the waitress serving the tables. It might even be one of the old men, or one of the working girls for all Kane knew, and in truth, it didn't matter. At this moment he was still planning to do what the Frenchman had tasked him with doing, and give Francois and his spies no cause for concern.

Kane checked his watch. It was a little after seven. That meant lunchtime in England. *Time to give the professor a call.*

Kane fished his mobile from his shorts pocket and rang John O'nians. When the call wasn't answered after two rings Kane knew his mentor wasn't home, as he always answered within two seconds if he was. *Try again later*, Kane mused as he nodded to the barman for another round.

Kane wondered what the professor would make of his decision to go to Oak Island. John was an adventurer too, and as a world-famous scholar and art historian in his own right, the lure of unearthing ancient lost treasures would surely appeal to the great man. The difference between Kane and O'nians, however, was that the professor wouldn't take any unnecessary risks. He was an astute organiser, and diligent in his tasks. He would leave no stone unturned in his research ahead of the mission, and leave nothing to chance. Thus, in reality there would be no way on Earth John would have accepted the offer made by Francois. Not in a million years. *So why am I doing it? What makes me so special?*

This train of thought led Kane to suddenly question his decision for the first time. Yet it was only a question, and as he had always done in the past, he asked himself what his beloved grandfather, the late great Hiram Kane Snr, would have done if offered the same opportunity. The answer was as straightforward as it always had been. Quite simply, Kane Snr would have said a resounding *Yes!*

The younger Kane was suddenly overwhelmed by sadness. Kane Snr had been murdered by a criminal organisation in Egypt a few months back. Again, it wasn't Kane's fault, yet like all the losses he'd been involved with over his career, he bore the brunt of the guilt on his sleeve and in his heart. The inevitable thing about it all was that Kane knew it was only a matter of time until it was his turn to die. It was so inevitable, in fact, that he knew he should probably walk away from this all now before it was too late.

There was the redemption he might achieve, sure, but what good was that if you were dead soon after? There was the issue of his love, Alex Ridley. She may have been AWOL from his life in recent months, but that didn't mean Kane had given up on her. He would never, ever give up on the love of his life, so that was another good reason to stay alive.

What am I doing? Why risk it all for something that until the last 48 hours I'd never given a second thought? Am I just plain stupid? Insane? Is my ego so out of control that I'll risk it all just to make myself feel better?

Kane found himself shaking his head at the absurdity of it all. At the absurdity of himself. He let his gaze drift out across the bay. The sun was sinking towards the horizon to the west, casting long shadows across the beach and turning the sky into a kaleidoscopic mix of oranges and pinks and purples. And then suddenly his mind was clear.

"I'm not going. I won't go to the States," he muttered to himself, "and I won't go to Canada."

Instead, I'll go home to England, he thought, *and I will sort my life out. I'll make contact with Francois, apologise, and tell him I've made a mistake accepting his generous offer and return the money. Once and for all, I will quit the booze, and turn things around. Then, most importantly, I will track down Alex.*

Unaware he was smiling, Kane turned back to the bar and grabbed his drink. He had planned to pour the rest of it into the sand as a symbolic gesture, but decided he didn't like to waste it and downed the last of his last ever drink in one long gulp.

He felt good about it. He was ready to take back control.

Which is precisely the moment when all control was lost.

Chapter Nine

Kane decided to seize the momentum of the positive decision and take himself back to the resort before his weaknesses could talk him out of it. The evening temperature remained hot but a gentle breeze whispered in off the ocean to keep the worst of the humidity at bay. He paid his bar tab and left a hefty tip for the smiling barman, and with a respectful nod in the direction of a cluster of the working girls sitting around in the corner, Kane left the bar and began making his way back along the beach.

As soon as Kane's back was turned, however, the barman's smile faded. He plucked his mobile phone from beneath the bar and placed a call. He spoke a few words, and waited for a response. It was swift in coming, and the message he heard was simple:

"Activate Encouragement Strategy!"

The barman confirmed the command and ended the call. He nodded subtly at one of the women, who nodded back and stood up from her barstool. She approached the bar and leaned in as the barman whispered something into her ear. Then, and casually, as if it were the most normal thing in the world, the woman stepped out from beneath the tiki bar's thatched roof and slowly followed Hiram Kane along the beach.

Kane was halfway back to his resort, successfully managing to ignore the pull of several more bars and making good progress along the beach. Just then, however, he sensed rather than saw that someone was following him. He knew he'd had quite a lot to drink, and after pausing to take a look around, he decided there was no one there to concern himself with after all and continued on the last few hundred yards to The Orchid Resort and Spa.

Feeling a little weary as he walked, Kane's hand slipped up to his upper arm, where an ache had taken root in his deltoid muscle.

Perhaps Francois can treat me to a massage at the spa, he mused, kneading his muscle with his knuckles. He then noticed an ache in his back, too, and a general weariness began creeping over him, starting in his eyes, and filtering through his body, until all of a sudden, a wave of dizziness crept over him and he stumbled, dropping to one knee on the sand beneath a towering palm tree.

"Mister, mister, you okay?" came a concerned female voice from somewhere behind him.

"Uh, yes, I... I think so. Just feel a little... woozy," Kane managed, slurring his words. *Must have drunk more than I thought.*

He tried to stand, but suddenly his legs felt like tree trunks and he couldn't move them.

"It is okay, I help you," the woman said, edging closer. "Do not worry."

He glanced up at the figure moving slowly towards him, but couldn't focus his eyes. It was a woman, though he could only tell by her voice.

"Do not worry," she repeated, very close now. Then Kane noticed another blurred form take its place beside the woman and an unbidden knot of icy concern took residency in his guts.

His blurry vision now faded to the point it was as if he were trying to see underwater, and the two vaguely human forms swam before his eyes. He tried to stand again but collapsed in a heap, and the last thing he felt before blacking out completely was two powerful arms reaching beneath his armpits and hauling him upright.

"Put your arm around him," the man told the woman in his native Khmer tongue, and she duly did as instructed.

Kane wasn't totally unconscious, but the huge amount of sedative they'd dumped in his drink back at the bar whilst he wasn't looking was enough to render him useless for at least the next six or seven hours. That was more than enough time to carry out his boss's plan.

Together, the man and woman leaned Kane against a tree, the woman keeping him in place with her arm around his shoulder. Then the man stepped back and snapped a few photos with his camera phone, and once he'd checked them, and was satisfied with what they proved, he helped the woman to walk Kane the short distance back to the resort.

Local women escorting drunk foreign men back to hotels was a common sight in Cambodia, and southeast Asia generally, and the security guards at the resort entrance barely registered the trio as they traipsed through the gate.

There were no other tourists or resort staff around, so the woman fished in Kane's pocket for a room key, and was relieved to find Kane had a luxury suite on the ground floor with a view over the gardens and a private deck adjacent to the main swimming pool.

She wasn't sure what she was going to have to do once they were in the room. This wasn't the usual gig with a punter. She knew he'd been drugged, but wasn't sure why. All she knew was that she'd been paid double her usual rate and told not to ask any questions, which was just fine by her.

Once they were safely into Kane's suite, they nudged off his flip flops, then stripped off his linen shirt and shorts, and laid him out on the large bed, spread-eagle, as if performing a snow angel.

"Get your clothes off and lie next to him," the man demanded.

"But he is unconscious," she began, then decided to play by the rules. Without fanfare, she stripped down to her underwear.

Satisfied, the man directed her to lie beside Kane with one arm draped across his chest. Once in position, he again took a few photos, making sure both Kane's and the woman's faces were clearly recognisable.

"Good," the man said, and stowed away his phone.

Kane began to stir. The man directing proceedings wasn't concerned. He would allow Kane to focus for a few seconds, and then send him back into opiate heaven. Kane groaned and eased himself up onto his elbows. It was time.

"And here's a little bonus for your efforts," the man said, before stepping towards the woman, who had sat up beside Kane on the bed. The man reached behind him, and as the woman's eyes widened in anticipation of the unexpected bonus, and after making sure Kane was watching, his hand shot forward and with one deft swipe of a wrist, he sliced her neck wide open with the business edge of a lethal blade.

Her hands flew to her throat as she tried in vain to stem the flow of blood, and as she stumbled forward in a futile effort to escape certain mortality, the man pushed her back onto the bed, where slowly, silently, she bled to a grim death within two feet of a wide-eyed Hiram Kane.

Before Kane could react, the man hustled next to him and plunged a syringe's needle deep into his neck.

Chapter Ten

Kane opened his eyes slowly and let them settle on the ceiling fan whirring gently above the bed. It was hard to focus and he closed his eyes again, regretting the headache firmly lodged behind his eyes. He breathed deep, sucking in cool air and noticed an odd aroma in the room. It had a coppery hint. Or was it bronze? Something metToullac anyway, but as he lay there, nostrils twitching, the smell became more pronounced as he became more awake.

What the hell is that? It was worse than he'd first realised and the stench began to turn his stomach. Not copper or bronze. It smelled like a fucking slaughterhouse and Kane sensed he might be about to throw up. He reached out both arms to his sides to stretch in preparation of easing himself out of bed, when his right arm touched something on the bed that wasn't the soft quilt he'd been expecting. Kane rolled over and found himself face to face with the glazed eyes of a beautiful young local woman.

It took one second to realise there was an unknown woman in his bed.

It took but one more after that to realise she was dead.

Kane yelled in shock as he stumbled and scrambled away from the dead woman until his arse slipped off the edge of the bed and he went down, one hip crashing into the unforgiving tiled floor. From his position on the ground Kane finally realised the true extent of the horrifying scene before him. There, lying on his bed in his hotel suite, was the near-naked body of a murdered woman. Someone had slit her throat, and so much blood had spilled from the horrendous wound that her half of the bed was now one dismal, dark stain showing up clearly against the once snow-white sheets.

"Ohmigod," Kane muttered repeatedly. "Ohmigod, ohmigod. What the hell? What have I…?"

No, no, not me. I don't know this woman. Why is she here? Who would do such a thing? Ohmigod…

Kane pulled himself off the floor, unable to take his eyes off the corpse. His hands went to his face, the true shock of what he was seeing only now fully registering. He knew he had to call the police. He would explain that he had woken up and found the woman dead. But who she was, and why she was in his room, Kane had no idea.

Kane's breathing became ragged as shock faded and panic began to set in. He couldn't call the police. What if they didn't believe him? He'd likely end up in a Cambodian prison, or worse. *Wait, does Cambodia have the death penalty?* He didn't know, but guessed it did. There's no way he could risk being accused of this. *Murder? Jesus, she's been fucking murdered here in my room. But how? I wasn't that drunk. I…*

Oh, shit.

Groggily, Kane recalled how he had suddenly felt ill as he'd walked home from the bar. He had stumbled, and found himself on the ground beneath a palm tree.

Did I bang my head? There was a voice. A woman. *Is this her?*

Kane glanced at her face. The caramel skin tone of her body did not match that of her face, which had paled significantly from massive blood loss. Kane gagged as a rush of bile caused him to retch. Once the impulse to puke had passed, Kane paced the suite, wondering what the hell he should do.

That's when someone knocked hard on the suite's door, and he froze mid-stride. "Oh no. Oh, shit, shit," he muttered, automatically backing behind a wall and out of sight from the floor-to-ceiling window next to the solid wooden door.

Kane's heart hammered against his ribcage, threatening to race out of control as more bile rose in his throat.

"Mr Kane? Answer the door!" called the man from outside the suite. "We know you are in there. You and your… friend." The voice was deep, the accent unmistakably French. *Not Cambodian? Not the police then.*

"Answer the door please. I have an important message for you."

It wasn't Francois, Kane was sure. And it clearly wasn't the local police. Francois had told Kane they'd be watching him. *Have they done this? Is it to set me up?*

Kane assessed his options. He could answer the door, explain to whoever it was out there that the woman lying dead in his suite had nothing to do with him, and hope everything got resolved in a peaceful, orderly and truthful manner. Or, he could call the reception and have the police come to the room, where he would wait, and explain everything when they arrived. Risky. There was a very good chance they wouldn't believe him, and that wouldn't be good for Kane at all.

Or the third option, that was sounding the best of a bad bunch more with every passing moment, was to simply run and take his chances of making it safely out of Cambodia.

There were only two ways out of the suite. The front door was the closest one. The other option was the sliding patio doors that opened onto a private terrace that led straight to the side of a swimming pool. He risked a glance around the corner. Through the sheer curtains hanging in front of the patio doors he saw the shadowy silhouette of a large figure. The other man at the door knocked and called out again.

So there are at least two of them. Fuck...

He realised he didn't actually remember getting back to the suite.

Must've spiked my drink at the bar. Brought me back here. Why would they kill the woman and pin it on me? Are they planning on blackmailing me? Yes, it's obvious now. Why, though?

Kane assumed it was in case he decided to change his mind and back out of helping Francois, so they'd killed this woman, probably taken photos of the two of them in bed while he was out of it, and would use the images to blackmail him into going through with the plan.

"Bastards!" Kane hissed through gritted teeth. He couldn't risk the police. Especially if these fuckers had incriminating photographic evidence.

There was nothing for it. He would have to run, and take his chances on the streets. He decided on the front door. If he made it past the first man, he could leg it through the resort's grounds and be onto the busy road into town before they knew what had happened. He could disappear into the shadows and head for the Vietnam border. The patio option meant he would have to negotiate the pool.

Kane grabbed up his few belongings and stuffed them into his backpack, and also put his man-bag inside it too, which contained the cash, the credit cards and his passport.

He stepped over to the slain woman. She looked no more than early twenties, and had been murdered simply to set Kane up. Kane didn't have words to express his grief, though he felt it in every fibre of his being. One more innocent victim, dead because of him. He thought about reaching out and gently closing her blank, staring eyes, but in a rare moment of clarity he thought about fingerprints and DNA and decided against it. "Bastards," he muttered again, then prepared himself to make a run for it.

"Okay, I'm coming out," he said from just inside the door, pulling the backpack straps tighter to his chest. There was no reply, so after a deep breath he silently unlocked the door, then in a rush of movement he swung it open, and sprinted.

Kane made it only three steps, when a tree trunk of a forearm slammed into his neck and dropped him in a crumpled heap to the ground.

"Where do you think you are going?" the huge man said, chuckling as he grabbed Kane by the feet and hauled him back inside the suite.

Chapter Eleven

Kane's hands clutched at his throat. He felt certain his windpipe had been crushed by the powerful forearm he'd taken from the huge man now towering over him.

The second figure had moved around to the front of the suite and now stood inside the locked door, eyeing Kane with cold, hard eyes. The two men looked alike and fleetingly Kane wondered if they were brothers. Big ones. Like the Mitchell brothers in the British show Eastenders, with lots of additional steroids.

The older looking of the two had a large foot planted either side of Kane's torso. Kane still had his backpack on so he was in a half-sitting up position as the thug spoke down at Kane in calm, French-accented English.

"You cannot escape, Mister Kane, and nor should you. You have a deal to work for our boss, and this little episode is to ensure you do not change your mind." He reached into his suit jacket pocket and retrieved an envelope, which he dropped to Kane. "Open it."

"No!" Kane said. He didn't want to see what he felt sure was inside.

The big man above him shifted his foot and placed it down hard on Kane's chest. "Open it. You need to know how serious this is."

"I can see how fucking serious it is…" Kane massaged his throat. It was difficult to talk, and painful. "You killed a girl and are setting me up." There was a wheezy quality to his words, as if he'd smoked a thousand cigarettes that morning.

"You are mistaken, Mister Kane. I did not kill a girl. You did. Look inside the envelope."

Kane sighed. He opened the envelope and slipped out half a dozen photos. In the first one, he saw himself leaning against a tree, looking shit-faced, with the now-dead girl's arms around him. His throat went dry as he realised just how much shit he was in. *Who the fuck are these people?* In the second image, the girl was lying on the floor on a deserted stretch of pathway. Kane was kneeling over her, his arm raised. There was no doubt it was him. He had no recollection of any of this, but there was no denying it was him kneeling aggressively over the girl.

The third and fourth photos were of the two of them lying in his bed. The girl was dressed only in knickers and a bra and had her arms draped around Kane's neck. And the last one, the worst, most shocking photograph of all, was of Kane laying in the bed, a knife in his hand, and a dead girl with a slit throat lying next to him. It didn't show Kane in the act of killing her, but it painted a pretty damning image of what had occurred.

It did not look good for Kane.

Just then he heard the distant rise and falls of police sirens. *Oh, bollocks…*

The thug looked down at him, malice in his eyes. "You have about three minutes to convince me you are going to stick with the plan of helping our boss. If you cannot convince me, I will keep you here until the police arrive. We have friends in the service. They will do what we tell them to do. Believe me, Mister Kane, you do not want to find yourself in prison in this country."

Kane was well known for his understatements, but that was right up there. He didn't know what to believe. These men had killed an innocent young woman. For all he knew, they might turn him over to the police anyway, maybe to scare him, perhaps to give him a taste of how things might be if he didn't cooperate.

One thing he did know was that he couldn't risk the police getting their hands on him. Who knew how that would turn out? No, the bottom line was, he had to get the fuck out of there. And now.

Kane slammed his right shin up so hard into the big man's groin that he actually whelped, and as he doubled over Kane thrust himself upwards, planting his forehead as hard as he could manage into the massive thug's nose, relishing the sound it made as the bone crunched beneath the skin. Using gravity to his advantage, Kane grabbed the man's jacket lapels and hauled him over to his right, at the same time leveraging himself to his feet. The entire exchange had lasted less than five seconds, fast enough that he managed to turn and face the other brother as he charged at Kane from the doorway.

Despite the fact Kane had just destroyed the first thug's manhood as well as his nose, he was surprised to see the younger brute grin, apparently relishing the chance to smash Kane to within an inch of his miserable life. Yet despite his superior size, the thug obviously hadn't done his research and as many had done before him, he had underestimated Hiram Kane.

Kane lowered himself into his favoured tae-kwon-do fighting stance, a move that amused the killer. As if it had inspired him even more, the thug launched himself at Kane with a ferocious right cross that whistled by Kane's ear as he sidestepped the huge man and spun on his heels, following up with a devastating left-right combo into the general area of the man's kidneys. Unperturbed, he turned and faced Kane, no hint of any burgeoning respect for his new foe.

Somewhere beyond the resort, the sirens wailed ever closer and Kane predicted he had about one minute to get the hell away from there before the police arrived, ninety seconds tops.

The thug surged towards Kane, agile for a big man, and with surprising dexterity grabbed Kane's shoulders and forced him back towards the hefty wooden door. What he didn't realise was that Kane had anticipated the move and had let it happen, and as he resisted the charge with just enough strength to trick the thug into thinking he was getting his own way, at the very last second Kane grabbed the bastard's lapels, dropped, and heaved backwards, slamming the thug face-first into the immovable door. Kane heard a definite crack and hoped it wasn't the man's neck snapping.

He eased himself out from beneath the big man's bulk, now lying still and prostrate on the floor. He did a cursory check to make sure the man wasn't dead, then hauled him away from the door. Then he hustled over to the other prick, who lay in a heap muttering something in French Kane couldn't understand. This guy was going to be okay, although Kane had seen to it there would never be any more kids springing from this fucker's loins. He also now had a nose ugly and gnarly enough to suit the rest of his face.

Kane heard the squealing of rubber on concrete and knew the police were just seconds away. He had to go. Now. He swung the door open and cautiously stepped out of the suite. A flash of movement to his left caused him to duck back into the doorway. It was too late to go that way. He went back inside the suite and locked the door, then raced over to the patio doors. He slid them open, and trotted across the patio towards the pool, then skirted around the pool using the palm trees as cover. A minute later he had left the resort and had joined the throngs of locals and tourists going about their days.

What might come next, he had no idea. For now, somehow, he had just gotten away with murder.

"No, you will not kill him. Is that clear?" Francois wasn't a physical specimen. He was a small man, lean and even effeminate looking, some might say, yet he wielded plenty of power over those who worked for him. Thus, when he spoke, people listened, however difficult it might be.

Clement seethed inwardly. The slippery Englishman had surprised him and his brother Claude, and had given them both a fair beating. Now the burly French-Canadian mercenary wanted revenge. It would have to wait. Neither brother dared go against their boss's commands, however frustrating. To do so would mean they would quietly disappear one day, their bodies found half-eaten by crabs and lobsters in Halifax Harbour.

"Yes, boss. It's clear. So, what do we do now?"

"You do what I told you to do. You follow him, wherever he goes next, and report back on his progress." Francois paused for effect, before adding, "Is it too much for you, Clement? Is the Englishman going to be a problem?"

Clement subconsciously touched a finger to his smashed nose beneath the bandages and winced.

Fucker! "No, boss. No problem. Looks like he's heading towards the bus station," Clement told Francois, following Kane through the market but keeping out of sight fifty yards behind.

"Good. Find out where he's going. Don't fucking hurt him, okay? Let him start searching once he gets to the States. Okay?"

"Okay," Clement said, nodding at his smirking brother as Kane entered the Kep Central Bus Terminal. *Fucking prick*, Clement thought but didn't say aloud as he ended the call. *My boss is a fucking prick!*

Chapter Twelve

After the narrow escape from the thugs and the incoming local police, Kane had to tread carefully. He still didn't really know who these people were, but all was definitely not what he'd first thought after meeting Francois. They were killers, that was now obvious, and they had slaughtered a young woman, using her as a tool to gain leverage over Kane. *Shit, what a waste!* All they had to do was threaten someone and Kane would probably have played ball. They did not need to kill her.

Kane felt the usual guilt as a lump in his throat and a broiling, burning fire in his belly. However, he had to hold it together for now in order to get away from there and out of the country. There was a chance they'd broadcast his photos across the wires as some kind of fugitive. On the other hand, perhaps the goons figured they'd done their work well enough, and would let him get away and proceed with the original plan.

What is my plan? Kane hustled in and out of the milling throngs at a local fish market. *Right, I don't have one.* Now he knew how callous and dangerous these people were, of course he didn't want to work with them. In fact, he should call in the authorities once he was safe and have the men arrested. But was there another path open to him now?

What was clear, was that Francois—*was that even his real name?*—believed there was something worth finding on Oak Island. Something of great financial and historical value. *So,* Kane thought, *why don't I go there and follow through with the plan, but have nothing more to do with Francois and his psycho sidekicks?* Maybe, he figured, there was some good to come from this nightmare after all.

Kane left the open-air fish market and ducked into a covered market area. The pungent smells of the fish and slowly rotting seafood had been replaced by tropical fruits, fresh flowers, spices, incense and an array of unrecognisable vegetables that looked more like aliens than anything edible. The crowd was thick here and it was so hot Kane's shirt was soon drenched in sweat.

He spotted one older hawker standing alone behind his table of carved wooden products, and angled towards him.

"Hello," Kane said, hoping the old man knew some English.

"Hello, mister," replied the old timer.

"Can you tell me where the bus station is please?" Kane asked, cautiously glancing over his shoulder.

The old man eyed Kane, somewhat suspiciously it seemed, then grinned. There were more gaps than teeth. He raised a bony hand and pointed. "One mile east. Bus station. Where you go?"

Well, that was a good question. Kane hadn't really thought about it, but knew he had to leave the country. Two options; Vietnam to the east and Thailand to the north and west. Vietnam was closer and he could probably make it to

Ho Chi Minh by bus in twenty-four hours. A third option was to stay here in Cambodia, and make his way to Phnom Penh and take his original flight. On balance, that was too risky. He had no idea if what the thug had told him was true, that they had people on the payroll in the Cambodian police. If they didn't, and it was just a bluff, then the police would definitely be looking for someone, and Kane had been photographed with a dead hooker. Innocent or not, he couldn't take that chance. He plumped for Vietnam.

Kane thanked the old man with a fistful of Francois' cash and eased back into the throngs, and just twenty minutes later he was making his way discreetly into the vast, swarming bus station. He hung back in the shadows a moment, and noticed a few police loitering about. They didn't appear to be searching for anyone, which Kane took as a sign the alarm had yet to be raised. Still, he couldn't take any chances. He spotted a woman selling various touristy items and made his way over. He bought a bandana, which he tied around his neck. He thrust a straw hat atop his head and paid too much for some genuine fake Ray Ban aviators, which he shoved on his face.

The last thing Kane did for his attempt at a disguise was a quick shirt change, switching out his manky, sweat-stained linen number for a ubiquitous I Love Angkor Beer t-shirt. It was too small, and super cheesy for a man the wrong side of forty, but if this didn't make him blend in with the crowds, nothing would. He thanked the lady and made his way to the ticketing booths, soon spotting tickets for Ho Chi Minh city.

Should I actually buy a ticket? He knew he'd have to show his passport, and if his name had been given to the authorities, would it show up so soon on the system? He didn't think so. A lot of stuff in southeast Asian tourist destinations was still done in the old-school way of ledgers and notebooks. There was probably nothing online to worry about yet. Still… something didn't sit right. His freedom was on the line, and he decided against purchasing an official ticket.

Kane stepped back against a wall and scanned the scene, eyes roving the swarm of humanity for a particular demographic of person. It didn't take long. Male. Thirty to forty years old. Tall-ish. Backpacker. Probably low on funds. Kane glanced around for any police presence, then made his move.

"Excuse me. How are you?" he asked.

The tall guy with shaggy blonde hair and a fully laden backpack eyed Kane suspiciously and clutched his backpack a little tighter. "Um, good thanks, mate. You?"

"I'm doing great," Kane lied. "Listen, did you just buy a ticket to Ho Chi Minh?" Kane knew he had.

"Yeah… what of it?" The accent was Australian.

"Want to sell it?"

"Uh, no. Why don't you just buy one?"

"How much did you pay for it?"

"Seven-hundred thousand dong. Thirty US bucks." The guy's eyes narrowed further, clearly suspicious.

"How about I give you two hundred dollars for it and you don't ask any questions?"

The narrowed eyes now widened, then narrowed again. Drug mules operated all across the region, and worse. "I'm not carrying any fucking bags. Mate, if you're into some weird shit, forget it."

"No, no, nothing like that. Use the money to buy another ticket. I don't care. No questions, and no bags. A simple trade. What do you say?"

Kane pulled an envelope of cash from the bag and counted out two hundred dollars, then added another fifty for good measure. "Here, two-fifty in exchange for your ticket. Deal?

The guy inhaled, then proffered his ticket to Kane. They traded and Kane thanked the guy.

Fifteen minutes later he took his seat on the crowded bus, where he pulled his new hat down over his eyes, and cried for the murdered young woman and a little bit for himself too.

Chapter Thirteen

Kane had let himself be lulled to sleep by the monotonous drone of the engine and the vibrations of the ageing bus over the rough road. It also seemed as if he was the only passenger who hadn't entered the loudest voice contest apparently going on all around him. Nevertheless, he was so physically and mentally drained that sleep was a welcome surprise when it came.

When he finally roused from his slumber a few hours later, rather than feeling refreshed he felt more exhausted than ever. Darkness had pervaded his dreams, and images of the murdered woman in Kep haunted his mind. *Who could do that to a young woman?* Perhaps she wasn't a saint, and was in some way complicit in Francois' scheme. But Kane assumed she didn't deserve to have her throat slit, and the barbaric nature of it made Kane cringe inwardly. He felt sick to his stomach. A headache had lodged behind his eyes.

His thoughts turned to Francois. The Frenchman had provided copies of the so-called letters of introduction he'd sent Kane in the recent past. In an attempt to learn more about the Frenchman, who claimed to be a good person but apparently was anything but, Kane pulled out one of the envelopes and read the note folded within.

Dear Mister Kane.

I hope this letter finds you well.

You don't know me, and for now I'd prefer to keep my identity a secret.

I'd like to start by saying that I've admired you and your family from afar for many years. In fact, several decades. The work your grandfather, and your great-grandfather before him, have done for the world of archaeology, and their staunch support of the preservation of the world's great cultures, has been both heartwarming and invaluable. I know you are cut from that same Kane cloth, and that you are a philanthropist by nature.

So too am I. However, I have a problem. For reasons I will explain more about later, I am unable to undertake what I believe is an adventurous mission right up your street. It is a mission which, if successful, will benefit many thousands of people as a result. I don't mean to sound overly dramatic, but the truth is, I'm not. This is all very real.

Thus, I have a proposal for you... and yes, I am flagrantly appealing to both your goodness and to your innate sense of adventure. For that I make no apology. You are a man after my own heart, Hiram. I think you'll like what I have to tell you.

I have recently learned of a great lost fortune, the details of which for now I'll keep to myself for fear this letter may fall into the wrong hands. The unimaginable worth of what I speak is the stuff of legend, yet known only to a few. Just months before his untimely death, the man who informed me of this treasure told me it is beyond anything ever discovered. He had spent many years searching for it, but alas, he failed. He has tasked me to continue the search. But as I already mentioned, Hiram, I am no longer able. I can think of no other person in the world to whom I would rather hand over this mantle, especially since it was the man who handed me the mantle in the first place who brought you to my attention.

You have no interest in personal fame or fortune. You are a seeker for seeking's sake. Thus, when you become the man to finally find this great lost bounty, you will do the right thing by it, and help me deliver it to the right and worthy organisation. That's why it should be you, Hiram. It MUST be you.

Intrigued? I truly hope so.

Enclosed is a first-class flight ticket from London to Paris. If you accept my invitation to meet with me, my driver will collect you and bring you to my house in the countryside near Versailles. There I will fill you in on everything else you'll need to know in order to find the lost haul and help thousands of lives in the process.

Time is of the essence here, Mister Kane. There are other, less savoury characters out there who may well be closing in on the bounty themselves. Thus, the air ticket is valid for tomorrow only.

I do hope you can make it.
Regards,
F. D.

Well, what a load of shit, Kane thought as the ancient bus clattered over a pothole, slamming his shoulder against the window and jarring his spine.

Only another twenty-something hours to Uncle Ho Town, he mused, his trademark wry grin curving his lips but the smile not reaching his eyes. There was really nothing to smile about. Kane straightened in his seat and gazed out the window. The dusty highway was flanked on both sides by mile after mile of the almost iridescent green of flooded, mature rice paddies. Water buffalo wallowed in deep ponds and mules pulled carts laden with vegetables, building materials and in some cases, they transported human cargo from one scrubby village to the next. Gaggles of kids in threadbare clothes played and squabbled at the side of the road. Flea-bitten street dogs scratched futilely around for any scrap of food as their ribcages protruded through thin, mangey skin.

In the distance to the west, a forested mountain range ran hundreds of miles south to north, and to the east. Though it was several hundred miles out of view, Kane imagined the Vietnamese coastline snaking with miles of golden beaches receiving the passive tides of The South China Sea.

So many places to run away to and hide, Kane thought. *To forget it all, and to live an anonymous life while drinking myself into oblivion...*

Kane quickly dismissed the notion. It was what he'd been doing these last months since Egypt, and in essence, it was what had landed him in this shit in the first place.

So, what to do? Francois was obviously a criminal, using Kane to get his hands on the lost treasure of Oak Island. Yet, as far as the Frenchman knew, Kane was still onboard. Yes, he'd battered the thugs, but Kane sensed Francois might secretly enjoy learning about that if he hadn't already. As Kane sat there on the bus speeding east across the lush Vietnamese countryside, he made a decision. He would stick with the plan. If there really were others out there with orders to keep an eye on him, they would find him soon enough and report back that he was in fact doing the right things. Then, if he later found anything at Oak Island—Kane thought that was highly unlikely—he would betray Francois, involve the authorities and do the right thing by his own moral code and hand the treasure over to the Canadian specialists.

Now he had come to a decision, Kane finally started to

relax. He felt certain no one knew he was on this bus. From the bus station in Kep he could have gone to a dozen destinations, and he hadn't even used his own ticket. Thus, he felt safe, and had made what he thought was the best decision he could under trying circumstances. For now, he was alone and free.

A moment later he was asleep, once more rocked into oblivion by the forwards motion of the bus and the dull rumble of an overworked engine.

Chapter Fourteen

With delays at the border crossing, in which Kane suffered a severe bout of anxiety at being rumbled as a murderous fugitive, and one laborious tyre change after a blowout on the highway, Kane's bus finally rocked into Ho Chi Minh a little before midnight. It had taken almost thirty-six hours, of which he had slept a maximum of four. Now he was exhausted beyond measure, hot, sweaty and hungry after declining a range of dubious unknown food items on offer at several pit stops en route.

Kane decided to go straight to the airport and see what flights were available and how soon, hoping he'd get lucky and be away from Asia within hours. For the first time in far too long, Kane did get lucky. After taking a taxi to the airport from the bus station and heading straight to the ticket offices, Kane learned there was a flight out of Ho Chi Minh leaving for Washington D.C. at 4 in the morning. And what do you know, there were a couple of seats left. With a recommended check-in time of three hours before departure, he was technically only an hour early.

With this in mind, he relaxed further and bought a one-way ticket on Francois' credit card, not worried that the Frenchman would learn of his whereabouts when his banking app pinged an alert. For all Kane knew, they somehow already knew he had left Cambodia and was now in Vietnam. He glanced about, almost expecting to see the two big thugs he'd pummelled watching him from somewhere in the departures hall, but he saw no familiar faces, and none with a bandaged-up nose.

He passed the time dozing after grabbing some recognisable food and two large waters, and quick as a flash, Kane was aboard his flight and jetting to Washington D.C. via Seoul in South Korea. It was a long and arduous flight, but in some ways, it was just what Kane needed. Once aboard, there was nothing to do except chill, enjoy the hospitality, occasionally snooze, watch the odd shitty movie or two and think about whatever shitty movie he was getting himself deeper into. At least he wasn't fidgety.

Back on the beach at Rabbit Island, he had never felt truly relaxed, despite his altered state of consciousness. There was nothing to keep him there other than his own desire for anonymity, and yet it wasn't in his nature to lay about drinking all day, though he'd become very good at it. There was always somewhere to go, some new place to explore, even if it was simply a new corner of the island. On the huge aeroplane, miles above the land and ocean, he had no choice but to stay put.

By the time the pilot announced to the crew to prepare for landing, Kane figured he'd managed a paltry six to seven hours of fitful sleep in the last fifty-odd. So, by the time he'd emerged from the rowdy immigration line and collected his single backpack from the over-crowded carousel, and negotiated the hordes of airport goers and found a taxi, against his better judgement Kane needed a beer.

First, he took a cab from Dulles International to the downtown hotel Francois had booked for him. The hour-long crawl through lunchtime traffic had done nothing to lighten Kane's mood, which had steadily deteriorated since touchdown. And, even though he didn't like this surly version of himself, he couldn't help but grunt his way through the tedious check-in procedure. The patient, polite lady working the hotel's reception desk gave Kane his digital keycard and directed him to the lift, which he took to the fourth floor and shuffled along the well-appointed corridor to his suite.

After a quick shower and a miniature gin from the well-stocked minibar, Kane made his way down to the lobby bar and ordered himself a pint of Samuel Adams, which seemed appropriate considering where he was.

Next he pulled out his phone and began a cursory round of research, typing in such keywords as *lost treasure Washington DC,* and *Masonic treasures in Washington. The Fantome missing treasure*, and *Masons on Oak Island* were also searched. After a few minutes, Kane had sourced a half dozen promising articles, of whose links he'd emailed to himself ready to print out back in reception. The plan was not to go too hard on the research today. He was truly exhausted, and decided a quiet day and a good night's sleep were in order to better prepare for a full-on day of research and info-digging tomorrow. It was a solid plan, though the way the gin and the pint had gone down so easily should have been a portent of things to come.

After successfully printing out his stack of reading material, Kane soon found himself back on the sunny streets of downtown D.C., feeling slightly better about life. With the promise of some excitement looming, and delving into the research, Kane decided to find the nearest upmarket bar—at lunchtime on a Friday in the nation's capital, it was too early to hit the dive bars. It should also help him stay focused and not get lured into the shadows, however tempting it was.

He settled on the Old Ebbitt Grill, a local landmark, and an institution for drinkers who spent the rest of their days behind large desks in the nearby financial district, pushing pens, making and breaking laws, and generally playing bureaucratic games. Just a couple of hundred yards from the White House, and literally across 15th Street from the US Treasury Department, there were bound to be those who considered themselves politicians, though Kane could do without those types today.

He entered the Neo-Classic-styled building and immediately felt underdressed, but decided no one would question his attire the moment he opened his mouth and spoke in his apparently posh English accent. Back in England he'd take it as an accusation. Here it was just cute. Apparently. His theory was proven correct, as a young waiter in tight trousers with fluttering eyelashes greeted him at the maitre'd station and escorted him to a seat at the long, expansive bar.

This will do nicely, Kane thought as he took a seat and was immediately served by a tall barkeep with a clipped yet distinctive Caribbean accent. "Certainly sir," he said, bowing slightly before hustling off to fix Kane's drinks.

A moment later, Kane's order of a pint of Sam Adams and a gin chaser arrived. Yet, as he reached to pull his research papers from his satchel, something made him pause.

Chapter Fifteen

Kane decided it was just the exhaustion making him edgy. That, and the gin, which he'd always known was a bad idea, but sometimes you just couldn't beat a good Bombay Sapphire on the rocks, no matter the often demoralising effects. Now on his third, with pints of Sam Adams chasers, he had grown weary of reading his so-called research papers, and instead was satisfied with a bit of people watching. It was late afternoon now, and the large bar was jam-packed with what could only be described as an extraordinarily eclectic cast of revellers. He couldn't be certain, of course, but if Kane were to guess, he was currently surrounded by politicians, lawyers, stockbrokers, professors (the ones wearing scarves, despite the sultry weather), plastic surgeons, police chiefs, TV presenters and at least as many out-of-towners… also known as tourists.

It was interesting to watch the dynamics of the crowd, and though it wasn't a surprise, the noise levels had increased exponentially, almost as if every single patron in the bar was intent on winning the latest in a series of loudest voice competitions. *That's okay*, Kane mused, unconsciously breaking into his trademark wry grin, *everyone has a right for their opinion to be heard.*

The effects of the increasing noise combined with the alcohol, plus his burgeoning jet lag, prompted Kane to pay his bar bill and head out for some fresh air. It wasn't far back to the hotel and the walk would do him good. He might even eat something before bed… it had been a while since he'd enjoyed food, and often he had simply forgotten to eat dinner in his time on Rabbit Island.

He paid the bill and negotiated the early Friday evening crowd, stepping out onto the bustling sidewalk, where it was at least quieter. He sucked in some revitalising air, had a quick glance left and right to make sure he knew in which direction the hotel was, got it completely wrong and headed in the other direction. After a mile of strolling along aimlessly, it dawned on Kane that he was probably not going the correct way. Had he meant it? Kane had no problem with getting lost in an unfamiliar place. In fact, he thrived on it. Perhaps subconsciously he'd deliberately chosen wrong… it was an excuse to make a pit stop at a bar or two. It was probably time for a dive bar anyway.

With this in mind, he soon found what he pretended he wasn't looking for, and ducked into the Ivy and Coney, a bar on 7th St NW, tucked between a grimy coffee shop and a food bank on one side, and a burger joint and barber shop the other. *What else does anyone need?* Kane pondered as he entered the dimly lit bar and sidled up to the greasy bar top.

"A beer, please," Kane said politely.

"Coming right up, mister," said the scantily clad waitress with peroxide hair and a cleavage to make a twenty-year-old Madonna blush.

"Oh my," Kane muttered, the wry grin returning, suspecting it wouldn't be long before the lawmakers and politicians left the Old Ebbitt and discreetly found their way here.

Chapter Sixteen

"Stop staring... be more natural," muttered Clement in his native French. His huge shoulders were as square as his stubbled jaw. His narrowed eyes fixed on his brother stood opposite.

"Stop whining. He doesn't know we're here," replied Claude.

Tucked into a small booth in the corner of the Old Ebbitt Grill, the brothers sat casually sipping their cappuccinos. One was reading a newspaper, while the other scrolled through an app on his phone, his eyes constantly darting up, then back to his phone, then up again. They weren't lawyers or doctors. Nor were they professors or politicians. They definitely weren't plastic surgeons, though they'd rearranged plenty of faces between them over the years. They were there in a working capacity, albeit a very different kind of profession to the other patrons, oblivious to the mercenary thugs among their throng.

Claude was right, though. Their mark Kane didn't know they were there, although a few minutes ago he had started looking nervously about the bar. Those apparent nerves had soon dissipated, however, and he'd returned to reading the papers he had on his lap, as he polished off yet another glass of what might have been gin or vodka.

"He likes drinking," Clement commented, his massive shoulders slumping a fraction. "Lucky bastard... I'm sick of these weak coffees."

"Whining again?" Claude chided. "Do you ever stop?"

"Actually, I don't," Clement said, leaning in closer to his brother across the table. "But I'll fucking stop you, if you continue staring at him. You might as well have a fucking tattoo on your forehead that says, 'Hey, look at us... we're here, and we're going to...'" Clement exhaled. "Idiot." He leaned back again, turned the page of his newspaper and settled back into the stakeout that had now lasted a good two hours, and who knew how much longer.

The thugs had a job to do; follow the man for a few days, or longer if required, and if needed, protect him from other nefarious characters... killing, if necessary. It was a simple task, and it had only just commenced, but the tension between the two brothers, French Canadians from Montreal, was already frayed. Clement, the older of the two and technically his brother Claude's boss, had been putting up with Claude as his sidekick for close to a decade. They made a good team, and were sought after by many unsavoury organisations across the east of Canada and the northeast of the USA. It didn't mean they had to get along. Usually, they didn't. Clement put it down to jealousy, and he understood why. There's no way he'd put up with a brother giving him orders all the time.

Most of the time, Claude accepted what Clement said... most of the time. Sometimes, he just couldn't, and let his feelings be known. He had always looked up to

Clement. He was a strong man, a good leader and lethal in a fight. Claude considered him a whinger, though, and knew he worried too much. For a few years now Claude's eyes had been on his brother's position as boss. Not enough to do anything about it. Not yet. But if Clement kept on fussing the way he did, kept on making things more difficult than they needed to be, perhaps then it would be time for a changing of the guard.

"Wait, he's moving. Looks like he's paying his bill," Claude muttered.

Clement edged his newspaper slightly to the right in order to subtly look in Kane's direction. He was indeed in the process of paying his bill. "Get our check," Clement said. Claude nodded, stood, then casually made his way to the bar.

"Keep your eyes on him," Claude muttered as he passed. "We can't lose him."

Clement rolled his eyes, then kept one on the departing Kane and the other on his newspaper. He watched as Kane gathered his papers up and slotted them in a satchel that he swung around his neck, then slowly made his way towards the main entrance that led out onto 15th St NW.

Claude caught his brother's eye across the room and nodded towards the outside, and Clement watched as Claude left the bar ahead of their quarry. Clement waited until Kane made it to the door, then slowly rose from the booth and followed a safe distance behind. He noticed Kane was remarkably steady on his feet, despite the amount of drinks he'd consumed in a relatively short space of time. *An experienced drinker. And he can definitely handle himself,* Clement mused as he stepped outside The Old Ebbitt, once again touching a finger to his nose and silently cursing. He spotted Claude across the street, leaning on a lamppost and smoking a cigarette. His brother dipped his head to the north. Clement turned that way and spotted their target fifty yards along the road.

The brothers set off after Kane, a good distance behind as the man ambled slowly northwards, to where, they didn't know.

This is too easy, Claude thought… *but when's the fucking real action coming?*

Chapter Seventeen

Rather than install himself at the bar, his usual preference, Kane occupied a small table tucked into the corner of the dingy pub. From there he had a view of the bar, the two pool tables and the main front door... not that he was worried about anyone following him any longer. For a moment back at the Old Ebbitt, he'd felt as if someone was watching him, but he soon dismissed that as an over-addled mind brought on by the months-long binge he'd been on. Even if someone was there, it was probably Francois' men keeping an eye on him. *Could those same clowns have tracked me here so quickly?* From his recent experiences, Kane knew anything was possible.

He also knew that for some people, alcohol acted as a depressant, and gin especially was known for it. Kane didn't think he was particularly affected by alcohol in that way, but it could sometimes make him a little edgy. He knew he'd have to dry out a bit if he were to continue on this... *what is this? A mission?* It seemed churlish to think of it as a treasure hunt, though essentially that's exactly what it was. Yet, now the game had changed. Now the mission was different. As always, some corrupt bastard with nefarious intentions was involved, and had gotten Kane involved under the guise of philanthropy, a serious endeavour, and technically a paid assignment working for a responsible employer. Kane now knew different, and he had to use that to his own advantage. How? As yet, he didn't know.

"Treasure hunt, or mission? Who am I kidding?" he mused. "Of course it's a treasure hunt." *And I'll lay off the drinks tomorrow.* He kept that lie internal as he tipped back the beer and immediately went to the bar for another. By the time he'd returned a couple of minutes later, he hadn't noticed Clement and Claude had entered the pub and had taken seats out of his line of sight beyond the busy pool tables.

Kane relaxed into his seat and pulled out some printed pages from his satchel. Ridley had once called it his man bag, which he supposed it was. Satchel sounded more... scholarly. Didn't it? *Or does it make me sound like the 1980s school kid I often wish I still was?*

The printed article had been written a decade previously by a Nova Scotian resident named John Wesley Chisholm, an apparent scholar on the Freemasons, and especially The Scottish Rites chapter of the organisation. According to a quick Google search, Chisholm was also an underwater archaeologist and a well-known documentary maker. *Fascinating guy,* Kane thought, and he made a point of trying to seek him out once he got to Nova Scotia. *Maybe he'll help me.*

As Kane scanned the document, his eyes seeking out buzz words he thought might be relevant to his mission, he paused. *Washington D.C. is actually a treasure map? Wait? The city itself is a treasure map? Holy shit!*

That got Kane's attention. He'd heard theories like this before. Many places in the world had hidden meanings, secret, coded messages within their architecture and symbolic meanings within their layouts. In fact, his beloved Cuzco, Peru, a place he'd adopted as his hometown for many years until recently, was one such place. The ancient architects who had designed the former Inca capital had used its natural geography, as well as their own magnificent structures, to create a giant puma, one of the culture's sacred animals. The massive fortress in the north of the mountain city formed the head of the puma, while the city itself outlined the shape of the animal's body. Kane had led groups of tourists around the city himself, as part of his work as a guide, and had certainly become convinced of the legitimacy of that particular theory.

Kane read on, learning that the basic layout of Washington D.C. was outlined by Pierre Charles L'Enfant, a French-American military engineer, a plan that is today known as the L'Enfant Plan, commissioned by George Washington in 1791.

Kane came to the first mention of the enigmatic Oak Island. Among Chisholm's many bold claims, he stated that there was an imaginary line running from the Temple Mount in Jerusalem, home to King Solomon's Temple, then to Versailles in Paris, and to Nolan's Cross on none other than Oak Island, Nova Scotia… home to the near-mythical Money Pit.

Since L'Enfant had designed the city of Washington D.C. based on the Palace of Versailles, this was certainly a link to all things Masonic and Templar, with lost treasures, and not to mention secret societies. The city design, Kane read, was thought to encode certain secret symbols of Freemasonry. Some scholars, Chisholm wrote, stated that the symbols, if ever correctly decoded, would unveil a cryptic history not only of the nation's capital but of the destiny of the United States as a whole. These rumours had been around a long time, Chisholm added, at least since the height of anti-Masonic paranoia under President Jackson's administration. According to the Masonic map theory, Chisholm continued, the Washington Mall was laid out in order to replicate a Masonic Lodge. A standard Lodge floor plan from the 18th century backed this up clearly. It was well known that many of the nation's founding fathers were Masons, including Washington, Franklin and Revere, and for two hundred years many conspiracists had considered them as a front for some other nefarious force—the Illuminati, or the Congregation for the Light, among others, all believed determined to undermine American sovereignty and her institutions.

Kane slipped out a map of Oak Island he'd printed, followed by a map of Washington D.C.

Before studying them in detail, he read on down the article. Chisholm mentioned a famous stone on Oak Island he claimed to be part of a bigger symbolic message. He went on to declare that in D.C., The Washington Monument, the White House and the Capitol Building were positioned at perfect angles on L'Enfant's original Washington D.C. blueprint. However, Chisholm then stated that the infamous stone on Oak Island was cut at a seven degree deviation, adding that if anyone simply went to Google Earth and checked this angle out for themselves, they'd find that the White House also actually deviated from the Washington Monument by...

"... seven degrees?" Kane heard himself mutter. *Hmm... interesting.*

In the article was a grainy black and white image Kane

couldn't quite make out. Whether that was because of the poor quality of the image or his now slightly alcohol-blurred vision, he couldn't be sure. *Might be enough research for one day,* he thought, but couldn't take his mind off the article's claims.

Though the image was unreadable, Chisholm declared that if you superimposed L'Enfant's blueprint of Washington D.C. over the map of Oak Island, and rotated it clockwise by seven degrees, then the obvious similarities in the layout were undeniable.

Holy shit… this is really something, Kane thought, yet another of his humble understatements. Without realising, Kane had finished his drink. He was about to head to the bar for another, when the Madonna wannabe arrived, placing down another pint.

"I took a liberty," she said, leaning over and offering Kane an eyeful of potential. "Was I right?"

"Um, yes, ma'am, thanks," Kane mumbled. He hadn't spoken to another woman in… how long had it been now? An image of Alexandria Ridley's beautiful face flashed in his mind, and he blinked to make it go away. He didn't need sadness to bring him down right now.

"Hey buddy, you alright?" Madonna asked.

"Huh? Oh, yes, sorry. I'm fine, thanks. Er, thanks for the drinks."

Kane offered a shy grin, which Madonna returned with something the opposite of shy before heading back to the bar. Kane took a long gulp of his beer and returned to his articles and maps. Chisholm said that he'd been amazed how well the west and south sides of Oak Island, especially the famous corner at Smith Cove, as well as the notorious swamp, fitted almost perfectly with L'Enfant's blueprint.

It could all be random coincidence. Then again, as soon as the thought had passed, he knew he hadn't really believed it. In art and architecture, Kane knew, nothing was ever really random.

Chisholm continued, and Kane came to the first mention of Samuel Ball, a name he vaguely recalled but couldn't remember why. Working on the assumption that the Capitol Building, the White House and the Washington Monument were the most likely search areas for any hidden treasure, Chisholm wrote, then he believed that Samuel Ball had purchased exactly the right lots back in the late 1700s.

Samuel Ball? Kane wracked his brains for references to the name. It was obvious from the article that the man had something to do with the mystery of Oak Island and the lost booty, whatever that booty was.

Kane pulled out his phone and opened the Google app, typing in Samuel Ball. Immediately, dozens of articles appeared. Kane selected one and read about an early Loyalist settler named Samuel Ball, a black man and former slave-turned cabbage farmer. Apparently, Ball lived for several decades on Oak Island and became one of the richest men in the province. The article suggested that many scholars believe any such treasure on Oak Island was found as long ago as the late 18th century and was immediately taken elsewhere. Samuel Ball was considered the most likely of all the suspected treasure finders.

According to the article, it wasn't until the mid-19th century that rumours began to spread about the alleged treasure on Oak Island, and deeply entrenched in any of those rumours was the name Samuel Ball. By the time Ball died in 1845, the article claimed, the man who had been born a slave owned more than a hundred acres on the island. He also owned another smaller island, back then named Hook Island. Today, the locals know it as Sam's Island.

Surely the treasure's not there? Kane thought, and knew it wouldn't be. If he had access to this information, so did everyone else.

Kane returned to the well-written article by the Nova Scotian scholar, John Wesley Chisholm. Chisholm summarised by saying that if he were to go and undertake a genuine search for the enigmatic lost treasure of the equally enigmatic Oak Island himself, he wouldn't even bother with the infamous Money Pit. It's just too obvious, he stated simply. If it ever was there, it's long gone by now.

So… where the hell is it?

Chapter Eighteen

The day rolled over into early evening as the sun set over D.C. in a fiery blaze of glory.

Kane's earlier weariness seemed to have passed and he was experiencing a second wind, at least in terms of having more drinks. Kane wasn't a partier... he hated nightclubs with a passion. He did like drinking late though, and decided he'd done enough research for one day and turned his attention to more pressing issues; blotting out his burgeoning misery and trying to ignore the weight of the shame that hung around his neck like a... like a Rosetta fucking Stone.

He glanced towards the bar, half hoping Madonna would be on the ball. He caught her eye and nodded; thirty seconds later she arrived with a fresh pint, beneath which she slipped a folded piece of paper. With a wink and a coy smile, she bustled back to the bar.

Kane scooped up the paper. Predictably, there was a name, a note and a number:

I get off in an hour. Cerise ;-)

It was definitely time to go. The last thing Kane wanted or indeed needed was to make a mistake tonight he'd regret for the rest of his life. Instead, he downed the pint in two long gulps, left enough cash on the table to cover two of his bar tabs and slipped out of the Ivy and Coney. He hoped Cerise hadn't noticed him leave.

Kane had a habit when it came to making decisions. He always flipped a coin. Sometimes they were unimportant decisions, such as what to eat for dinner. Sometimes, too often in recent years, they were life or death choices. So, he flipped a coin. Heads meant right. Tails, left. It was always tails. Always. He slid a quarter from his pocket, and knew it would land on the eagle, and not the first president's head. As he caught the coin and flipped it over, Kane was actually shocked to see George Washington on the back of his hand. *It must be a sign*, Kane mused, offering no one in particular his trademark wry grin.

Shaking his head in genuine disbelief—it was the first time he'd ever flipped a head—Kane turned right and soon found himself in an even divier dive bar, Jake's Tavern, this one across the street. Ready and willing to continue his quest to blot out the sad reality his life had become, Kane waited for a gap in the steady flow of traffic and darted across the road. Unlike in the movies, he didn't get hit by a taxi. A few moments later he was inside Jake's and sitting at his customary position at the end of the bar, beer in hand and a shot waiting in the wings.

The two thug brothers, who'd left the bar just moments behind him, paused. "Is that all he fucking does, drink?"

grumbled Clement, which elicited an eye roll from his brother.

"Is that all you fucking do?" Claude shot back.

"What?"

"You know what."

Clement stepped closer to his brother. He stood half a foot taller than Claude, and though Claude was tough, a vicious street fighter when it came to that, a fight between them would be no contest. "Shut your mouth, motherfucker."

Claude smirked. He was easy to wind up. Still, no point getting into a fight here on the street. They needed to get this assignment finished first. Then there might just be a power struggle.

"Go on inside," Claude said. "I'll wait out here. Get yourself a shot of something strong."

Clement managed to keep his mouth shut. He crossed the street and lingered at the bar door for a moment, making sure Kane had sufficient time to get a drink. A moment later, he stepped inside.

An hour later, and four more pints and a couple of shots to the wind, Kane's mood had inevitably slumped. He had tried engaging various bar mates in light conversation, but for whatever reason, they had politely... in most cases... made their excuses and moved away.

As they often did, dark thoughts swirled in his mind when deep into a drinking binge. Images flashed as his pulse quickened. Kane knew he should get back to the hotel and sleep it off. He knew that, but the lure of the next drink was a powerful force; lately, he hadn't the strength to fight it.

In his mind's eye, he was suddenly on a cliff edge in

Peru's Sacred Valley, clinging to life as his best friend Evan lost his. Then he was pulling dead bodies from a raging river in Japan. Being shot by gangsters, and a mad neo-Nazi. The Valley of the Kings, with gunshots and screams, and murdered children in Mexico. His brother, Danny, missing for decades, and it was all Kane's fault...

That, at least, had seen a happy ending, and he subconsciously cuffed at a tear that had escaped the corner of one eye as his mind settled on an image of Alexandria Ridley.

After the troubles in Egypt, and after they'd returned home to recuperate, he had been about to propose to Alex. He never got the chance. He had held a ring in his hand, his grandmother's antique engagement ring, when a helicopter had landed in the grounds of the Kane Estate on the Norfolk/Suffolk border. A man had approached, and had made Kane an offer he couldn't refuse. Ridley had encouraged him, and Kane knew he would get his chance to propose again soon.

The work opportunity had not materialised in the end... a chance to hunt for the true Dead Sea Scrolls after the existing ones had been revealed as an elaborate hoax. Kane had raced back to England after his wasted trip to the Sinai Peninsula, but Ridley had gone. She had not returned a single phone call in the months since, and he had no idea where she was. Hence, he'd fled to the anonymity of Cambodia, for sorrow drowning and self-pity wallowing, things that, to his shame, he'd become very good at.

"You okay sir?" Kane didn't hear the bartender's concerned question.

Why am I here? Kane wondered. *All this way for some wild goose chase. You're an idiot... Dad was right.*

"Sir?"

Kane heard this time. "Yes? I'm sorry, did you say something?"

"I asked if you were okay."

"Oh, thanks. Yes, I'm fine… gin… double… on the rocks."

Kane took out his mobile phone and, with shaking hands, made a call.

Chapter Nineteen

Clement was impatient. The man they were tasked with following—and later, dispatching—was, quite simply, on a mad bender. The urge to take him out tonight and be done with it was strong... especially since Kane had broken his nose in half. Just then he spotted Kane take out his phone. He knew Kane knew they were going to be watching him. However, Francois had explicitly warned them not to hurt him, and if Kane got spooked knowing they were close, he might do a runner and disappear; that would not go down well with the boss. Clement needed to find out who Kane was cToullang.

"Hey, buddy," Clement said to a young guy walking by. "Want to earn a hundred bucks? It'll take you two minutes, and no funny business."

The guy eyed Clement suspiciously for a second, then greed got the better of him. "Sure."

"See that tall guy at the bar, cellphone in his hand?"

"Yeah, I see him. What about it?"

"Go stand next to him, find out who he's cToullang. I need a name. Details about what they discuss. Got it?"

The man nodded and held out his palm. Clement stuffed a hundred into it. "Go, and don't think of running off with the money."

The guy grinned and went to the bar, nudging his way next to Kane. Clement grunted and returned to his seat, never taking his eye off Kane and his new spy.

Sizing up Kane now, it was obvious the man was a drunk, though he was still clearly in good shape and Clement knew how well he could handle himself. He would need to remain cautious, but one day, once Francois gave the word, Clement would relish smashing the limey bastard to a pulp and feeding him to the fishes.

Against his better judgement—he knew it would leave him disappointed—Kane called Ridley, but after only two rings he'd ended the call. *Why would she answer? What would I say if she did answer, which she wouldn't? Who the hell do I think I am? I should never have attempted to propose.*

Kane had known it was risky to propose to Alex. Her fierce independence was one of the things he'd always loved most about Ridley, ever since they'd first met almost two decades earlier. She had to have known that's what he was doing that afternoon at the estate. There had been no official mention of an engagement, and she hadn't even seen the ring he'd held secretly. But Ridley was smart, much smarter than Kane, he knew, and super-intuitive. She had worked it out, and he had scared her off. It had to be that. Didn't it? The worst was, maybe he'd never know. Perhaps he'd never even see the love of his life again.

I'm so fucking stupid… so, so stupid.

Kane took a deep breath then polished off the double gin. He checked his watch… 8:45 pm. Quarter to two in the morning in the UK. He made another call anyway. It was answered on the first ring.

"Hiram? Is everything alright?" came Professor John O'nians' smooth voice. "Where on earth have you been the last couple of months? Are you okay? You've had people worried sick."

"Hello, John. Listen… I'm sorry for cToullang so late… I hope I didn't wake you or Elizabeth?"

"Elizabeth is fine. You, however, do not sound fine. Give me a minute… I'll pick up again in the study." Kane heard the phone click and imagined John scrambling quietly out of his bed, putting on slippers and a dressing gown, and making his way downstairs to his vast study and picking up the receiver of the phone on his antique desk, which Kane had sat at himself many times over the years.

"So, my boy, what is it? It's unlike you to call in the middle of the night… especially after so long." John's voice had lost its frantic edge, and for Kane suddenly everything felt a little better.

He didn't answer for long moments. He wasn't sure what to say. Didn't even really know why he'd called. Then he realised he simply needed a friend, and John was about his only friend left in the world. "I wanted to ask you something."

"Wait, are you in a bar? Where even are you?" John asked, concern now back in his voice. "You know I won't judge you. None of us will."

Kane nodded. "I'm sorry I just disappeared after… you know, after Egypt. It's been a difficult time."

"It wasn't your fault. None of it!" the professor declared. "Come home, Hiram. Come back to England and we'll get you sorted out."

How does he know I'm not in England? John O'nians was a world-renowned professor and knew people in every corner of the globe. Still, Kane didn't think anyone knew he'd gone to Cambodia to hide away from everything. Certainly, no one knew he'd just arrived in D.C. Did they?

"I'll come back soon, John, I promise. First, I'm into something here…" A long pause followed, only broken when John spoke next.

"Into something? Son, you're always into something," he said, but his tone was light. Kane almost smiled. "What is it? Why don't you fly to London and we can talk about it over a… a cuppa?"

Kane exhaled. He could always rely on the prof to make him feel better. He could rely on John for anything. "I can't come home, John, not yet. I'm on a… what the hell, I'll just come out and say it. I'm on a treasure hunt."

Kane heard the professor audibly exhale, as if in relief. "Well that's fabulous," John said, sounding genuinely relieved. "That's what you do, Hiram, and your grandfather before you. He, and you, are two of the very best."

Was one of the best, Kane mused, but decided not to say it.

"Oak Island. The Money Pit. The *Fantome*," Kane listed, knowing the prof would definitely be familiar with them.

"Ah yes, the mysterious lost treasure," John said without missing a beat, almost as if it wasn't even a surprise. "Fascinating story, isn't it? So intriguing. Such an enigma. Of course, it's been all over the TV in recent years. However, I have to say that I don't think it's there anymore… I mean, any treasure."

Kane was relieved to be speaking to someone familiar. John had such a gentle manner about him, and had the ability to put anyone at ease. It was Kane's turn to exhale, meanwhile raising his empty glass to the bartender, who swiftly refilled it with two more neat gins. Kane took a long swig, then continued.

"Do you really believe that, John? There's no evidence any treasure was ever removed from the island, right? No artefacts have ever turned up in any museums, have they? Nor on the blackmarket, as far as I know?"

If anyone on the planet had heard of such news, it would be John, with his vast network of contacts in all levels of the art world. "Yes, that's true," he conceded, "but you and I both know, that doesn't prove anything. It's a mystery over two centuries old. You really believe that in all that time, no one has found anything? Oak Island isn't very big. If there was something there, it would have been found by now. No, my boy, I'm afraid I can't tell you anything more positive. So why don't you just come home, eh? Everyone will be glad to see you."

Not everyone, Kane thought. "I can't John, I just can't!" Kane said, a little more firmly than he'd intended. "Sorry. Listen, humour me for a moment. Let's say I insisted, and nothing you could say or do could dissuade me… what's my next move?"

John exhaled. Kane heard it, and a smile twinkled his eyes. He knew that sigh. It meant resignation.

"I might have a friend," John said simply, and now Kane grinned. "I'm giving you a number. New Orleans. Are you writing this down?"

"Yes," Kane lied.

John O'nians ended the call with Kane. Then he grinned, and immediately made another one.

Moments later, as the spy returned to Clement and explained all he'd heard, Clement also grinned.

Chapter Twenty

Kane's late-night arrival into the heart of The Big Easy had proven impossible to ignore. He took a cab from the airport in the direction of his hotel in the French Quarter, yet before they were even within a mile, the driver told Kane there was no way he could get him any closer.

"Mardi Gras, man… biggest and best party of the year in the entire country. Prolly the world. You chose a good night to arrive, buddy."

Kane had to admit he'd had no idea it was Mardi Gras. Didn't stop him smiling when he stepped out into the humid evening air. The hotel operated a 24-hour reception, so he decided to stay out.

As it was, Kane edged slowly from one bar to the next, sometimes taking his drink—a Sazerac cocktail, a Mardi Gras favourite—outside into the wild party atmosphere amid thousands of Mardi Gras revellers. Kane had seen images and videos of the annual festival before, but found himself in no way prepared for just how raucous it was. On every corner, jazz bands blasted out their tunes, with dozens, even hundreds of partiers singing along. The drinks flowed as fast as the time, and before long Kane had closed in on his hotel, the famous Maison de la Luz on Carondelet Street, just yards from Lafayette Square. It was Francois' money... why not go for the best?

Just one more cocktail, he lied to himself. *Just one more.*

Several beers and a dozen Sazeracs later, Kane stumbled into the hotel. It was almost four in the morning, yet outside it was as frenetic as when when he'd arrived at nine. Kane was a good drinker, able to hold more than most. But the spirit pours in New Orleans were large and strong, and the quantity of alcohol was taking its toll. By the time he'd slurred his way through the laborious check-in process and made his way to the first-floor suite, he was almost done for as he kicked off his shoes, pulled off his clothes, tripped and almost put his head through an antique glass coffee table, then fell into bed. He was asleep in seconds.

Kane rolled over and dry-heaved. Dribble followed, sparkling on his chin for a moment before plummeting to the floorboards. He looked down at the spit abstractedly and knew there were no floorboards in his house. Nor were there floorboards in his apartment in Cuzco.

This time the heave wasn't so dry, and he puked up a bizarre orange, almost golden liquid, then puked again.

A memory flashed in his brain, which thudded, causing more nausea to roil in his guts. The image fluttered and flashed, like a dangling bulb swarmed by blinded moths. Then it blinked out. Gone.

Kane rolled back onto the bed and stared at the ceiling, which he also didn't recognise. The memory flitted again. Faded. Buzzed in his ears instead. Then, silence.

"Alex?"

Kane heard the word, though he didn't realise he'd said it himself.

Alex? Where...? Why...?

"There he is. Grab him," came a harsh voice from the doorway. "Grab him. The boss said to shake him up a little. So let's shake him up."

Instincts launched Kane from the bed. He landed solidly on two feet. So far so good.

One foot slipped in the combination of spit and vomit —*is that blood?*—and he crunched down onto one knee.

He risked a glance over a shoulder. Over the other shoulder he spotted two huge men. Familiar faces. A big, crooked nose. One held a gun in front of him.

What the fuck?! Where the hell am I?

Kane regained his balance and stood on powerful legs. Automatically grabbing his backpack, he ran bare-footed for the French doors across the space. He reached them and yanked them open as a bullet destroyed the glass of the left door.

"What the fuck are you doing?" yelled Clement. "We can't kill him yet."

"I... fuck, Clement, it was an accident... I didn't mean to shoot," growled Claude. "I was just pointing it to scare him."

Kane stepped out into torrential rain on the first-floor balcony. Below, New Orleans' carnival-goers had outlasted him by several hours.

In a fleeting moment of rare clarity, Kane figured he had less than two seconds to make a choice. Two seconds not to die, unaware the bullet hadn't been meant for him.

"Fuck it!" he muttered, and jumped.

Didn't land well. Not well at all.

Could've been worse.

Mardi Gras revellers had filled the skip with so many empty plastic cups and beer cans that his fall was somewhat broken. *Better a somewhat broken fall than a really broken ankle or skull,* he mused as he dived out of the skip and crouched behind its bulk.

Reams—not reams, squadrons—of partiers marched past. Not a single one of them paid the almost-naked Englishman a second glance.

Kane dared a look back up at the balcony. *No one there. That's good. Isn't it?*

"There! By the dumpster. Go! No more shooting," Clement demanded.

Oh, shit.

Kane stood and ran, letting muscle memory usurp his desire to crawl into a ball and accept what he knew was coming. What he knew he deserved.

What he wanted?

Do I?

No. No, I…

No!

"Not dying today," he muttered. *Move, you idiot!*

Move he did.

Three yards…

Shaquille O'Neil—or a man as big and strong as the NBA legend—proved awkward to negotiate… an impenetrable barrier.

"Hey, man," the huge guy yelled at Kane. "Be careful!"

"Sorry," Kane mumbled as he scraped himself from the glistening cobbles of Bourbon Street. "I'm sorry, it was an—"

The behemoth swatted Kane away as if he were nothing more than a drunken wreck. *Actually…*

"Hey, who you pointing that gun at, muthafucka?" Kane heard over his shoulder as he slipped and stumbled into the shadows and tumbled into a side street, down which he ran flat-out for five minutes, focusing only on planting one bare foot in front of the other and getting far away from whoever it was that wanted him dead.

Only one person knew that Kane was in New Orleans. One woman.

Which meant...

No!

With a mile in the legs and the Sazerac more or less sweated from his system—Kane learned quickly that the Louisiana humidity was good for detoxing; he'd also learned that the Louisiana humidity was equally adept at encouraging the libation of more toxins—Kane felt almost human again. Well, almost human. Normal-ish? Yeah, he'd take that. For now.

There was just the small matter of men with guns trying to shoot him dead. Which was usually a problem when you enjoyed being alive.

Do I enjoy being alive?

Alex?

Kane placed his sweaty palms on a damp red-brick wall and inhaled greedily of the moist air. Each breath felt like a gulp of water as it went down. Quenching. Revitalising. Lifesaving.

Alright, what's next?

Wait...

Kane dug deep into the annals of his addled brain. Was it pickled yet? He thought it probably was.

The professor... John O'nians'... his friend?

Kane knew of only one person in New Orleans. She was the reason he was here. The one the professor had told him to visit. *The bayou?*

Yes, the university on the bayou.

Despite recent evidence suggesting this as yet unknown woman was somehow involved in trying to kill him, Kane knew that it simply couldn't be the case. She was John O'nians' friend. There was no way she'd be involved in anything like this. With little choice other than to trust the professor, and his own instincts, Kane reached for his mobile phone, then remembered with stark clarity he was wearing nothing more than his boxer shorts and his rapidly diminishing dignity.

Oh, bollocks.

He glanced about, getting his bearings. To the east a weak sun battled up through brooding swathes of threatening clouds. An hour until day-break.

Where the hell am I?
What the hell am I doing here?

Chapter Twenty-One

Kane didn't like stealing... he had never stolen anything in his life before. Yet, walking around almost naked before any stores were open, and with not more than a few dollars on his person—he had been cognisant enough to have grabbed his backpack but hadn't recalled the bulk of cash before he'd escaped the suite—he had good reason to swipe some clothes he'd spotted hanging on a line in a garden as he made his way cautiously towards town again. The clothes had been a huge stroke of luck. Then, when he spotted a five-dollar note fluttering in the breeze near a gutter, he almost smiled. Almost, but not quite. An hour ago two men had tried to kill him and he was lucky to be alive. He snatched up the five bucks and shoved it in his pocket. Well, not his pocket, exactly... someone else's pocket. But still...

Now feeling just about ready to tackle the day, though still shoe-less, Kane made his way back towards the edge of the city. He needed shoes and a phone box... the order didn't matter. It was still early... not even six by his best guess, and no Goodwill stores would open for a few hours.

A phone was more pressing than shoes anyway, and he soon came to a beaten-up yet seemingly functional public phone booth. *It's a wonder they still exist*, Kane thought, yet wherever in the world they were, they still reeked of piss. *Everyone has mobile phones these days.* Now he grinned. *Except me.*

A five-dollar note was useless at a phone box, but in another stroke of luck he spotted an all-night diner along the road, and hustled his way to it. The dour-faced waitress —*unsurprisingly dour after pulling an all-nighter,* Kane mused— grunted as he approached the counter. Whether she'd seen his bare feet or not, he wasn't sure.

"Coffee to go, please," Kane said, trying to keep his accent neutral. "Hold the milk."

"You got it," the waitress mumbled back, pouring coffee from a large urn into a takeaway cup. "Buck twenty."

"Thank you. Could I get some change for the phone?"

Now the waitress eyed Kane. *Who the hell uses pay phones these days?* her expression intimated, but she didn't comment. *Washed up bums,* Kane assumed she thought, looking him up and down. Whatever it was, she kept it to herself. "Sure thing."

He was back at the phone box, feeling better after the welcome hit of caffeine. Kane didn't exactly have hyper-thymesia syndrome—basically, an unusually high ability to memorise or recall event details. However, he was someone who almost always remembered phone numbers, even if he'd only read it once. It had served him well as a younger man, when dating was a thing and before mobile phones were commonplace. It served him well now. Despite his condition, he recalled the number John O'nians had given him. Glancing around, still very aware the gun-toting brothers were out there somewhere, no doubt keen to once again make his acquaintance, he stepped into the battered phone booth. It was early, but Kane decided to make the call. It answered after two rings.

"Allo? This is Professor Peerdeman," came a woman's European-accented voice. *Belgian?* Kane mused. *Dutch?*

"Ah yes, hello. Erm, sorry to call so early, but—"

"Hiram Kane," the professor said. It wasn't a question. "I've been expecting your call."

"Yes, I'm Hiram. A mutual friend said I should—"

"John told me you call. He did not say at five in the morning." The tone was flat, yet Kane sensed a hint of mischief.

Only five? Oh, shit. "Um, sorry," Kane said, feeling bad in case he'd woken her.

"Don't worry... We Dutch are early risers." *Yes, Dutch.* "How can I help you, Hiram?" she asked. "Where are you?"

"Sorry to call so early, but I'm in some deep shit. And..."—Kane glanced around for any obvious landmarks—"I don't know where I am. There's a diner... Lou's All Nighter?"

"Ah, yes... Lou's. What the hell are you doing all the way out there? It's a little... unsavoury in that area."

"Long story," Kane answered simply. As understatements went... even by Kane's standards, that was a good one.

"Listen, it's a thirty-minute drive. Don't move. I'll leave now."

"Okay, great. Thanks a lot, um, professor...?"

"Call me Anja."

Twenty minutes later, Professor Anja Peerdeman slowed her antiquated Volvo to a stop near the diner and gave a couple of short, sharp honks of her horn to get Kane's attention. He'd taken up residence in a quiet corner of the diner, and believing himself safe, for now, he'd played the posh English accent card on the now chirpy waitress, Susannah, explaining how he'd been beaten up and robbed. She had taken the bait, and told Kane she would pay for the breakfast herself. A few minutes later she had served him a large plate of eggs hussarde, and Kane promised to mail her a cheque; a promise he would keep if only he could stay alive long enough.

He thanked Susannah, and made his way out to the professor's car, swung open the door and climbed in.

"Nice shoes," Anja quipped through a wry smile as she sped away, apparently eager to leave the area as soon as possible. "You can explain why you're bare-footed later," she said. "First let's get you home and cleaned up."

Small talk mostly revolving around their mutual admiration for Professor O'nians filled the short drive. It transpired John had been mentor to both Anja and Kane, though almost a decade apart. They were of similar ages, but Anja had started at university later, during the professor's years up in Boston, at Harvard. She had followed her studies through, all the way to PhD level, and was now Professor of Symbolism at Tulane University.

She soon pulled off the main highway and through a stand of old-growth cottonwood trees, down a bumpy, muddy trail, finally coming to a stop at a large but humble-looking nondescript wooden structure surrounded on three sides by huge trees, and with a clearing that led down towards a large swampy pond.

"Home," Anja declared. "Come on in."

Kane followed Anja inside through a well-secured front door, complete with electronic key code panel. "Can't be too careful," she muttered as she locked the door behind them. "Shower's through there. I'll get you some more suitable clothes," she added before striding off along a corridor and out of sight.

Kane glanced around. If ever there was a classic, stereotypical look to an art world professor, and their private space, this was it. Piles of books sat on tables and chairs, including some of John's, he noted. A map of Europe lay spread out on a large table. Paintings by a variety of Flemish artists hung on the walls. It was organised chaos, and felt very familiar to Kane.

He made his way to the guest bathroom and stepped eagerly into the shower. As he stood under the revitalising flow of hot water his mind drifted to the reasons he had travelled to the States in the first place. The Frenchman. Francois's men had tried to kill him last night. But why? He hadn't given the bastards any reason to make them think he was betraying their boss. It didn't make sense. As far as they knew, he was still working with Francois. Yet, no one else knew he was even in the country. *Did they?* Maybe after a shower, things would start to make sense.

He stepped out of the stall, surprised to find a pile of clothes and some slippers placed on a side table. *Hmm… I'm sure I locked the door?* Kane dried himself and got dressed, then made his way along the same corridor Anja had taken. He found her sitting at a large dining table in an open-plan kitchen.

Without asking, she poured him coffee.

"Thank you," Kane said. "And thanks for picking me up. So, uh, do you know why I'm here?"

Anja nodded. "John mentioned you were on a fool's errand. He apparently likes fools, and asked me to help." That mischief again, twinkling in her eyes.

Kane nodded. "Fool's errand, eh? Maybe. The man…

the contact I'm working with... he doesn't think so." Kane wasn't sure what to think anymore.

"What about the hundreds of people before him? Before you? Maybe even thousands. Empty handed. No proof of any treasure. Certainly not on Oak Island. Were they fools?"

"Maybe they were unlucky," Kane countered. "Maybe they were—"

"Fools?" Anja finished. "Look, I understand why you would want to go after the Oak Island treasure. I know about you. I've known about you for a long time, and followed your career ever since I first met John. He loves you, you know? Thinks of you as the son he never had."

Kane nodded. "He's a special man," he said quietly, yet another of his exceptional understatements.

"John has asked me to help you. I would normally stay well clear of anything to do with the Oak Island enigma. And anything to do with the legend of the *Fantome*."

Kane noticed Anja gulp. She was also a little fidgety, as if the conversation was making her uncomfortable.

She continued anyway. "Believe me, nothing good can come of a new quest to get to the bottom of that mystery. But..."

Kane fixed his eyes on Anja's. There was a definite sparkle there. Or was it something else? Concern? "But what?" he asked.

Anja held Kane's gaze. Appraising. Contemplating. With a subtle nod, almost as if to herself, she arrived at a decision. "Grab your bag and come with me... there's something I'd like to show you."

Chapter Twenty-Two

Anja led Kane back along the hallway and paused at a nondescript door. Sliding down a discreet metal hatch revealed a digital keypad, and when Anja turned to see Kane staring at it, wide-eyed, he turned away in embarrassment. A moment later, he heard a gentle pneumatic hiss, and the normal-looking pine door swung open. He turned back to see Anja stepping through into a dark stairwell, beckoning him to follow. Once inside, she depressed a switch on the wall and the door eased silently closed, then a series of locks clicked shut.

"Cool, huh?" Anja said matter-of-factly.

"Um, yes. Wow," was all Kane could manage. He followed Anja down one flight of stairs, and stepped into what he expected to be a basement.

That's what he'd expected. It is not what he saw.

At first glance it looked like the bridge of the Starship Enterprise. Banks of large, flat-screen monitors filled one wall. A series of desks loaded with high-tech computer equipment stood off to the right. A few glass cabinets dotted about the large space contained a variety of artefacts, ranging from some gold ornaments, a couple of ornate sculptures, and a ceremonial sword Kane thought to be Samurai, something he had witnessed close up once before and never wished to again. He blinked away the unwanted image of a shamed Yakuza man's head being liberated from its body, and tried to take in the rest of the room.

"What is… Why do you… wow," Kane mumbled, feeling suitably impressed—no, blown away—by the surprising underground treasure trove. That's when he spotted something that really caught his attention. On one wall, set apart from other artefacts and displays, was a piece of parchment. Set behind glass, it was about A4-sized and in its centre was a faded diagram. Kane stepped closer and tried to discern the markings, but it was too faint. The only thing he was certain about was that it had something to do with the Masons, as he could just make out the iconic carpenter's square and compass associated with the mysterious group. Only two words were evident, and he had to strain his eyes to read them: *The Allegiance?*

"What is—"

"We all need hobbies, right?" Anja said, noticing Kane's intrigue in the ancient parchment and leading him swiftly away by the arm. "I can't tell you about everything I do here," she added. "Nor for whom I work. Just assume I really like investigating secret societies and cults, and their so-called hidden messages in wider society. It's better to keep this kind of stuff hidden away."

"Sounds like you're a conspiracy theorist," Kane said, a little too easily. "Not that there's anything wrong with that," he added, quickly digging himself out of the hole he felt sure he'd just dug.

"Something like that," Anja said, grinning, apparently

enjoying watching Kane squirm a little. "So, now you know a little about me, why don't you ask your question?"

"What question?"

"Look, John sent you here for a reason. He knows that I know a lot about the kinds of people who might be looking for the same thing you are."

Kane nodded. He exhaled, and fixed his eyes on the Dutch professor. "Who the hell is trying to kill me?"

Anja looked sympathetic, as if she knew, but couldn't say. That didn't look good to Kane. "The man... the French guy I mentioned, he seemed so convincing. He explained he was unable to search for the treasure himself, so is paying me to find it. It did all seem odd, especially when he gave his scarcely veiled warning. And there were the bastards who tried to kill me. Anyway, I... well, I needed a kick in the arse, and meeting Francois was it. Are you saying he is definitely *not* a simple treasure-hunting philanthropist? Certainly seems that way now, doesn't it."

"Listen, Hiram, I can't be certain who they are," she told him. "There are a few possible organisations that don't want the enigma surrounding Oak Island to be solved."

"But why, though? What harm could come of it?" Kane couldn't understand why anyone would need to hide information about a long-lost ancient treasure. "It doesn't make sense."

"No, it wouldn't make sense... if it were only simply lost treasure in the physical sense. What if it were more? What if the treasure were actually not chests of gold and pearls?" she said, an unreadable look in her eye.

"What do you mean? You're not suggesting it's like *The Da Vinci Code*, when the treasure was actually the fact that Jesus had got his rocks off at least once in his life?"

Anja chuckled. "Not exactly like that, no, but you're on the right track. What have you learned in your research so far?"

"I've read that the treasure, whatever it actually was, was allegedly stolen from The White House by the British, after which they burned down the building. And that the treasure might very well have been looted from the Holy Land, removed by the Knights Templar and later placed under the care of the Freemasons."

Anja nodded. "That's certainly one of the most popular theories. Assume that theory is true. Also, assume there is no longer any lost treasure on Oak Island. Hiram, you're one of the world's foremost explorers. Right? You find things others haven't been able to. Imagine then, if you were allowed to go to Oak Island, and if you of all people couldn't find anything, then clearly there is nothing there. That would be highly embarrassing, wouldn't it, for a certain organisation that you have read is highly involved. So, I ask you again… who would not want that secret out? Who might want you dead?"

Kane shook his head. "The Masons? Are you saying the Masons sent two men to try to kill me?"

Anja's lips pursed. "Like I said… I can't be certain."

"Come on, Anja. John sent me here for a reason, as you said yourself. Why, if not to get any info?"

Anja exhaled, then nodded gently. "Could be, yes."

"Could be, or probably?"

"Could be… probably," Anja conceded, exhaling again but now with concern creasing her brow.

"Well, shit, that's not good," Kane said, taking his understatement game to a whole new level.

Anja suggested Kane take a walk down to the lake, to get some air and to try and relax a little. Kane agreed and as she watched him stride out beneath the cottonwoods towards the lake shore, she made a call.

John O'nians picked up on the first ring.

"He's here," she told him.

"How's he doing?" John asked.

"People shot at him, John. I'm worried about him. I don't know who it was, but it doesn't sound like the usual suspects. And I'm sure of that, because if it was them they wouldn't have—"

"Missed," O'nians finished. "Very true. So who do we think it is?"

"Don't know. My guess is that they're a new player, John, someone not on the organisation's radar. It could even be the benefactor's men gone rogue. It's happened before."

"Don't remind me."

"I tried talking him out of going to Oak Island, as we discussed. He's adamant he wants to go." Anja exhaled. "So I guess we're on track. Good job he's stubborn, just like you, and just as you said he would be. What do we do?"

Professor O'nians was silent for many moments, and Anja knew he was considering the best course of action for his beloved protégé. She had known the professor for close to two decades, and his long silences usually meant things were very bad.

Anja heard John clear his throat, and braced herself for what was to come. She had come to like Kane in their few short moments together, and she knew John loved him. Thus, Anja feared the worst.

John said, "We let things play out. He's on the course we hoped for. But Anja?"

"What is it, John?" She didn't like the sound of this.
"I think it's time to call in The Squad."

Chapter Twenty-Three

Clement had always considered himself the smarter of the two brothers. Not just because he was older, and more experienced in the ways of the world. It was simply because he thought Claude was stupid.

Clement had been reluctant to take on this assignment. Following people wasn't their usual gig... they were more used to finding people and killing them, end of story. But Francois, their new boss, was paying them well—too well for this kind of work, it seemed—and it had been too good to refuse. They had no idea what organisation Francois represented, though Clement suspected it was bigger than just the man himself. The huge fee was to ensure they didn't ask any questions, and so far he'd refrained.

The way Claude was behaving though was getting a little hairy for Clement... and putting the bonus payout upon successful completion of the mission at considerable risk.

It had been Claude who had burst into Kane's room, alerting him to their presence and thus affording him a momentary chance of escape before they'd applied a little more pressure and roughed him up a bit. Clement had instructed his younger brother to use the skeleton digital keycard they'd stolen from a terrified maid and sneak in. He had seen first-hand the inebriated state the man was in back in the bars and on the streets, and didn't think they would have woken him by entering the suite quietly. They were to go in, take care of business and be long gone before anyone found the man's beaten body.

Claude was often impatient, however, and lately had been acting up, and coiled like a spring. In the moments outside the suite, his impatience had won over and he simply couldn't wait any longer, so he had kicked the door in, risking them being caught. A moment later, they'd watched on as an almost-naked Kane had launched himself off the balcony and disappeared into the throngs of Mardi Gras revellers. Despite giving chase, they had lost him. Clement only hoped they'd successfully disconnected the swanky hotel's CCTV system, and hadn't been picked up on camera.

So the Englishman had escaped a beating. However, after a quick call back to headquarters, Clement felt they knew where Kane had gone. His tech guy had revealed a well-known link between Hiram Kane and his former professor and mentor, John O'nians, and then found a subsequent link between O'nians and a symbology professor by the name of Peerdeman.

"It has to be her Kane's here to see," Clement said, proud of his investigative skills. He typed the name Anja Peerdeman into the online app Spokeo and waited while the results pinged in. There were only two. "One in Philadelphia, and what do you know, one right here in New Orleans. Bingo," he said, flicking Claude a smug grin.

"Well done, Columbo. Now let's go, before I die of boredom."

The brothers climbed into their rented SUV, not before depositing their special ops bags in the trunk. Clement activated the Satnav and typed in the location provided by the Spokeo app. It didn't give an exact address, but since there was only one property registered within a five-mile radius, Clement felt pretty sure he knew where to go. "Thirty minutes," Clement declared.

Claude grunted. "Make it twenty or I'm driving. Listen, I know you're my boss and older brother, and I sometimes give you shit. But I—"

"Sometimes? Ha, what a fucking joke," Clement spat.

"Okay fine, I give you a lot of shit. But hear me out. I don't like this. I don't trust Francois anymore and I don't like how this is shaping up."

Clement turned to face his younger brother. He didn't really like it either. "What're you suggesting?"

"Listen, this Kane guy. He's well connected. He knows our faces. What if he's playing us? Setting us up somehow? He seems too smart to have been tricked by Francois. He's tough, too… we can't deny that."

Clement nodded, glancing at his busted nose in the rearview mirror.

"He could be using us for this job, then he could easily set us up too. I just don't like it, so I suggest we take Kane out, and then go to Francois and take him out too."

Clement didn't answer for several seconds, pondering his younger brother's words. Claude rarely spoke so earnestly, and it gave him pause to think. Finally, a smile creased his eyes. It was the first time he'd agreed with anything Claude had said in years. He turned to him, and said, "Brother, you're right. Let's kill Kane and Francois. It's time we took over the business."

"So what do I do?" Kane asked as he rejoined Anja in the basement treasure hall. He noticed her eyes had lost their sparkle.

"I've given this a lot of thought. I don't think it's safe for you to stay here," she responded. "The more I think about it, the more I realise it was a mistake for John to send you to me. Don't worry though. This old place is more secure than it looks. In terms of what's next, there is only one obvious choice. Since you're ignoring the advice of both John and I, you need to go to Nova Scotia, to the archives in Halifax. I think that's your next step. I highly recommend you don't go directly to Oak Island."

"What will I learn at the archives? What can I find out there that you can't tell me now?"

Anja inhaled, as if it were a good question. "Listen, I—" The professor's voice trailed off, and her head cocked to one side, as if she'd heard something. Her eyes narrowed in concentration.

"What is it?" Kane hadn't heard a thing.

Anja held a finger to her lips, remaining silent. She closed her eyes, listening intently. Kane noticed her head shake just a tiny bit.

"What is it?" Kane asked again, his pulse quickening slightly.

Anja exhaled. "Nothing. It's nothing. So, to answer your question, the archives, that's—" Anja cut herself short again and strode over to a cabinet against a side wall and pulled it open, revealing several hunting rifles on a wooden rack. "You need to leave. Now. They're here!"

Chapter Twenty-Four

Clement made it to where he believed the professor's property began. There was no obvious boundary to the vast area, but a forest of cottonwoods, swaying under a stiff breeze, and a snaking series of narrow waterways served as a natural border to the 4-acre spread. "This is it." Clement glanced at his watch. "Nineteen minutes."

Claude ignored him and nodded forwards. Clement edged the SUV across a shallow ditch and onto the property, slowly following the muddy track towards where Google Maps told him the main structure was located.

"We do it my way this time," Clement stated flatly. "We go in quietly, and as soon as we see him, we take him down. If the professor sees our faces, she dies."

Claude didn't answer, but a subtle nod of the head confirmed he'd understood.

Good, the older brother thought, *a little fucking respect. Finally.*

After a couple of minutes of slow progress along the

winding trail, Claude spotted the old structure ahead. "Stop here... we should walk the rest of the way."

"Agreed." Clement edged the door open quietly and stepped out of the SUV, and went to the rear to retrieve the weapons bag.

Claude followed suit, but just as he exited the vehicle a sudden gust of wind slammed the car door shut.

"Jesus," hissed Clement, his face screwing up in anger. "Why don't you hit the horn a few times too, eh?"

Clement then realised he had left his own door open too, and hustled around to close it. Too late. Half a dozen seconds after Claude's door had slammed, Clement's did the same. "Fuck."

"So smart, big brother," Claude spat, his mouth curled into a sneer. "Fuck your way... I'm going in."

"Who is here?" Kane asked. "What's going on?"

"I haven't had a single visitor all the way out here in the last three years. And now, on the day you show up? It isn't the fucking Avon lady. You have to go."

"Go where?"

Anja flicked open a latch in the back of the rifle cabinet, and pulled the back wall forwards, revealing a brick-lined tunnel. "Through there. Follow it for five minutes and it'll take you to the eastern edge of the property. There's a small wooden shed, hidden behind some thick undergrowth. Inside you'll find a motorbike. Key's in the ignition. Here's your bag," she said, thrusting it at him. "Get out of here. Go, now!"

Kane's wide eyes stared into the dark tunnel. *What the fuck? Who is this woman?* "What about you?"

"I'll follow behind you in two minutes. I have to stay to

send an important message. Don't worry about me. We Dutch women are very resilient. Go on, get out of here. These people don't mess about. Believe me, if they find you, they will kill you. Now go, and don't look back."

Anja practically shoved Kane through the tunnel entrance before he could protest. The moment he was inside, she shut the door, slid the rifle rack back into place and closed the cabinet, locking it behind him.

After hustling to a computer console across the room, Anja flicked a switch and waited two seconds until a green light blinked on. "Call Caesar," she instructed the system. A series of electronic beeps sounded, and then a click as the line connected. "John, it's me. Someone's here. I don't know who. Can't take any risks. I'm shutting us down."

Clement and Claude had made it into the house undisturbed. They had encountered some decent security measures, but they weren't stupid—well, sometimes they were but they had smart people on the end of a phone call —and had disabled them easily.

The same was true of the secret door down to the basement, and as they tiptoed down the stairs, they heard Kane's voice.

The door behind Anja exploded in a burst of splintered wood and brick fragments as first Claude then Clement charged into the room, their weapons raised. The two men scanned the space, searching for Kane. He was nowhere in view.

"Where is he?" demanded Clement.

Anja stared in disbelief at the intruders. They didn't know who she was, but she definitely knew who they were, and the disbelief came from the fact that she had fucking hired them to protect Kane. And that could only mean one thing: Kane was now fending for himself.

She forced the shock from her face, and despite the fact that the organisation's plan was unravelling before her very eyes, she commanded herself to remain calm.

"Where is who?" Anja replied. She'd made the inexcusable mistake of placing the rifle down when making the call. Now it was out of reach.

"Last chance… where is Hiram Kane?" asked Clement, his eyes narrowing on the professor.

Anja tried stToullang for time. She knew now that the hired mercenaries had gone rogue and were betraying the scheme's pseudo benefactor, Francois. It had been risky hiring unknown people for this gig, but since they were operating outside of the law, they had to dig a little deeper for the right help. Thus, Anja knew what these men were capable of and she already knew her fate. So, now, assuming the worst, she exhaled, then smiled, hoping Kane could make it safely away, and certain Caesar would take care of the rest.

She took a step towards the gun-toting intruders, then paused and placed her hands on her hips. Still smiling, she said, "Hiram who?"

Claude shot her in the head from point-blank range.

On the other end of the still open phone comms line, John O'nians, A.K.A. Caesar, closed his eyes.

Chapter Twenty-Five

What the fuck was that?

Kane had found himself in enough dark tunnels over recent years that he'd believed if he never saw another one it would still have been too soon. Yet here he was, abruptly making his way along a dark man-made passage underground, apparently escaping two psychopathic killers. Suddenly a deafening, echoing blast rattled through the tunnel, and he froze.

What the hell just happened?

His naïve heart hoped it was just a door slamming. His wise head told him an entirely different tale.

There had been something in Anja's urgent tone that had troubled him. She had remained amazingly calm, but there was determination in her words and steely resolve in her eyes. In fact, unless Kane was mistaken, there had been no surprise evident in her attitude. To Kane it was more as if she had almost expected people to come. If true, who the hell were they? Surely not Francois' goons? And who the hell was Anja herself? No ordinary symbology professor keeps a secret stash of weapons in a high-tech, secret underground space. What the hell was that room? A museum? A science lab?

There was also the way she had hurried him away from the odd Masonic parchment on the wall. Whatever that room really was, it also served as a cover to hide an equally secret tunnel.

Escape tunnel? From whom? Who wants me dead? Who is Professor Peerdeman, and how is she involved? John? Kane knew she was close friends with Professor O'nians, who had sent him to her.

So, what's the link?

There wasn't time to analyse any of that now... he had to get away from the people apparently trying to kill him, whoever they really were.

There was very little light in the passageway, just a few sporadic naked bulbs hanging from the ceiling of what might have been an old mine shaft, though Kane doubted this was a mining area, deep in the Louisiana swamp land. Anja had said the tunnel would emerge at the edge of the property. He obviously didn't know how large the property was, but with so much water in the area, with rivers, lakes and bayous, it couldn't be much farther. As if on cue, he suddenly came to a dead end. Attached to the wall—solid earth reinforced with thick timber beams—was a ladder that led up to a wooden hatch. He paused, fToullang silent to listen in case he was being followed, but all was quiet. Something scurried at his feet, making him jump; it was just a rat. Kane exhaled, trying to regain some composure.

Jesus, who the hell are these people?

He scrambled up several rungs of the ladder, enough so he could reach the hatch, which he gave a gentle shove. It wasn't locked, and he eased it open enough to allow a stream of faint natural light into the shaft. Easing his eyes above the ledge, Kane scanned 180 degrees and, satisfied he was alone, he clambered through the hatch and closed it behind him. As Anja had told him, in the small shed stood a motorbike, hidden beneath a large cover draped over its bulk. He edged to one of the two small windows, which let in just enough light to see within. There was literally nothing inside the shed other than the motorcycle, making it seem to Kane that this was indeed a purpose-built escape route.

Who the hell is Anja Peerdeman?

Suddenly Kane heard an engine start somewhere, perhaps half a mile away, which seemed about right based on how far he'd travelled underground.

Shit!

Wasting no time, Kane yanked the cover away, revealing a Honda CRF450X trail bike. Kane wasn't a motorcycle aficionado but he knew his way around bikes. The body of this machine had been detailed in camouflage paint, rather than the red and white he imagined to have been its former colours. As promised, the key was in the ignition and a helmet sat on the seat. There was also a small bag containing a stack of dollars. He pulled on the helmet and the gloves he found inside it, and tightened the chin strap. Then he quietly swung open the double doors of the shed, and stepped outside, scanning the dense wooded area. Seeing nothing, he returned to the bike, and for the first time spotted a folded sheet of paper attached to the handlebar. He opened it and saw a hand-drawn map of the area, with a series of green arrows illustrating the way to the nearest highway.

Okay, useful.

A flash of light caught his eye and his head shot up.

Through the trees, several hundred yards away, a window or a mirror glinted beneath the sun. An SUV.

Bollocks!

Kane's heart began pounding as a memory flashed like a strobe in his mind. Bali... the temple... the forest... the rice terraces... the mad motorcycle chase around the island to rescue a kidnapped little girl. The girl had lived, but not because of his motorcycle skills.

Got to get out of here. Now!

Kane straddled the seat and turned the key, and the powerful bike roared to life at the touch of a button. He took a few deep breaths, trying to memorise the map he stared at. Two miles, more or less, to leave the forested swamp area and get on the highway. He wondered if he could make it before being caught or cut off by those chasing him. As he gazed at the map, aware he was wasting precious seconds, he didn't think he could.

He twisted the throttle, getting a feel of the first motorcycle he'd been on since that fateful day back in Bali a few years ago. That time he was desperate to save a little girl.

Now it was his own life on the line.

Chapter Twenty-Six

Kane disengaged the clutch and with a last deep breath, he flicked down the visor and accelerated out of the shed, just as the black SUV came tearing up alongside, almost crashing right into him. By mere feet had he avoided a collision, and a quick glance in a rearview mirror suggested another was imminent. Realising he was probably in a life or death race, he threw all caution to the wind and accelerated at full throttle towards a narrow gap in the tree line up ahead, one he hoped the SUV couldn't break.

Momentarily pulling away from his pursuers, Kane thundered over the sodden ground, glad of the choice of motorcycle, no doubt specifically selected, which ate up the yards with ease. He powered through the gap, essentially a natural arch formed by two low-hanging boughs, and sped away, leaning into the curves and relying on muscle memory rather than innate riding skill. A further hundred yards up the winding trail, he dared a look back over his shoulder. No SUV in sight. He couldn't hear it either, and wondered if the chasers had turned back. He slowed the machine to a stop and arched his neck, scanning in all directions, and saw no sign of the sleek black vehicle. Unwilling to rest on his laurels, he pulled away again, heading for where he believed the exit onto the highway was marked on the map.

Seconds passed and Kane had no further sighting of the SUV, nor had he heard it, which was odd in the otherwise near-silent forest. He slowed a little, now anxious the pursuers had somehow gotten ahead of him and were waiting in ambush. He didn't know the terrain, and doubted they did either, though it was all guesswork at this point. Still, with no engine noises or visuals, Kane decided to go all out for the highway. Twisting the throttle towards him, Kane angled through the forest on a direct trajectory towards the road. That's when he realised his mistake; the thick branch came arcing from out of nowhere and slammed into his helmet, flinging him from the motorcycle.

Kane flew through the air as the motorbike's front wheel locked to the left, causing the machine to cartwheel forwards several times before coming to a juddering halt at the base of a towering cottonwood. Somehow, the engine still ticked over.

Kane lay still for a moment, wondering if he was dead. When it became clear he wasn't—his fall was broken by landing in a shallow, marshy stream—he scrambled to his feet, ready to face his would-be attackers. He immediately spotted one trotting towards him, a large man with massive shoulders and a shaved head. Francois' man... the older bastard. He had a revolver in his right hand, raised and pointing in the general direction of Kane's face. Twenty yards to that man's left was the other brother, striding with intent towards him, and forming one half of a two-pronged pincer movement.

Kane's eyes darted in all directions, desperately

searching for an escape route. He glanced back at the men, now clearly recognising their gnarly mugs. Kane had already proven to them he was no mug himself, and could handle a fight. But two of them, both with guns?

No, not this time.

However, he could outrun them. Almost as if they'd anticipated his imminent flee for his life, both men simultaneously fired, the rounds zinging harmlessly past Kane's head, still ensconced in the helmet.

Time to go. Kane yanked off the helmet and dropped it at his feet, then turned on his heels and sprinted for all he was worth, his body aching from the violent impact with the ground beneath the shallow stream, but thankfully not injured. Kane had let his fitness dwindle over the last months of wallowing, yet he was still a fine athlete, and soon pulled away from the killers, darting left and right, around and between the dense trees, initially aiming for the highway which was still half a mile away.

He knew he could outrun the men. Then what? He had no idea how far along the highway he'd need to run to find the next town. So he needed wheels. On a whim, he changed plans, and with that, also changed direction. He veered right, flying over the ground as if his life depended on it, which very clearly, it did. He sprinted perhaps two hundred yards east, then glanced over his shoulder. No sign of the chasing pack, so he angled south and back towards the motorcycle, surely his fastest way out of there. His best hope was that the two men hadn't second-guessed him, and he actually made it back to the bike unmolested. That's what he hoped.

Things never went as planned.

He spotted the motorcycle still lying at the foot of the tree. Yet now, standing next to it, clutching a huge log, was the bigger, slightly older-looking thug. Smiling. Kane didn't spot the man's gun, though he surely had it on him.

What's he playing at? Kane wondered. *He actually wants to fight?*

Other than back at the suite in Kep, it had been several months since Kane had found himself in a similar scrape. On that occasion in Egypt, he had defeated his adversary. This man was bigger, though, and though he had surprised him last time, Kane had to assume he wouldn't be so lucky again. Also, for whatever reason, things had obviously changed; now they wished him dead.

Kane came to a stop. The other man was nowhere in sight. If he could take this bastard out in short order, he believed he could get away. Kane inhaled, then exhaled slowly through his nose, repeating the action several times before stepping towards the huge thug, who in turn stepped towards Kane. Kane paused at the helmet he'd discarded. Anything he could use as a weapon now might just help him, as long as the big guy didn't pull the gun.

"Es-tu prêt à mourir?" Clement growled, ready to dish out a fearful beating before killing his opponent.

Kane's French wasn't perfect, but it was good enough to answer the question. "No, I'm not ready to die. By the way, how's the nose?"

Kane lunged at the thug's feet, swept up the helmet and threw it as hard as he could at the man's head. He was big, but a little slow, and only managed to deflect the helmet at the last second. It was the moment Kane needed, and he launched himself at the monster rugby-style, slamming his shoulder into Clement's waist, sending him backwards, until his feet slipped on the moist ground and he went down.

Kane was upon him, unleashing a series of right crosses down onto the man's considerable chin. Clement was strong and powerful, and absorbed the blows with some ease. He managed to get one hand up, grabbing Kane around the throat and squeezing his windpipe. He was even stronger than Kane had imagined, and Kane had to grapple with all his strength to force the man's hand away.

He sent out a solid left hook, which rattled the man's jaw, then another, and heard a sickening crunch as his already broken nose once again exploded into a pulpy mess of blood and bone fragments. Clement roared through gritted teeth, and shoved upwards with his immense strength, forcing Kane up and away, and scrambling to his feet on powerful legs.

"Motherfucker," he yelled in English, spitting blood onto the ground. He lunged forward, seemingly confident he could defeat the smaller man in a brawl without pulling the gun. It was a mistake borne of ego and of dominating those he had previously faced in one-on-one combat.

From some deep reserves of energy, a welcome discovery after a few months of living like a slob, Kane found a second wind. He easily side-stepped the onrushing thug, spinning and smashing him with a right hook to the chin as he passed. He followed up with two straight jabs, one of which caught Clement's excuse for a nose, forcing him backwards, then Kane fired off a left cross which shattered the right cheekbone and forced him back further, his momentum slamming him into the trunk of an ancient cottonwood. Like the tree, he remained standing.

Tough bastard, Kane conceded, striding forwards until he was a mere four feet from his wannabe killer. The two men eyeballed each other for several seconds. Kane remained on high alert, watching the man's hands for any movement towards a concealed gun he felt sure was imminent. He strained his ears for any sign of the man's brother, but heard nothing. Didn't mean he wasn't closing in discreetly.

Clement's eyes glanced over Kane's shoulder, as if to intimate they weren't alone. Kane didn't fall for it. The man's fingers twitched, and Kane readied himself. Despite his size and injuries, the man had surprising dexterity, and his hand flew to the inside pocket of his jacket. Yet, even before he could remove the gun, Kane had taken one step back, and then sprang forward with lightning speed, powering off his left foot and launching into a flying *twio yeop chagi*, the flying side kick from his beloved martial art discipline, skills he'd mastered over two decades of taekwon-do practice.

Kane's right foot hammered into the man's chin, which in turn slammed his head back against the immovable tree trunk. His knees buckled and he crumpled to the ground, one arm crunching beneath his bulk, and the cruciate ligaments in one knee exploding.

Kane had landed cleanly and stepped back, immediately on alert for the second assailant. With no sign of the other man, Kane, breathing deeply from the exertions of the fight, trotted over to the helmet, slipped it on his head, and ran to the motorbike, its engine still running. Hauling the machine upright, he slid onto the seat and with a final look around, Kane accelerated off into the woods and towards the highway, hoping beyond hope he wouldn't be picked off by a hidden sniper.

Chapter Twenty-Seven

Kane made it to the highway without further incident.

He cleared the last section of cottonwood forest, and after following the highway along what seemed to be a farmer's dirt track for a mile or so he found an open gate and joined the highway on a slip ramp, merging into the mercifully light traffic. Now all he had to do was get to the airport and find a flight to Nova Scotia.

It seemed clear now there was some kind of organisation determined to stop him making it north. How much did they know? Enough to have tracked him to New Orleans, even though it had been a last-minute hotel choice. Then they'd found him at the professor's house, when even Kane himself hadn't known where he was.

What the hell is going on?

He needed to call John O'nians as soon as possible. Surely John could fill him in? First things first... get to Halifax.

Kane made it to the airport in half an hour. As far as he

knew, he hadn't been followed. He dumped the Honda in short-term parking and made his way to the ticket offices, selecting the counter with the fewest people waiting. His thoughts returned to Anja Peerdeman. Had that escape route, the motorcycle and the cash been made ready for her? From whom would a respected professor from a top-end university need to escape?

As he thought about it now, Anja had been pretty insistent he kept his bag with him as they'd gone below ground to the basement. It was a good job she had... Kane's passport and credit cards were all in his satchel, which he'd stuffed in his bag as he'd fled from the hotel in downtown New Orleans. Had that just been the professor's intuition? Had she already known those men were coming?

More questions than answers, Kane mused, a situation he didn't like one bit.

Anja? Kane wanted to call her, check if she was okay. Something niggled though, and he already suspected what had happened. Could he just leave without checking on her? If he called her home number, the one given by O'nians, would these people be able to trace him to the airport? He simply had to call... more out of respect than any hope she was okay. In his heart of hearts, he knew it had been a gunshot he'd heard while running through the underground passage. She remained there, defending her property, while he ran away?

It had all happened so fast. Throughout his life, Kane had been fearless in his professional work as an explorer, expedition leader and as a mountain tour guide, especially when those expeditions went pear-shaped, which they often had in recent times.

Far too often.

He'd faced down callous, murderous gangsters, religious terrorists, crazed cult leaders and heavily armed criminal gangs. Perhaps worse, he'd had numerous scrapes with Mother Nature herself, and yet he'd never fled any challenge. Never shirked the innate responsibility to do the right thing. Yet this time, he'd run away along that tunnel and left Anja to fend for herself.

Kane's head hung in shame, mortified at whom he'd let himself become in recent months. How he had slipped. How he'd let himself go. What would Professor O'nians think if he saw him like this? Worse still, what would his late grandfather think of him in this state? Kane's grandfather, Hiram Kane Snr, had been a world-renowned art historian and a senior figure at the British Museum in London. They'd been on many adventures together, and the love and respect the two men shared ran deeper than blood. This is not how his grandfather would have behaved, whatever situation he found himself in.

Where's your pride and dignity? he imagined Kane Snr asking, disappointment in his voice, though he knew the great man had never judged him.

Where's that famous Kane resilience?

Kane shook off his growing angst towards himself for just long enough to approach the ticket counter. He found a flight to Halifax on Air Canada, which boarded in a little over two hours.

Time for some self-pitying in the bar, Kane thought with zero levity as he negotiated the check-in desk and security line, which was surprisingly short considering he was in a major U.S. city. Ten minutes later he was at a bar in close proximity to his gate and gulping down a double gin courtesy of the Frenchman's credit card.

Kane had promised himself he would have a few days off the juice. He needed to stay sharp, especially since realising the sobering reality that people were literally hunting him down. Yet here he was again, the all-too familiar sensation of that first hit of alcohol doing its best to dampen his shame, even though he knew it would only lead to deeper feelings of shame and guilt with each vanishing drink.

Once this is over, I'll get myself sorted out, Kane thought, probably lying, while sipping at the last of the gin and ordering another. *Get to England. Hole up at the estate, and replenish. Try and contact Alex…*

In truth, it was since Alex Ridley had apparently disappeared off the face of the earth—at the very least, she'd disappeared out of his life—that things had begun to unravel, and had been unravelling ever since. He'd always considered himself an independent man, a free spirit who needed only his health and access to the great outdoors to be at one with the world and at peace with himself. His time spent wallowing on Rabbit Island had instead proven to him with great clarity he was nowhere near as independent as he'd once thought. Not even close. He needed friendly faces around him, a good support network. He needed his late grandfather. His brother, Danny, who had come back into their lives after two decades of absence. He needed Professor O'nians, a mentor and father figure, and as influential in his life as his beloved grandfather had been.

Most of all, though, Kane now knew, he needed the love of his life. He needed Alexandria Ridley. Yet, she was gone. He was alone. He didn't know if he would ever see her again, and the hole that had created in his heart was bigger than anything he'd ever had to negotiate before.

Kane didn't think he was capable.

He checked his watch, then ordered another drink.

Back in the departures hall, Clement and Claude stalked towards the ticket offices. Clement had a severe limp, and a bandage wrapped around his face. Claude wore a smug grin and cast a sideways glance at his brother.

"You're too old for all this," he said quietly as they walked. "Time to move aside and let the young guys step up."

Aboard the aircraft, Kane began to feel a little better. He had, after all, just survived an assassination attempt and had seemingly shaken off his would-be murderers. Since Francois was paying, Kane had booked a seat in business class, and willingly accepted the glass of champagne from a tray the flight attendant had offered him. Before the man could leave, Kane reached out and grabbed a second.

"That bad, eh?" the steward asked, a knowing look in his eyes.

Kane looked up at the young man, surprised at the question, almost as if he'd momentarily forgotten where he was. From the expression on the man's face and the direction of his gaze, Kane glanced down at his shirt, the front of which he found smeared with several small bloodstains.

Oh, man.

He placed the two flutes of bubbly down on his tray table and sat upright, zipping up the hoodie Anja had given him. "Uh, yes… something like that," he muttered.

The steward simply nodded and started to leave, then paused and said, "I'll be along with something stronger shortly… if you'd like?"

Kane nodded. "Thanks," was all he said, and the steward turned and made his way to the next passenger.

Jesus, sort yourself out, man, Kane thought, cursing his sloppiness under pressure.

Who the fuck am I?
What have I become?

Chapter Twenty-Eight

The flight to Halifax from New Orleans totalled almost eight hours and included two short layovers, one back in D.C. and the second in Montreal. Kane would have preferred a direct flight, but since that wasn't an option, he'd sucked it up and in turn sucked down as much of the complimentary booze as he could. By the time he reached Halifax it was early evening and any thoughts of a productive visit to the archives building would have to wait until the morning.

Kane had summoned enough foresight to have reserved a suite at The Barrington Hotel, downtown near the waterfront, just a fifteen-minute walk from the archives.

Surprising even himself, just fifteen minutes after he'd checked in at the lobby desk and after a quick shower, Kane curled up on the suite's large sofa prepared for a quiet night of research. It was a good plan and was exactly what his mind and body needed.

Not surprising at all was the fact that his best-laid plan lasted less than five minutes. Kane was soon hustling out of the hotel and along Barrington Street, enjoying the cool salty air of the historical Halifax waterfront and, using an almost inbuilt search engine, was very quickly entering the Beer Garden, a rustic dive bar that, had there still been daylight outside, would have afforded views over Terence Bay. Instead of a view of Georges Island, named after King George II and, if rumours were true, remained haunted by a thousand ghosts of the soldiers and inmates to have fought over and been imprisoned on the island over the centuries, Kane saw only twinkling lights on the far side of the wide harbour.

Kane was numb. He'd been sitting in the same spot outside for hours, other than several visits to the bar and the gents' loo. His body ached, sore from inactivity and the cold, and his legs tingled from what he believed was a compressed disc in his spine.

I'll get that looked at back in England, he mused, but doubted he would. In truth, his mind was in worse shape than his body. That too was numb, though Kane innately understood it was a defence mechanism, trying to blot out all he'd seen and witnessed in recent years. Most troubling was what might have happened to Anja, an innocent friend of a friend who had only been trying to help.

There may have been more to the Dutch professor than met the eye, but Kane didn't know that for sure, and didn't really know anything about her at all. Except that she'd been determined to keep her underground secrets safe.

Kane's mind drifted, flickering loosely on the professor and her link to John O'nians. *The Frenchman? Is he involved with either or both of the professors? The archives? The Fantome? Is it all part of a bigger picture I'm simply not understanding?* Kane wondered. *Or that I'm not meant to understand?*

That made more sense. It was starting to feel as if he

were being used. But by whom? And to what end? Surely his friend and mentor John wouldn't use him?

He wouldn't do that. Not to me.

Until a couple of days ago Kane would never have believed something as ridiculous as that, and he almost felt ashamed for letting the thought slip into his mind. John O'nians was as honest and forthright as any man Kane had ever known. He would never betray anyone, not least his protégé.

Then again… what the hell do I know? Kane conceded as he left the table and made his way to the bar via the loo.

Kane pondered his mentor, and realised there was every chance John was involved in things he didn't know about. He was an internationally important scholar in the world of art history, and wasn't it those kinds of people who ended up holding leading roles in secret societies? Like Mark Twain, Sir Isaac Newton and Leonardo da Vinci? Kane knew it wasn't just in the movies, and the more he thought about it, someone as quietly influential as his friend and mentor Professor John O'nians fitted the bill of a secret society member exactly.

When he returned a few minutes later, his mind reeling with thoughts of cults and shady secret organisations, he downed the last of his existing pint and set about the new one with relish, determined to not over-think things for the rest of the night and head back to the hotel after this final beer.

Kane had been tired all day, both mentally and physically, but now he was suddenly overcome with exhaustion. His mind became foggy and even his eyesight was turning blurry.

A knot of fear began forming in his gut as the familiar sensation of having been drugged kicked in. Kane stood and immediately reeled against the table, knocking the collection of glasses to the floor with a crash. He placed his palms on the table to brace himself, certain he was about to keel over. Then, through the brain fog and his blurry vision, a flash of colourful movement caught his attention.

Kane knew he'd been the last person out on the terrace, but now two figures approached slowly from the wharf end of the fenced-in patio, and not from within the pub. With a sleeve he cuffed at his eyes, trying to clear his vision, but it didn't work and Kane came to a certain, undeniable conclusion that his beer had been spiked and the movement was almost inevitably that of two men closing in to kill him.

It's been written that under extreme fear and duress, humans are capable of unimaginable acts: magnificent displays of courage, unfathomably good decision-making under pressure and superhuman feats of insane, incredible strength. That may have been true for some. Sadly, it didn't factor in a two-month hardcore binge of epic proportions.

So when Kane tried to run, his legs simply gave way beneath him and he crumpled to the floor, dragging the wooden picnic table over with him in a desperate attempt to remain on his feet.

Yet, that was to be his saving grace. For now. The commotion of the smashed glasses and fallen table had bought the bar manager running. It had in turn halted the stalking progress of Kane's would-be killers, who had now shied away and skulked off into the shadows of the alleyway down the side of the bar.

Kane mumbled something to the burly bar manager, who didn't understand and reached down to grab Kane and lift him into a sitting position.

"What the hell, man?" he yelled. "You gonna pay for that damage, eh?"

"Yeah... I will," Kane grumbled, right before he puked on the concrete at his feet.

"Jesus, you alright dude?"

Kane's vision had almost totally clouded over now, and his head pounded like it never had before. He had no doubt he'd been drugged, but he couldn't risk trying to explain that to this bar manager, who'd probably call the police... or an ambulance.

Got to get out of here.

Kane reached into his pocket and fumbled for his wallet. He hadn't had a chance to get any Canadian dollars yet, but grabbed out a fistful of greenbacks and thrust them in the general direction of the bar manager.

"S-sorry," Kane managed, "I hope... hope that's enough."

"Whoa, man," the huge bar guy said, eyeing the wad of cash. It was about a thousand bucks. "I, uh, well... yeah, alrighty then. Hey, let me get you some help," he said, taking the money and scurrying back into the bar.

When he returned a couple of minutes later, his customer was gone.

Chapter Twenty-Nine

The concrete at Kane's feet was obliterated as the first few rounds struck. Somehow he wasn't hit. Yet.

He dived for cover through a doorway to his left, rolling forward, then scampered back against a wall as more bullets zinged his way.

Kane dry retched on the floor. His eyes watered. His stomach was empty and nothing other than bile emerged. The smell made him gag.

What the fuck's going on? He still didn't know where he was. In front of him was a stack of boxes, shrink-wrapped on a pallet. They were so dusty it was as if they'd been abandoned there years ago.

Kane scrambled forward and ripped at the plastic packaging. *Tuna?* A pallet of tuna fish. That was irrelevant. He looked closer at the writing on the boxes. Two languages; English and French. *Hm, where am I?* Kane made a quick mental list of countries that spoke both languages. A dozen nations in Africa. Several islands in Polynesia. Canada, obviously. *Canada?*

Yes!

Faint recollections formed in his frazzled mind. He'd been in the United States, after travelling from... *Where? Asia? Probably. Cambodia?* Yes, Cambodia, on an island. *Drinking.* He'd met a man. *Francois?*

Then he'd been in Washington D.C. New Orleans? Now he was in...

Nova fucking Scotia?

The door frame exploded in a storm of splintered wood and concrete fragments. Kane threw himself behind the pallet of tuna as more rounds screamed his way, peppering the walls and destroying the pallet of canned seafood. The stench of fish and brine made him retch again. There was nothing left to throw up.

Nova Scotia? Really?

Kane knew it was a big island. *Where, exactly?* He wracked his brains, though lucid thoughts seemed a million miles away at that moment. He wracked anyway.

Some kind of harbour? Tall trees? Yes. A bar? Obviously. A fight? Hmm, why was I fighting?

Kane wasn't a fighter, at least not in the childish bar-scrap-kind-of-way he'd once been good at. Now he only fought for worthy causes and against injustices, not for cheap thrills.

So, why a fight? I'm forty something for fuck's sake!

No, not a fight. Kane's ragged memory finally hit on something.

I'm groggy now. I was groggy then. I was drugged.

He'd worry about the details later. Someone was trying to kill him. Right now, that was an altogether more pressing concern.

More rounds whizzed his way. Some hit the tuna. Others hit the wall and floor.

One ripped right through his thigh.

Kane had been shot before. He'd had a finger removed by a bullet fired by a Yakuza gangster in Japan a few years ago. That had hurt. Or so Kane had thought then. Being shot in the leg was a whole new level of agony.

He gritted his teeth, desperate not to yell out for fear of broadcasting his exact location to his unknown adversaries. That would mean more bullets. More pain. Probable death.

Hm, no, not here. Not this way.

Sweat poured down his face, stinging his blurry eyes. Blood soaked his leg, blossoming darkly on his jeans.

Fuck that hurts!

He closed his eyes and took several deep breaths, mentally analysing the extent of his injury. Hadn't he read somewhere that more blood meant a wound was less serious? Didn't sound logical to Kane, but he hoped it was true anyway as he opened his eyes again and gazed down at his thigh. The pain had eased a little with each inhale, so he kept it up, inhaling long, deep breaths through his nose and letting them out through pursed, dry lips.

Somewhere in the next room he heard muted voices. French accents. Two men. Not happy. At least the shooting had stopped. For now.

Perhaps they're out of bullets…

In truth, as Kane's heart rate slowed and faint moments of clarity seeped into his mind as the blood seeped into his jeans, it all became clear. The memories began flooding back in.

Oh shit, that's not good. That's not good at all.

Kane was suddenly sober, both from the booze and from being drugged. Extreme blinding pain and a sudden, stark realisation one's mortality was on the line could do that to a person. To say the last few months had been a bender would be doing a very great disservice to the Herculean drinking session Kane had been on since the events in Egypt.

In Egypt, he'd lost almost everything. His life. His reputation. His love... They were in ascending order of importance. He hadn't cared much for his life in a long time. Outwardly, he'd never knowingly show that. Yet inwardly, he'd been on a downward mental spiral ever since Peru, when too many people had died on his watch, including his best mate.

His reputation had once been important to him. Well, the reputation of his family name, at least. And yet, the moment terrorists had spoiled the party in Egypt, he'd felt that his reputation had been spoiled with it, damaged beyond repair. Now, that once proud reputation meant nothing to him.

Hiram Kane?

Hiram what? Kane who?

That man was lost. And he didn't care.

Only that last category truly mattered now. His love. Her name was Alexandria Ridley. Kane knew she was lost to him forever.

He shook thoughts of Ridley from his mind, difficult as it was. He wanted to see her again. Tell her he was sorry for letting her down. Say he was sorry for everything.

However, he couldn't say sorry if he was dead.

So, survive, idiot! You must survive. You can die later if you want, but survive this day first.

He glanced down at his leg again, wiping at his eyes, which remained blurry, no matter how foten he cuffed them with his sleeve. There was so much blood soaking his jeans that it was hard to see anything resembling a wound, but it had at least seemed to have stopped flowing. It still hurt like a bastard, but less now than before.

Kane held still, listening, but heard nothing. He doubted his pursuers had given up. He knew what these people were like, based on too many similar experiences. They wouldn't quit until he was dead.

Kane remained confused. Why would they kill him? Francois had sent him on a mission, and these were Francois' men. Weren't they? Had they deviated from the plan? Had Francois been full of shit? Was there more going on than Kane realised? Is there a third party here? A fourth?

Chapter Thirty

As his senses and faculties returned, Kane recalled how he'd come to be there in the dilapidated warehouse. He'd been sitting outside the pub on the waterfront. He knew he'd downed plenty of beer and a few shots... plenty... though not enough to have felt so wretched. He was sure of that. He recalled feeling dizzy, kind of out of the blue, and noticing the two figures approaching and the realisation that his drink had been spiked. Again. He hadn't had a chance to chide himself for his sloppiness, as he'd fallen and glasses had smashed as he'd crashed into a table.

I gave the bar manager some cash. Then what?

He recalled he couldn't see properly due to the blurred vision.

My legs felt like jelly. How the hell did I get away?

He knew the pub was in a dark corner of the waterfront and surrounded by industrial buildings on all sides except the actual harbour's edge. Kane couldn't see well enough to safely run. Neither did he know exactly where he was, so he couldn't simply scurry along the back streets like a rat back to The Barrington Hotel. He remembered thinking that he didn't need his eyes to swim.

On a whim, Kane had scrambled along the pub's low perimeter fence, using the wooden top rail as his guide in lieu of his eyes. He recalled the edge of the harbour wall was perhaps only twenty yards away. There wasn't much to see along that stretch of the docks, not in the dark, and he'd only seen a couple of late-evening dog walkers in the hours since he first sat on the terrace.

Kane made it as far as the dock edge and paused, ducking down behind the fence and listening to see if he'd been spotted. He recalled hearing a deep French-accented voice ask a question in English.

"Where did he go? The Englishman? He was just here."

"Your guess is as good as mine, buddy. Looks like he just, um, disappeared, eh?" Kane heard the big bar manager say.

Kane then heard the thug grumble something, then heard two sets of footsteps striding towards the edge of the dock. All fell silent then, and Kane imagined the two killers disappointed to see nothing other than the twinkling lights across the bay, and hearing only the same as he could; the gentle lapping of the waves against the concrete harbour wall, to which his body was pressed against too.

"Merde!" the younger thug growled. *Shit!*

Six feet below the thugs, Kane had held his breath.

It had felt an eternity, clinging there as he'd waited for the killers to give up and search elsewhere. His muscles burned. His head throbbed and his eyesight wouldn't clear. He had slowed his breathing, remembering his tae-kwon-do practice and forcing some Zen into his body and mind. Finally, he'd heard the footsteps edging away from his precarious position, fading until they were out of earshot altogether.

Remaining on full alert, and using his hearing as his primary sense, Kane recalled hauling himself up the rusting steel ladder he'd been clinging to and easing himself over the edge. He remembered expecting his senses to have let him down, and that he would be dragged over the edge of the dock by the two thugs and beaten to death where he lay. But no rough hands grabbed him, and no blows had been forthcoming. He'd inhaled deeply, trying to force enough oxygen into his bloodstream to clear his mind and his vision, but nothing had worked.

He knew he couldn't stay there. He knew he needed to get somewhere secure, somewhere out of sight. The hotel wasn't safe, which he'd learned after his experience in New Orleans. Whoever these men really were—other than killers—he figured they probably knew where he was staying.

He needed another option.

He made his way back along the pub fence, this time taking the northern edge, which he knew ran down a side alley, across from which was the outer wall of some kind of warehouse.

He remembered thinking he just needed to get inside.

Kane had shuffled across the alleyway, keeping one arm outstretched to prevent an unfortunate collision. Once he'd reached the crumbling wall, he used his hands to work along its surface, hoping to come across a door or a low window. He was in luck. After just a moment, he had jimmied open the apparently long-redundant fire exit and ducked inside. Kane's eyesight had worsened; he was now totally blind. He didn't know much about drugs, or what kind of chemicals criminals used to incapacitate their victims. Whatever it was, they'd chosen well.

Exhaustion had threatened to overwhelm him, and he felt certain then that if he didn't find somewhere to hide, he would simply collapse. If they were still looking for him—he knew they were—then of course they'd search the abandoned warehouses along the quayside. Including this one he'd ended up in.

Kane had scrambled blindly through the warehouse, occasionally colliding with a wall or a stack of pallets. Finally he'd found a staircase and carefully, one step after another, he'd ascended, coming to the top and taking a left turn along a corridor, which lay in all-consuming darkness. Added to the fact his eyes were as useless as a chocolate teapot, instincts were going to be critical to his survival.

That's when he heard the voice.

"He must be in here," one of the men called out. "This door is open."

So, Kane ran.

Straight into a brick wall.

Head first.

Chapter Thirty-One

Kane staggered, somehow regaining his balance as he careened through the doorway like a pinball, banging into each jamb as if it were some kind of obstacle course for drunkards. *Actually...*

That was the moment the first shots were fired. Somehow the bang on the head had jolted his brain enough to have cleared his vision, at least enough to make out where he was.

"Son of a..." Kane muttered, as nausea-inducing pain in both his leg and head threatened to elicit a scream. Instead, he swallowed it down and exhaled through gritted teeth.

There was no time for screaming. The men were closing in. His head now throbbed worse than anything he'd ever known, and though instincts pleaded with him to curl up in a ball and forget the world, and maybe find some peace, if only for a short while, Kane knew that would mean certain death. Any thoughts of the men not actually wanting him dead were dismissed as a further flurry of bullets peppered the walls, floor and pallets around him. Kane wasn't a praying man and had never believed in miracles. Yet, even he had to admit it was some kind of miracle he was still alive.

Got to get out of here…

Wincing, Kane rose to his knees, then his haunches, and ducked behind the pallet of tuna, where he took a series of rapid yet deep breaths. At last, the intake of oxygen cleared the remaining fog from his mind and the last of the blur from his eyes.

Got to get out of here now!

Kane believed that though he was only on the first floor of the warehouse, it still meant he was about thirty feet above ground level. Or sea level…

Yes. Sea level…

The men had blocked off the way in which Kane had entered the building, so he had to continue deeper into the vast structure. Where he'd entered was perhaps forty or fifty yards from the harbour wall, but since it had once been a seafood canning establishment, Kane felt certain there must have been some kind of loading dock, perhaps with a conveyor belt system directly over the water. If he was correct, from there he could jump into the harbour and make a swim for it, hopefully out of sight—and the firing line—of the would-be killers.

After a couple more deep breaths, Kane felt ready to run. That's how he felt. That was not his reality. He'd somehow forgotten he was a drunk and drugged, with a cracked skull and a bullet hole in his leg. As he pushed off from his 'good leg' he soon realised with horror that his good leg wasn't that good any more, and it crumpled beneath him, stretching his medial ligament the wrong way and causing another white-hot blast of pain to sear up his leg and into his spine.

"Fuck," he seethed through gritted teeth, fighting desperately to remain quiet. He knew that he had perhaps twenty seconds before the men discovered his exact location. Twenty seconds to make his escape.

Twenty seconds before he died!

He scrambled to his feet again, ignoring the lightning strikes in his left knee and the cricket bat pummelling his right thigh. Kane glanced around. Left or right? Right was back towards the men. Left was to the waterfront.

Left = possible survival.

He steeled himself against the incoming fire he expected, and darted left, stooping low and ducking through the nearest door, which led into a long open space running parallel to the harbour's edge. Street lamps from the docks below illuminated the huge room in an orange glow, enough that he spotted what he was hoping for up ahead.

He threw a glance over his shoulder and saw nothing, though he heard voices yelling to one another in French. He couldn't make out the words as he set off in a limping shuffle along the outer wall, closing in on the prize of escape up ahead.

Thirty yards separated him from the hatch in the wall that allowed the now-redundant hydraulic conveyor belt to pass through, once upon a time loading and unloading goods to and from boats down below.

Just ten yards now.

Five.

A metToullac crash sounded as a bullet dinged into the metal hatch just a dozen feet ahead. Kane ducked instinctively as a second and third round sailed harmlessly by.

Good job these clowns are bad shots, he mused as he reached the machinery. Then his heart sank as he spotted the industrial-sized padlock hanging from the hatch. Then hope soared as he realised it was hanging open.

Kane ignored the fire in his lungs and legs, and scrambled over the wide belt and towards the rusting metal hatch in the wall. It was a three-foot square and he could easily scramble through there and drop into the dark harbour water below. Except the stupid hatch wouldn't open. The padlock came away easily but, such was the build-up of rust on the hinges, the bastard wouldn't open.

Kane dared a glance over his shoulder and saw the two large men closing in. They had stopped running, seeming to realise he was cornered and at their mercy. They came to a halt ten feet short and stood there, panting. Each thug wore a smug grin.

"You are a slippery man, Monsieur Kane," Clement said. "Like an eel."

"A slippery eel, but soon dead," spat Claude, the smug expression now gone, replaced instead by one of undisguised bloodlust.

Kane's eyes flashed from the men who wanted him dead, to the stubborn door, and back to the men again.

Well, shit!

It was obvious the hatch would be of no use. With the state of his leg, he couldn't kick it open. He wouldn't get the chance anyway. If the men thought he might escape, they'd simply shoot him, of that he was now sure.

He glanced through the window to the right of the hatch, realising he was actually over the water. This part of the building was in fact a giant mezzanine which extended out and over the harbour by at least twenty feet. Unlike the door hatch, which was a solid, steel-framed fitting, the windows were wooden and rotted from years of exposure to the harsh Nova Scotian elements.

He glanced back at the men, who stood expectantly, waiting for Kane to make his move. Claude, the younger, angrier of them, looked about ready to end this right there, right then. Kane couldn't wait another moment. He turned back to the window.

I can make it, he mused. Then a dark thought flicked unbidden into his mind.

Don't really give a shit if I don't.

He cast his eyes back at the men, then nodded suggestively over their shoulders. To Kane's great surprise, both men fell for the oldest one in the book. Kane seized the moment. In one slick movement, he closed his eyes and slammed his shoulder into the rotted central muntin, then in what seemed like slow motion, cold air whistled and rushed around him as his stomach stayed where it was and he plummeted a full forty feet into the icy Halifax Harbour below

Chapter Thirty-Two

The impact with the water felt like hitting solid ice. It was ice cold anyway, and so black it was all-consuming. Kane was a strong swimmer, borne of a childhood incident in which he'd have died were it not for his friend's help. He'd taken it as a sign and over the years had become a fantastic swimmer and expert scuba diver.

The gelid water numbed any pain in his wounded leg, and he was soon paddling furiously to get into the lee of the high harbour wall. Seconds later, Kane was pulling himself up an ageing rusted ladder when he spotted a small boat tethered to the dock about thirty feet south of his position. In a flash he knew it was his best chance of getting away. Rather than climb out and risk exposure, he dove back into the inky water and used his powerful arms to propel him towards what he hoped would be his saviour. He'd need a little luck. Gas in the outboard motor, for one. If there wasn't any fuel, he wasn't going anywhere.

He occasionally glanced up at the dock edge, fully expecting to see the killers stalking him and waiting for a clean shot. They were nowhere in sight. It was only a matter of time...

He reached the small boat and paused for breath. He'd let his conditioning go in recent months and it had taken it out of him more than it should. After waiting a few seconds he scrambled into the boat and went straight to the outboard motor. Kane wasn't a boating man, but knew enough to turn on the fuel switch, release the choke and with a final glance up at the wall—

Oh shit!

Kane threw himself to the deck as several rounds crashed into the boat and the harbour water around him. He lay still as everything fell silent for a few seconds, then dared a glance up. One of the men, a mere silhouette in the glow of the harbour lights, was making his way down a ladder towards the boat.

Gotta go.

Kane launched himself up and yanked on the pull cord, hoping beyond hope there was enough gas in the tank to at least get him away from there. Nothing happened.

"No, no... come on..." he muttered, one eye on the ladder and the other on the engine, willing it to play fair. He yanked again. Again, nothing.

A bullet slammed into the fibreglass hull at his feet, and a flow of icy black water began to flood the bottom of the small craft.

Fuck! Come on baby... be nice, he mused as he pulled a third time, and with something like wonder as the engine roared to life, Kane exhaled and pushed away from the harbour wall and accelerated out into the bay.

It wasn't a second too soon. The thug was only a few rungs short of the boat and Kane heard him roar in frustration as he fired a few more rounds in Kane's general direction. The second thug on the dock had fired a half dozen rounds too but none had damaged the boat any further. Kane glanced left and right, and was relieved to see no bridges anywhere close by. He just needed to get across the bay, and he'd be away and safe.

Just a little further please, he pleaded with the boat, eyeing the rising water level at his feet. If the gas held, the water wouldn't be a problem.

Kane afforded himself a moment to breathe in the briny air of the harbour, and unbidden memories of his childhood in Lowestoft came flooding into his mind as the water flooded over his feet. Summers at the beach or on the Broads. Fish and chips. Ice cream. Seagulls stealing both. Happy days… the best of days…

Then the boat stalled, out of fuel and still fifty yards shy of the opposite harbour wall. Other than being hunted down and shot at by two unknown gunmen, this was the least surprising thing to have happened to Kane in a while. Of course there wasn't enough fuel. Of course he'd have to brave the frigid waters of Halifax Harbour again.

There was no one there to witness it, but Kane's trademark wry grin—more of a prize-winning girn, if he could've seen a mirror—appeared as he slipped over the side of the abandoned boat and once more powered through the icy blackness for two minutes until he reached the other side.

Freezing cold, drenched through and now without any money or travel documents, Kane couldn't help but chuckle as he trudged into the shadows of another industrial building, more or less grateful to be alive, but wondering what the hell he was going to do next.

Chapter Thirty-Three

The men wouldn't give up. It was only luck he'd survived what had been nothing less than an assassination attempt. The reasons why they wanted him dead could wait. What couldn't wait was his desperate need to get the hell to safety.

But with no money, and no travel ID should he need it, Kane had no choice but to risk returning to the hotel, though he suspected the men knew where he was staying.

Dangerously cold, and now on the wrong side of the harbour, Kane figured the only option was to walk back to The Barrington via a bridge he spotted a couple of miles north of his current position. Probably a ninety-minute walk, he estimated… time to get warm, dry off a little and, more importantly, gather his addled senses. He'd just have to take his chance with the bad guys.

Kane headed north from the Irving Woodside Industrial Wharf, as the sign called it, and through a woodland area, remaining within the shadows as best he could and ducking into the trees any time a car passed somewhere close by. It was the small hours of the morning now and traffic was almost non-existent, but those men were somewhere in the region and would still be out looking for him.

He skirted along the waterside edge of some kind of campus, still and quiet at this hour, and half an hour later found himself at the Angus L. Macdonald pedestrian bridge. At the start of the bridge, beneath it, a group of young men smoking weed and drinking beers eyed Kane with sideways glances.

Kane exhaled. He didn't need any trouble from these guys now. He was cold and tired, as well as exhausted from the events of the evening. Besides, he had nothing to steal and didn't want to fight. Then he had an idea.

He approached the group of half a dozen youths cautiously. "Evening," Kane said. "Um, sorry to bother you, but I need a favour and I'm willing to pay for it."

They shared suspicious glances. One of them took a step towards Kane. "Get outta here, you sick fuck. We don't want your kind 'round here."

Kane realised his error. *Oops.* "No, no, nothing like that. Sorry," Kane said, exhaling. "Listen. There are some bad men looking for me. I've lost them for now, but my money and my gear is back in my room at The Barrington. I've got five hundred dollars for the guy who can go to the hotel and get me my stuff."

The glances now became curious and amused. With his eyes narrowed, the leader stepped closer to Kane, and said, "Look man, if these bad guys are so... bad?... then five hundred ain't gonna cut it. I'll do it for a grand."

Kane had been expecting that. It wasn't even his money, and he didn't care how much the man wanted. "It's a deal... but I get your hoodie as part of that deal." Kane shrugged, shivering. "I'm serious." The men hunting him knew what he was wearing; the black hoodie would be a useful disguise. He'd always quite liked Run-DMC anyway.

The leader looked incredulous, but Kane imagined the thousand bucks coming his way was too good to miss. He could get another DMC hoodie for thirty.

With the deal agreed, and Kane now warming up tucked inside the large Run-DMC hoodie—hood up—Kane and the young gang member set out across the bridge en route to The Barrington, a further twenty minutes on foot.

They moved in silence for a while. Kane had nothing to lose by trusting this guy. His buddies hadn't followed, and it was just the two of them. The guy, who hadn't offered his name, noticed the blood seeping through Kane's wet trousers.

"Bad guys, eh?" he asked, motioning to Kane's leg as they stepped off the far side of the bridge onto Barrington Street.

Kane glanced down. He'd forgotten about the bullet wound, which the cold had numbed to the point he hadn't felt it in a while. Now though, the adrenaline had waned and he suddenly realised how much it hurt. "Um, yeah, something like that," Kane admitted.

"The hell you into man?" the guy asked. "Don't look like no criminal," he added, eyeing Kane up and down. "You English?"

"I am, and it's a long story. If you read about it in the news, that'll mean I'm either dead, or famous. Or both." Kane grinned, to which the guy shrugged.

"None of my business, bro. I just want my thousand bucks."

"Which I promise you will get when I get my stuff. So, how're you planning to get into the room without a key?" It was a legitimate question.

Now it was time for the other guy to grin. "I have my ways... which will remain my ways. Just give me the floor and room number. I'll do the rest."

"No one gets hurt," Kane said, his voice level. "I mean it."

"Hey man, don't worry. You watch too many movies. Besides, this is Canada man... this ain't the States. Be cool. No one gets hurt, you have my word. Name's Joel."

That was good enough for Kane, who sensed the man wasn't as tough as his demeanour had first suggested. Resourceful maybe, which is what Kane needed right now. "I'm Kane. Nice to meet you."

"Cain, like in the bible?"

Kane laughed. "No, not like that. Kane with a K. Like the wrestler." Now it was Joel's time to laugh.

"Listen Joel, the hotel is two blocks farther along this road," Kane said. "Best if I don't go any closer. If I wait here, will you bring my stuff?" Kane knew there were several thousand dollars in cash in his bag in the room. He had no choice but to trust Joel now.

"Just wait here. If I'm not back in twenty minutes, your bad guys got to me."

Kane inhaled and let it out slowly. He didn't want to put this apparently decent bloke at any risk. "Listen, Joel, they're looking for me, a white guy. They won't have any reason to suspect you. Get into the room, however you see fit, and please just grab my bag from the table. It's got everything I need. You'll be in and out in seconds."

Joel nodded, and his expression was something between

excitement and the hint of opportunity. Then he was gone, trotting off towards the hotel at a rapid clip.

Kane backed into the shadows of the Brunswick Street Mission Church and waited, unsure whether he'd been wise to let a stranger have access to his things, especially a stranger who appeared to be comfortable operating outside of the law. A few minutes passed. Kane had spent the time assessing his leg wound. In truth, although he was no doctor, it didn't seem that bad. He'd had worse injuries before, and though it would need attending to at some point, there was no immediate danger of infection.

He was just pulling his trousers back up when he saw a black SUV cruising slowly along Barrington Street, windows open and two men eyebToullang the street... searching for him. Kane gritted his teeth. It was the killers, heading towards the hotel. They'd get there at the same time as Joel. He had to warn the guy. It wasn't Joel's problem. There was no need to risk his young life for a thousand bucks.

Kane was just about to set off when the big gang member came trotting up the road, Kane's satchel over his arm.

"This it?" he said, handing the bag to Kane.

Kane nodded. He needed to check the contents but didn't want to appear suspicious.

Joel seemed to notice, and said, "S'aight man... go ahead. I know what I look like."

Kane nodded. He opened the bag and after a brief inventory, confirmed that everything was there. He counted out the cash and handed it to Joel, who took it without a word.

"Well, thanks," Kane said. "So, how did you do it?"

Joel smirked. "It's helpful to have a *brother* who works the night shift at The Barrington. In our world, no one asks questions. He owed me a favour. Now we're even. As are we."

"Yes, we are."

"You gonna be alright?" Joel asked, nodding at Kane's leg? "I know someone who could take a look."

"You do? Who?"

"My girl's a nurse… got some medical gear back at the crib… you know, for when shit sometimes goes down. Want me to call her?"

Twenty minutes later a car pulled up and Joel and Kane got in, and twenty minutes after that, at the couple's apartment, Joel's girlfriend was carefully tending to Kane's wound with such skill it seemed as if it were something she did regularly. He decided not to ask and instead just told them how grateful he was.

"Look man," Joel said after his fiancée had finished bandaging up Kane's wound, "if you want me to, you know, help you get rid of the bad guys"—he did the quotation sign with his fingers—"I have the means."

"No!" Kane said a little too forcefully. "I mean, no, thanks. I don't really know who they are, and I don't want anyone else involved. You've done enough for me already. You both have," he added. "Thank you very much. Actually, there is one more thing."

"Shoot."

"No, don't shoot," Kane said, which elicited a little laughter. He glanced at his watch. "Look, I have somewhere I need to be in the morning but the place won't open until at least nine. If I could just lie low here for a few more hours then get a ride there, that would be very much appreciated."

"No problem," Joel confirmed. "Hey, you look like shit,"

he added. "There's a spare room through that door. Get some sleep and we'll see you in the morning."

Joel's words were like music to Kane's ears, so he thanked them once more and made his way to the bedroom.

He was asleep in less than a minute.

Chapter Thirty-Four

The rest of the night passed without incident and Kane was grateful to the universe for a few hours' quality sleep. Physically, he felt better. Mentally, still unsure. Everything had happened so quickly. Meeting the Frenchman in Cambodia. Landing in D.C. Onto New Orleans. The first attempt on his life and the probable murder of Professor Peerdeman. Now here he was in Canada, having jumped through a third-floor window into a freezing Halifax river to escape being shot, after which he'd recruited a gangster to rob his own hotel room.

And for what? That was the crazy thing. Kane still didn't understand what he was into. One thing was certain now; it wasn't just a simple treasure hunt. Kane knew better than most how valuable the antiquities market could be, especially the shadowy blackmarket. He'd been the victim of a very daring artefact robbery himself; inadvertently, it's how he'd ended up here now.

Was it redemption he was after? A search for dignity? A

futile attempt to eradicate the shame and guilt he felt after his recent failings?

Kane wasn't sure, but he was too invested now to back away. Too deeply involved to turn his back. There were higher forces at work here. Powers mightier than himself. Not in any spiritual sense. That, he could handle. In higher forces and mightier powers, Kane imagined shady organisations and ancient institutions. Criminal enterprises. Possible cult involvement. Perhaps even governments...

In fact, the more he pondered it, standing at the window of Joel's spare bedroom, governments sounded likely, though he couldn't pinpoint why, or even which government. French, based on Francois' involvement? The US government? Canadian? Even his own British government? After all, it was the ultra well-connected scholar John O'nians who'd sent him to Professor Peerdeman, a woman who seemed to know more than she let on.

A knock at the door startled Kane and shook him from his musings.

"Coffee?"

Kane opened the door to find Joel proferring a mug of coffee. "Yes. Thanks a lot."

"Mia's making breakfast... ready in ten."

"Very kind, thanks," Kane said, and really meant it. He knew well never to judge anyone by their appearance; it had cost him plenty in the past. Despite his display of expensive jewellery and neck tattoos, and his hints at violence, Joel was a good man with a good family. Kane wouldn't forget it.

An hour later, wearing the Run-DMC hoodie and a cap donated for his discretionary cause by Joel, Kane entered the Archives section of the Nova Scotia Provincial Library, located on the corner of University Avenue and Robie

Street. He tried his best to remain anonymous and keep a low profile. Kane had to assume the thugs were still hunting him. Why couldn't they find him here?

Second, he just didn't want to be recognised. It wasn't many months ago Hiram Kane was a well-respected, world-renowned explorer and expedition leader. His face was recognisable to many thousands of people across the world, ever since he'd been the man to rediscover the lost Inca city of Vilcabamba and Atahualpa's gold; the archaeological discovery of a generation.

Now, his reputation lay in tatters; with it, his own dignity. The way Kane saw it now, he'd been presented with an opportunity to recapture some of that lost pride and dignity, and more importantly, to replenish the reputation of the Kane family name. He'd always been so proud to have followed in the footsteps of such tenacious explorers... brilliant men, like his great grandfather Patrick Kane, and his grandfather, Hiram Snr.

Yet, he'd been the first of the Kane dynasty to have failed, the first to have ever had his abilities and character questioned. And it hurt. Despite his grandfather correctly insisting he was not to blame, that external forces had conspired against him, the younger Kane just couldn't see it that way. It had been his duty, his responsibility, and it had all gone horribly wrong.

Kane would never get over the loss of innocent lives on his watch. Never! Yet, if he could just do something good, something positive for the world of antiquities, perhaps then, and only then, might the self-imposed stigma of failure begin to fade. At the very least, he could hold his head just a little higher in public.

As soon as Kane entered the main Archives room, he

began to feel eyes upon him. *Probably just my imagination!* He kept his hood up as he took a seat behind a public internet station.

Where to start? Kane had done plenty of research on all things Oak Island. He'd read about the *Fantome*, the infamous British ship, wrecked somewhere off the Halifax coast. He'd read articles on Samuel Ball, the former slave-turned-farmer, who some scholars believed was the man to find the lost treasure before spiriting it all away and off the island. Kane had read about the treasure's origin, which some claim was stolen Aztec gold and silver, while others claimed it was from the Inca culture, pillaged by the conquistadors half a millennium ago. Kane knew with absolute certainty that wasn't true. He'd seen the evidence with his own eyes.

Other so-called experts suggested the treasure wasn't gold at all, but more modern items, such as late Renaissance paintings, jewellery traded among European royalty, even legendary lost texts that contained earth-shattering secrets. This last one appealed more to Kane than any actual treasure ever could, though it seemed the most unlikely. The Dead Sea Scrolls were one thing... he had in fact been involved with those just months ago. But if there were other infamous ancient texts scholars claim contained writings of such unrivalled magnitude, and cultural and historical significance, why weren't more people looking for them?

Kane felt it again, an eerie sense someone was watching him, and without realising, he reached for the gold Inca sun disc that swung from a leather strap around his neck, as he often did when anxious. This *was* a public building, already bustling with staff and visitors. Two armed security officers were guarding the entrance lobby. He was safe here. Yet he couldn't shake the feeling. On a hunch, he suddenly spun away from the monitor he was facing and caught the eye of a young woman, who seemed to be staring at him, her eyes wide, a rabbit caught in headlights.

However, the blonde woman recovered quickly and hustled across the room, disappearing through a door labelled Staff Only.

Chapter Thirty-Five

Kane shook his head. Someone *had* been watching him. At least it wasn't the killers. When he realised he was holding his sun disc, he smiled wryly and tucked it back beneath his shirt.

He decided to focus on the infamous shipwreck, the *Fantome*, searching again for the article he'd printed out in D.C. Kane was warm beneath Joel's hoodie and pulled the hood down. He inhaled deeply, holding the breath for long seconds, before exhaling between pursed lips. Something just wasn't jiving with Kane about the available information surrounding the *Fantome*, certain he was missing something important.

What it was, he couldn't even guess. Kane was more adept at in-person, tactile searching, being out in the wilds and using his own intuition and physical senses. He was considered smart, and the odd professor or two at university might once have labelled him scholarly, though he'd always laughed off such compliments. Still, online detective work just wasn't his thing.

After a frustrating hour poring over the same few articles about the *Fantome* and the surrounding legends, Kane rose from the chair and stretched as he checked his watch.

To his surprise it was already lunch time. In truth, he was more thirsty than hungry. Kane had promised to himself to lay off the booze for a few days. It had caused too much anxiety in the last weeks and had left him sloppy. He'd let his guard slip, which resulted in him being unaware he'd been followed on at least two occasions. Still, as his frustration grew over a lack of progress, the thought of a cold beer burgeoned in his mind. He'd have to be careful. Those bastards were still out there somewhere, and Kane's instincts suggested they weren't that far away.

As he turned to leave, he spotted a cluster of people, staff, huddled in one corner of the Archives room. Several seemed to have recognised him. Two even smiled sheepishly before nodding in his direction and going about their duties. One older man pursed his lips, as if disappointed, and seemed to huff slightly before shaking his head and disappearing along an aisle between two shelving units. Only one remained; the young woman Kane had caught watching him before. She cleared her throat, and remained there for long seconds, as if deciding whether or not to approach.

It was clear she knew who Kane was. That wasn't unusual. In an establishment like an Archives office, his name would be known. Kane's relative fame had mostly been earned in South America and Asia. Still, his family name was legendary in the field of exploration and archaeology, and there would be many records of his own and his family's spectacular achievements in the field.

The woman seemed to take a faltering step forward, as if to approach, then she thought better of it and hustled out of sight.

What the heck? Dividing opinions as usual, Kane thought as he pulled the hood up and headed for the door.

"Excuse me. Nearest quiet bar serving food?" Kane asked the security guard standing just inside the entrance.

"South down Robie a couple blocks, then left on Inglis. Hit the Gorsebrook. Best brunch in town."

"Thanks a lot."

"Watch ya back, bud... some interesting, uh... characters down there." The huge guard chuckled, then tipped his cap and watched as Kane stepped outside onto Robie Street.

Kane soon entered the gloomy interior of the Gorsebrook Pub, loosely affiliated with the Saint Mary's University, and unofficial drinking hole for the uni's American Football team, the Huskies.

Despite the relatively early hour, perhaps a dozen patrons were dotted around. A handful sat scattered along the bar, who each wore an expression that suggested they thought the world might end that very day. A few other drinkers sat at tables in dark corners engaged in muted conversation.

Spears of light cut through ancient-looking shutters and danced with fluttering dust motes. Despite a smoking ban in public indoor spaces in Canada, the aroma of stale tobacco drifted on the air, generously laced with weed. A pool table stood in one corner, the torn playing surface half covered in stains.

"Perfect," Kane muttered as he approached the bar. "Beer, please," he told the bartender, "and do you have a sandwich?"

"What kind?"

"Anything." It was more for his conscience than his hunger.

"Coming right up," replied the huge barman, who Kane guessed was a defenceman for the Huskies, based on his size and age. "Here's your beer. Food'll be ten minutes. Tab, eh?"

"Tab, please. Thanks a lot," Kane said as he turned and found himself face to face with a familiar face.

Chapter Thirty-Six

"There's nothing left on the wreck."

To Kane's relief, the familiar face didn't seem to want to kill him.

It was the woman from the Archives. Toulla, as her name badge suggested.

"I'm sorry, pardon?" Kane said, wondering what the hell was going on.

"Sorry. Sorry, you're right." The woman took a step back, a little embarrassed. "I didn't mean to startle you. Let me try again. Hi… my name's Toulla. Toulla Corti. I work at the—"

"The Archives. You were spying on me."

"I was not spying on you… well, maybe a little." Toulla glanced nervously over her shoulder, as if she were talking to someone she shouldn't be.

"Just kidding," Kane said, his grin putting the woman at ease. "What do you mean there's nothing left on the wreck? You mean the *Fantome*?"

"Yes, the *Fantome*. It's all gone."

Kane nodded. The way the young woman spoke, with gentle authority, as if she were fully convinced of what she'd said, had Kane intrigued. He needed a lucky break. Maybe this was it. "Um, can I buy you a drink?"

"No, thanks." Toulla inhaled nervously. "Beer. Thanks."

Kane grinned. "Food?"

"Whatever you're having."

Kane placed the order, then led Toulla to a corner table away from curious ears and eyes.

"I'm sorry for following you. I recognised you as soon as you came into the Archives. I kind of guessed why you're here, and it was confirmed when I—"

"—when you spied on me," Kane finished, smiling.

"Yeah. I saw your online search for the *Fantome* and knew you were here to look for the Oak Island treasure. Since I know who you are and what you've achieved, I have to ask… why haven't you looked before?" A reasonable question.

"I've been busy," Kane said. A reasonable answer. "Let's just say this… something recently piqued my interest, so I thought I'd pay a visit to Nova Scotia."

Toulla nodded. Her long, blonde hair hung over her shoulders and her pretty face held eyes that had seen much, despite her young age. Kane sensed she was a troubled soul, wise beyond her years. He also saw a spark there, a sense of adventure, and despite the age and hair colour differences, Toulla had a touch of the Alex Ridleys about her. He ignored the thought and took a long sip of his beer.

"As I was saying," Toulla continued, "it's all gone. The treasure. If it was ever there in the first place."

"Are you saying the whole thing's a lie?"

"No, not at all. I'm certain that treasure once existed in the area. A lot of it. More than anyone could imagine. But it's obviously not on the *Fantome*. Hasn't been for a long, long time."

"I believe that." Kane nodded, sipping his beer. "So, what happened to it? Is it really in the Money Pit?" Kane asked, grinning again. Of course it wasn't. People had been searching for two centuries and no one had ever found anything more than a few coins and some rather tenuous evidence of man-made tunnels. "Is the Money Pit even real?" Kane asked before Toulla could answer. He'd seen and read enough bullshit in his time to know that most mysteries, myths and legends surrounding archaeology were just that.

The woman held his gaze, as if unsure how much to say. She hedged her bets. "I believe there once was such a thing as the Money Pit, yeah. I also believe it actually once contained unimaginable riches." She glanced around again, clearly on edge.

"There's no one here," Kane assured her, though he wasn't certain.

Toulla exhaled. "There was treasure. Was. Not anymore."

"What do you mean, not anymore?"

"It was stolen."

"That's generally what happens with ancient buried treasure," Kane teased, flashing the wry smile. When Toulla didn't smile back, his faded.

"The thing is," Toulla continued, "none of the theories people believe are true. Modern treasure hunters, like those brothers on TV, have never found anything. Their predecessors never did either, other than a handful of coins and a truck full of timber. If there was something on Oak Island, considering the number of holes these people have dug over the last century, they would've found it. I'm certain!"

"Meaning, it's been gone a long time," Kane stated.

"That's what I think, yes."

"Yet people still believe it's there, right? And treasure hunters and wreck salvagers still come in their droves, certain they'll find something and get rich?"

Toulla nodded.

"But these kinds of searches can be dangerous. Especially diving on ancient, unstable shipwrecks. If you're certain, then the government must be pretty sure too. Why don't they stop it?"

Toulla nodded again but now there was a glint in her eye.

"The authorities make a lot of money… a lot… issuing salvage licenses, and also by leasing plots of land on Oak Island. The treasure hunters lease the land for a month, even two or three months, at huge cost, then dig it up, find nothing and give up, then someone else comes along and leases the very same land that's been leased dozens of times before, and the cycle continues. The Canadian government makes a fortune and the treasure hunters and salvagers spend a fortune to find nothing."

"You have to agree it's a pretty good business model," Kane said.

This time Toulla smiled. "They actively encourage it. That's the only reason they allow documentary makers and shows like *The Curse of Oak Island* to exist. It all serves to perpetuate the myth and keeps the conversation alive, and the people lap it up, as they always have. The tourists still come in their thousands… and never get to see anything."

"Like the Loch Ness Monster, eh?" Kane said, adding the colloquial 'eh' for good effect.

"Just like it. The government knows for a fact there's nothing there. They've always known it." Toulla exhaled, and to Kane, unless he'd misread the situation, what Toulla had said was also a statement of fact, as if she somehow knew the Canadian government was a part of the theft.

How can she be so sure the Canadian authorities know it? Unless they stole it?

He was about to ask her outright, when the waiter arrived with their lunch. Realising how hungry he was, he tucked into the food and for just a moment, Kane forgot about treasure and killers and Oak Island and the probably slain professor, and even John O'nians.

"Many people think the treasure was lost when the ship sank," Toulla mumbled between bites. "And that it was never recovered. Others think it was removed from the *Fantome* before it went down and safely taken ashore, where it was hidden, and the boat was then deliberately scuttled to cause confusion."

"Like a red herring?" Kane asked.

"Yeah, I suppose you could look at it like that… plenty of herrings in Halifax Harbour," she added, and Kane laughed. Then he turned serious for a moment.

"And what do you think?"

Toulla didn't answer for a long time. Kane noticed her chest rise and fall as her breathing quickened. She was suddenly uncomfortable, and still clearly nervous. "I think we should leave here," she said. "Talk somewhere more secure."

"It's fine," Kane said, "there's no one here to worry about… unless the old-timers in the pub are listening, hoping for a hot tip?"

Again, Toulla didn't smile at Kane's attempted joke. "The people who search for the Oak Island Money Pit treasure are serious. Often criminally backed. They mean business. We should get out of here. There's much more to all of this than you know. More even than I know."

"You seem to know a lot," Kane said. He looked around, wondering why Toulla was so nervous, but didn't spot anyone who seemed to pose a threat. "Okay," Kane relented, "where should we go?"

"I know a man."

Chapter Thirty-Seven

Toulla led Kane back towards the Archives building, and then down into the underground parking garage where she kept her 1983 Jeep Cherokee during work hours. She walked fast, and despite Kane's long strides he had to hustle to keep up. He remained alert on the short journey, but saw no one ton be concerned about.

Kane wondered if Toulla was always this tense, of if his arrival had brought the anxiety upon her? He decided to wait and let her speak when she was ready.

They climbed into the well-maintained classic Jeep and, after nervous glances in all the mirrors, Toulla negotiated the exit ramp and accelerated towards the Fisherman's Memorial Highway, heading west out of Halifax and, Kane knew, in the general direction of Oak Island.

"So, where exactly are we headed?"

"There's someone I'd like you to meet." Toulla glanced at the dashboard clock. 1:22 pm. "Perfect timing," she muttered.

"Perfect timing for what?" Kane asked, intrigued.

"Veteran's Happy Hour."

The hour drive west through a largely featureless landscape passed with little more than small talk. Although Toulla seemed apprehensive to discuss Oak Island or the *Fantome*, she was curious as to why Kane had chosen now to come and investigate. Kane also didn't want to divulge too much information as to the whys and wherefores he was there. In truth, he was still working it out for himself. He really wanted to speak with Francois, the enigmatic Frenchman who had set this entire thing in motion. What Kane hadn't realised when he and Francois had parted was that Francois hadn't provided any way through which to contact him. He had given Kane money and credit cards, but no phone number or email. Kane hadn't noticed because he was…

I was fucking sloppy, he chided himself, something he'd been altogether too much of in recent months. Had it been deliberate by Francois, though? A simple oversight? The mercurial Frenchman didn't seem to be the kind of guy to forget something as rudimentary as that. *Just one more thing that doesn't add up. Oh, and the killers on his payroll.* Or were they? Kane realised he knew nothing about anything anymore.

The highway now arced south for a few miles before crossing what Kane noticed was named Gold River. He had to ask.

"Gold River, eh?" he said through his wry smile, adding the 'eh' for good measure.

Toulla shrugged. "There was always gold in the area. Doesn't mean it's treasure," she added, though the glint in her eye suggested otherwise.

"Sure thing." Kane nodded. "A river named Gold River, the mouth of which just happens to lie ten miles from the scene of… the world's greatest treasure mystery. Alrighty then."

"I'm just a local girl who works in the Archives. What could I possibly know about such things?" Toulla retorted playfully, and for the first time since they'd met, Kane sensed Toulla had finally relaxed.

"Where does the river lead to?"

"De Adder Lake, twenty-three miles from Oak Island. Four-hundred fifty-six feet above sea level," she replied immediately, proving that she did, in fact, actually know a lot. She turned to Kane and shrugged. The glint in her eye was unmistakable.

"Is it considered part of the Oak Island enigma?" Kane pushed. "In your opinion, at least?"

Toulla's eyes flicked up to the rearview mirror. For a fleeting moment, her eyelids fluttered, then her eyes narrowed.

Kane didn't miss it, and craned his neck to look out the back window. The traffic since Halifax had gradually thinned as they'd moved farther from the city. Now there were very few vehicles on the road. Just as he turned, he spotted a flash of black turning off the highway a few hundred yards behind them. A sudden icy knot of apprehension formed in his gut.

"SUV?" he asked casually.

"I… I dunno. Might've been. Yeah, SUV."

Shit! "Plenty of those kinds of vehicles out here, right? I've seen several since we left the city."

"Yeah, very common," Toulla agreed but the smile was gone and her knuckles had turned white from gripping the steering wheel so tight.

"I'm sure it's nothing," Kane said calmly. He wasn't a

good liar. But what could they do? He wasn't paranoid enough to make them hide behind a bush. The chances of that particular vehicle being driven by someone with bad intentions were slim at best. He needed to remain in control. Not let irrational fear get the better of him. It wasn't irrational, though. Two men had almost killed him. Twice, now. He was lucky to be alive. It could easily be the two thugs from before. He inhaled slowly, held in the breath until he felt a tiny bit dizzy, then let it out through pursed lips.

Okay... think...

"How far until we reach where we're heading?"

"Couple of miles. It's a bar, kind of an unofficial retired vets' club but anyone can go."

"Will it be busy?"

"One forty-five on a Monday afternoon? Prime time for the local vets. Yes, packed."

Ten minutes later Toulla indicated and swung off the highway towards Zwicker Cove. After negotiating a couple of smaller roads, she indicated again as The Salty Dog Tavern came into view.

"No," Kane said, a little more abruptly than he'd meant as he spotted the overflowing carpark. "Sorry. Don't park here. Pull into one of the small side roads. No need to advertise our position... you know, just in case."

Toulla nodded and continued on another hundred yards, then turned a sharp right away from the waterfront and right again, easing to a quiet stop behind a row of lock-up storage garages, well out of sight of the main road.

She stared straight ahead, as if steeling herself, then inhaled deeply, puffed out her cheeks and climbed out of the Jeep.

"I'll introduce you to my uncle," she said. "Jeremiah Samuel Ball."

Kane's jaw fell open.

Chapter Thirty-Eight

Jeremiah Samuel Ball? No... it couldn't be? Kane was incredulous.

"Well hello, darling," said a scruffy old fella at the bar as Toulla approached. "Lovely surprise. You should be at work." It wasn't a question. The old man eyed Kane with undisguised suspicion.

Kane glanced about the large pub. It was a classic wooden structure and Kane suspected much of the timber had been reclaimed from stricken vessels. His mind flickered on an imagined visage of the *Fantome* lying bereft at the bottom of Halifax Harbour. Paintings of sea battles and fishing boats lined the walls. In one corner a handsome middle-aged guy sat at a piano playing and singing Sinatra songs no one was listening to, yet he seemed oblivious behind his aviator sunglasses, useless while inside, and on an already grey day. The faded poster on the wall behind him declared his name was Johnny Favourite. Sadly for the talented yet wobbly musician, he wasn't a favourite today.

Lobster pots hung from ceiling beams. Bleached shark

jaws protruded from walls. Upturned whiskey barrels served as tables and a general aroma of saltiness drifted around the atmospheric barn-like structure. Kane half smiled as scenes from the bar in *The Perfect Storm* movie came to mind.

Toulla ignored her uncle's accusation about where she should be. He was of course correct. "Hiram, this is my uncle, Jeremiah Ball. Uncle Jerry, this is Hiram."

Kane held out his hand. Jeremiah didn't flinch.

"What about it?" the old man grumbled. "Why're you here?" Despite his gruff countenance, Kane sensed the old-timer wasn't being too serious. The two kin shared the same eye twinkle, if not the same demeanour.

"Jerry, Hiram's here to... well, to find out more about—"

"I know why he's here, Touls," Jeremiah cut in. "It's why everyone's here. It's why you're still here. There is no single other reason on Earth why anyone would come to this cold, grey, dreary and God-forsaken island if it wasn't to buy me a beer." With that, Jeremiah Ball erupted in a stuttering, phlegmy fit of laughter that jiggled his beard and set his large shoulders wobbling. Kane couldn't help but join in, and took his cue and ordered the three of them a beer.

Toulla continued. "I hope you don't mind, but I thought you might like to talk to Hiram a little. He's an explorer by trade... a famous one. He could do with your help."

Despite the bout of laughter, and the fresh pint now nestled in Jeremiah's chubby hand, his eyes retained their scrutiny of the new guy having wandered into Jerry's own personal corner of the world. He clearly didn't care who Kane was.

Jeremiah turned to the bar. "Chuck, table out the back free?" he asked. Chuck nodded to a curtain at the end of the bar. A sign hanging above it stated *Private*. It apparently wasn't private for Jeremiah Ball, a man Kane guessed had more personality and gravitas than Jim Carrey, Celine Dion and Mike Myers put together.

"Follow me," he said without ceremony and disappeared through the curtain with a flourish.

Toulla glanced at Kane, who raised his eyebrows in bemused curiosity. Toulla winked, and muttered, "Happy Hour in the Private room can only mean one thing: Uncle Jerry is ready to talk."

The two of them followed, any fear of being followed themselves now temporarily forgotten.

Once they'd all taken seats around a small circular table, beers in hand, Jeremiah fixed Kane with a hard, uncompromising stare. "Let me tell you right now, son. Leave Nova Scotia today and never come back."

Well, Kane wasn't expecting that. However, by the expression on Toulla's face, it *was* exactly what she'd been expecting. He held the old-timer's stare and calmly took a sip of his beer. He'd met dramatic old fellas before, men who were larger than life and smart as tacks, but who held within them a passion for adventure and a taste for the flamboyant. Jeremiah Ball fitted that bill exactly. It hadn't been declared yet, but it was becoming apparent to Kane that Jeremiah wasn't simply some quirky old salt dog with a story to tell. Kane suspected he was in fact a descendent of the infamous Samuel Ball, who many believed was the last person in possession of the *Fantome*/Money Pit treasure.

Jeremiah cast a sideways glance at his niece, then looked back at Kane. After a long pause, he declared: "If you don't leave, they'll kill you."

He stated the simple words with such calm sincerity Kane had no doubt he meant them. As he had so often in recent months, Kane briefly contemplated his life. He thought about what he had done, and who he had once been. What was left? Not much. His reputation and self-worth lay in tatters. So, he rolled the way he always had lately…

Fuck it.

"Listen, I appreciate your concern, I really do," Kane said, "but I have no intention of leaving. I'm not sure why Toulla brought me here, but I'm not asking for help. I'm going to attempt to uncover the enigma surrounding Oak Island and the lost treasure one way or another."

The old man sat quietly, appraising Kane, seeming to consider his next words. Jeremiah sensed Kane notice this. "Son, you think I'm weighing you up? You think I'm worried about you and why you're here?"

Kane shrugged. That's how it seemed.

"You're wrong. There're only two things I care about in this world these days. One is my beautiful niece, Touls." He pulled Toulla in for a hug, which she melted into, as if she were still a child. Kane waited for the second thing Jeremiah cared about. It wasn't forthcoming.

"Can I guess the second?" Kane asked after an uncomfortably long pause.

Jeremiah nodded. He knew what was coming.

"The Oak Island treasure?" Kane offered, and the old man's beard twitched above a burgeoning smile. Toulla grinned too as she leaned out of the hug.

"Can I tell him?" she asked, to which her uncle again nodded. "He only cares about his Monday Happy Hour… probably more than he cares about me."

"Not true, my girl… not even close. But it is true I no longer care about Oak Island and its so-called treasure."

Toulla glanced at Kane with an expression suggesting

her uncle had spoken a load of bollocks, but she didn't need to correct him. It would come out soon enough.

"I repeat," Jeremiah said, "you should leave here, son. Leave this place for good. It would be remiss of me not to say that to you now. Remiss indeed."

"Okay," Kane replied. "I understand why you believe that. I can vouch for the fact my being here might be dangerous. It's already happened. Two men. First in D.C. Then in New Orleans. I think they killed a professor I was with. They tried to kill me and I only narrowly escaped." It sounded dramatic as he said it. It sounded true. "It's possible we were followed, but they won't find us here."

Kane watched Jeremiah closely, the old man nodding yet again, though his eyes betrayed him. Kane sensed he didn't believe that at all.

The truth was, Jeremiah had appraised Hiram Kane. The moment he'd walked in with his niece, Jeremiah knew Kane was different. He'd seen it in his eyes. In the way he stood. Jeremiah considered himself good with characters. Good at understanding people. Reading them. He saw much of himself in the man, especially his younger self. He also sensed in him fear, perhaps not a fear of physical pain, or of bad things happening. More an inner, innate fear of himself, and of what he was capable of. He felt more than saw that Kane had experienced much, and not all of it good. Yet, Toulla had brought him here. She trusted him. She'd said she knew who he was, and that he was a 'someone,' whatever the hell that meant.

Despite his weary features and dark eyes, and the telltale shaking fingertips that spoke of someone who'd been drinking far too much for far too long, Jeremiah sensed that beneath that exterior was a humble, decent man with great integrity and an unshakable moral code. Kane was a good man. Jerry's kind of man.

He inhaled, and in exactly the same way Toulla had in the car, Jeremiah puffed out his cheeks and exhaled through pursed lips.

"Look, son," he said, "I know I'm wasting my time telling you to leave because it's dangerous. I see it in your eyes. You won't do it. Let me tell ya, neither would I."

The glint in his eyes had returned, and Kane sensed Jerry was about to divulge some crucial information. He was getting closer to unravelling the Oak Island enigma. He could feel it, and his anticipation rose.

"There's another reason you should leave," Jeremiah added. "This time I'm deadly serious."

Oh. Okay, I also wasn't expecting that, Kane thought. He didn't answer. He knew he didn't need to. He glanced at Toulla, who for the first time seemed a little confused. She offered Kane the slightest hint of a shrug. Kane turned back to the old man.

"You should leave, because the thing you seek, and the thing everybody else comes here seeking, simply isn't here. It hasn't been here for two centuries."

Chapter Thirty-Nine

"So where is it?" Kane asked.

That's exactly what Toulla hinted at back in Halifax, that the treasure was long gone. Kane hadn't really been convinced, though he believed she was herself. Yet, the sincerity with which Jeremiah had declared it had proven much more powerful in convincing him. Didn't mean it was good news.

Jeremiah seemed suddenly uneasy, as if he'd let his guard slip and had said too much.

Like uncle, like niece, Kane thought, and pressed the man for answers.

"Where is it, Jeremiah? Do you even know *what* it is? Was it stolen, as Toulla believes? If so, by whom?" Kane was calm, but persistent. "It's all very well being mysterious, but"—he turned to Toulla—"you brought me here. I think I at least deserve some answers. Eh?" Kane added, and it softened Jeremiah's stony face for a brief second.

Jeremiah said, "For the last time, I think you should leave… if you stay it will almost certainly get you—"

"Killed? Yeah, I know." Kane had already weighed up those costs. He didn't care.

Jerry's eyes darkened and a haunted expression shaded his weathered face. "Too many have died already."

"You don't believe in curses, do you?" Kane asked, then laughed. The old man did not.

"Curses in the magical, gypsy sense? Like those fools spout on about on that idiotic TV show? Spells cast by goddamned witches? No, son, I do not believe in those curses. I believe this curse is worse than that. Much, much worse."

Kane felt a wave of exasperation, but swallowed it down. "Look, I'm not leaving, because, even if you say the treasure isn't here, unless you tell me where it is, I won't believe you. So tell me, who stole it? The MDT? (Modern Day Templars) The Illuminati? Some religious cult or other?" Kane paused for a second, watching Jeremiah, who had turned his head away. Finally, Kane asked, "A government?"

Jeremiah turned sharply back to Kane. His eyes flashed between Kane and his niece, then back again. For her part, Toulla suddenly looked guilty, as if she'd let her uncle down.

Now with a resigned look on his wise, sun-beaten face, Jeremiah exhaled. "Meet me tomorrow morning, eight sharp. I have a humble cabin on Vaughans Lake, down Sandy Cove Road. I'll have some answers for you, but I'll tell you now, and I'll even tell you for free, you won't like what you'll hear." He looked at his niece, almost glaring. "Don't come."

"But... Uncle Jerry, you know I—"

"I said no! You know what..."

Jeremiah's voice trailed off. Sadness replaced the resignation, and as the old man looked away, Kane suspected there was more to this relationship than he knew.

With great reluctance, Toulla agreed not to go to her uncle's cabin the next day. After the old salt dog had ducked back through the curtain into the main bar, she glanced at Kane. There was something in her eyes, some hidden message there she wanted to say but couldn't for fear of betraying her uncle.

Just then Jeremiah poked his head back through the curtains. "Not another word of this out in the bar, okay?" Both Kane and Toulla nodded. "Come on, let an old coot buy you kids a drink. It is happy hour after all."

Chapter Forty

After a few more beers for the men—Toulla abstained as she was driving—the afternoon morphed into a fine evening but, unusually, Kane thought, the pub began to empty out. By eight it was just himself, Jeremiah and Toulla, and a handful of other patrons dotted around in twos and threes. Somehow, Johnny Favourite was still managing to play his tunes. Kane was impressed with the man's stamina.

"Alright kids," Jeremiah said, "I'm going to get on home. Touls, would you give me a ride, darling?"

"Of course. Hiram, would you like a lift back to the city?"

Kane thought about it for a moment, but he caught a glimpse out the window across Mahone Bay and as the sun was setting behind them to the west, the orange glow across the lake and the peace and quiet of the pub made it an easy decision to stay. "No, thank you though. I'll get a room nearby, and that way I'll be closer to Jeremiah's place in the morning."

"Fair enough. Good idea," Toulla answered, and Kane

sensed a hint of disappointment in her voice. "I'm sorry I, uh, spied on you this morning," she said, grinning. "I hope you find the answers you're looking for. And hey, I'll pop in and reserve you a room at the motel next door. Just turn up when you're finished here."

"You're very kind, Toulla, thanks. I'll see you around, and thanks for hooking me up with Jerry."

"Don't be late," Jeremiah said as he turned and led his niece out into the dusky evening.

"Here to find the lost treasure, eh?"

Kane turned and found Johnny Favourite next to him at the bar.

"Is it that obvious?"

"We don't get too many visitors, but ninety-five percent of those we do get are only here for one thing. Just speculating, of course."

Kane chuckled. Johnny was right. Yet, it seemed the two people he'd met since arriving in Nova Scotia were utterly convinced he was in the wrong place.

"Guilty," Kane said and Johnny nodded knowingly. "Hey, by the way, great playing mate and I love your voice. Buy you a drink?"

"I'm glad someone noticed. I only still play because, you know, what the hell else would I do? And I get the occasional drink bought for me. Scotch on the rocks. Thanks."

Kane ordered Johnny's drink but hesitated for his own. Things were getting interesting on his quest, but just as he'd begun to feel he was getting somewhere, Toulla and Jeremiah had thrown almighty spanners into the works. But, he was halfway in the bag already, the vibe in the pub was good, Johnny had kept him entertained and, like Johnny, what the hell else would he do all the way out here? Thus, he ordered himself a Scotch too, then wondered why he'd ordered singles and made them both doubles.

"What do you think about it all?" Kane asked Johnny. "Oak Island, I mean."

"I knew what you meant. To be honest, it's all folks out here talk about. You know, I haven't always been a musician. I studied archaeology for a while too, but I got tired of the cold here in the east and went south to sing on the cruise ships. Went really well for a couple of decades, until" —he wafted his glass in Kane's direction— "until this all took ahold and before I knew it my showbiz career was over. I came back north after a few years running bars down in Mexico. Anyway, I digress," Johnny said, slurring his native Newfoundland accent, which sounded somewhere between Canadian, Irish and Scottish, and which Kane found charming.

"Back to your question. I saw you speaking with old man Ball and his niece. You know who he's related to, eh?"

"Samuel Ball? The man with the money?"

"The very same. Yeah, old Jerry is a direct descendent of the richest man Canada has ever known, and yet most people prefer to believe the fairytale that the treasure is still buried somewhere on the island."

"I take it you don't believe that?" Kane asked.

"If I were you," Johnny said, his eyes narrowing ever so slightly, "I would believe whatever the old man tells you. There isn't a person alive who knows more about it than Jerry, except maybe his niece," Johnny said, adding a wink. "Ah, Toulla Corti… Johnny Favourite and Toulla Corti does have a nice ring to it, doesn't it? Or it would if she'd just accept the rings I've been offering her for years now."

"You asked her to marry you?"

"Four times, maybe five. Fine, it's eight. 'Not my type', she always says. She's just wrong, that's all. But don't worry, my new friend, it'll soon be my birthday and I shall ask the future ex Mrs Favourite again."

Kane laughed, enjoying Johnny's friendly manner, and wondered how much he really knew. He didn't want to spoil the moment, however, and instead bought another round and before he knew it, it was closing time and he was suitably wasted. Wasted enough to make a terrible decision.

After saying farewell to the wonderful Johnny Favourite, he set off on the hour-long walk to Old Man Ball's cabin on the lake.

Chapter Forty-One

It seemed like a good idea, but after stumbling at the first hurdle... the bottom step out of The Salty Dog... he wisely changed his mind and was soon checked in at the motel. The receptionist hadn't been at all surprised at the time of his arrival, as if she'd been tipped off somehow.

Thanks, Toulla, Kane mused. *Have I become so readable?*

He found his room and, suddenly exhausted, he curled up on the bed, his mind flitting between thoughts of Jeremiah and Samuel Ball, Professors O'nians and Peerdeman, all things Oak Island, and of course Ridley, and how shit his life was without her in it.

Kane didn't get hangovers. He occasionally woke a little foggy, sometimes even sluggish. But a quick, cool shower and some deep breaths of fresh air was always enough to launch him into a new day. Today was no different. He always awoke naturally and by seven o'clock, after a cup of tea he'd made in the room and a stale sandwich he'd snagged from a vending machine in the downstairs lobby, Kane was making long strides inland from Zwickers Bay en route to his meeting with the mercurial old-timer, Jeremiah Samuel Ball.

As he approached the cabin, nestled remotely among the trees at the end of Sandy Cove Road with a commanding view over Vaughans Lake, something felt off. Unbidden, the hairs on the back of Kane's neck tingled, and instinctively he backed behind the slender trunk of a jack pine. He waited, listening, but heard only the gentle rustle of branches above and the occasional cawing from an unseen crow or two.

He poked his head out slowly from behind the trunk. Nothing looked untoward. No visible cars. Nobody anywhere in sight. All was quiet and still.

What the hell's wrong with you? Kane chided himself, wondering if the booze had finally rendered him too paranoid.

He took a deep breath, then stepped out from behind the tree and strolled casually towards the cabin. He kept his eyes and ears alert but otherwise remained calm and measured.

He checked his watch. 7:56 am. *Close enough.* Kane knocked on the sturdy timber door and stepped back, waiting for Jeremiah to answer.

After receiving no welcome for a full two minutes, Kane knocked again and waited. When he'd knocked a third time with no response, the first knot of unease formed in his gut. His throat was suddenly dry, and he took a swig from his waterbottle. Inhaling, he stepped down from the porch and headed round the back of the cabin, glancing in each window as he passed and keeping his senses on full alert. The house was built on a slight incline, which sloped down towards the lake, meaning the house was essentially constructed on two levels. When he reached the rear of the cabin, from which the passive waters of the lake could be viewed from a wide, expansive deck, he was at the lower floor of the house.

Kane sensed he was being watched. He paused, listening, yet heard nothing other than the birds and the distant hum of a small motorboat.

Stepping up onto the deck, he edged towards the back patio doors. They weren't fully closed, and a thin curtain within fluttered on the gentlest of breezes. Unclosed doors probably weren't that unusual all the way out here, where Kane suspected crime rates were low if not zero. *Still…*

He downed the rest of the water and discarded the bottle on a wooden bench. With a couple of deep breaths, and focusing his mind, Kane silently slid open the patio doors enough to step through and enter the cabin.

The hum of an approaching motorboat grew louder but Kane barely registered it now he was inside. At the same time, somewhere in the cabin a dog whined, and it was such a mournful sound it send adrenalin fizzing through his veins.

Chapter Forty-Two

Something in the air told Kane things weren't right in the cabin. The atmosphere felt heavy, as if closing in all around him. Suffocating. Stifling. On top of that, the dog whine was unlike any animal noise he'd ever heard. Traumatic. Distraught.

Kane shrugged off his own burgeoning anxiety and raced from room to room searching for the dog, and what, or whom, he feared he'd find with it. Moving at pace but with soft steps from the main reception room and up the narrow stairs to the kitchen, then into one bedroom followed by another, Kane found nothing. No sign of any disturbance, no hint at any struggle. He didn't want to call out and alert any possible intruders.

There were just a couple more rooms to try. First he trod gently to the bathroom and found it empty. Last of all he found a study room, and a swift glance around showed him walls lined floor-to-ceiling with bookcases filled to bursting.

Kane froze when he thought he heard a door click shut

somewhere in the house, but only silence followed and he dismissed it as the kind of sound all old wooden houses made.

He recalled seeing one final door back down the stairs, and he hustled down them, ears straining for any sounds other than those he himself made. Again he heard the dog, and knew now it was behind that final door. He stepped quietly up to it, and after a deep breath, turned the handle and stepped inside.

No! No, no, no!

Lying on his back, arms splayed out at his sides and legs crumpled beneath him, was old man Ball. Jeremiah's eyes remained open, staring lifelessly at the ceiling above. The dog was laying at his side, head resting on Jeremiah's thigh and growling so quietly Kane could hardly hear it.

Kane spotted the blood.

He stepped cautiously over to the body and knelt down beside it.

"Hey boy," he said gently, letting the dog know he was a friend. The dog growled a couple more times, then fell quiet, sensing Kane meant no further harm to his master.

There was no more harm to be done.

"It's okay... I won't hurt you."

Kane reached out and clasped Jeremiah's bearded chin and tilted his head gently to one side, certain of what he'd see. The old man's throat splayed wide open and he had been left to bleed out. The blood on Kane's hands was still a bit warm and he realised whoever had done this to the poor old boy could still be close and probably was.

A bead of sweat trickled down Kane's back, but then he felt eyes on him and a cold shiver bade the hairs on his neck to stand up. Kane rose from his crouch and turned, expecting to come face-to-face with a killer. Instead, Toulla was standing there. As Kane had moved, he'd cleared Toulla's view to her stricken uncle. When she saw he was dead, she screamed, and it was the haunted sound of complete devastation.

She rushed to Jeremiah, dropping to her knees and wrapping her arms around him. Huge, wracking sobs caused her shoulders to rise and fall as tears streamed onto Jeremiah's cheeks, now pale from lack of blood.

"I knew it," Toulla muttered. "I knew it."

Kane didn't know what to do. His thoughts had already moved on, from shock and sorrow, to survival. If the killers were close by, and he had to assume they were due to the warm blood, then they had to get the hell out of there.

"We have to go, Toulla. It's not safe here."

"I knew this would happen. I knew it," she said, her voice raw with emotion. "I knew it."

It wasn't only sadness Kane heard in those words, though. He sensed anger there, frustration, as if Toulla had known this would happen, and it was only a matter of when, not if.

"As soon as you turned up, I knew something bad was coming," she said, turning and looking at Kane. He sensed no blame there, no accusation towards him, yet he felt it anyway. Bad things happened to good people when he was around. There were many reasons he had taken himself off to a remote island off southern Cambodia. That was one of them.

"It was always going to end this way," Toulla said. "Uncle Jerry knew too much. He knew this would happen too, but he was too stubborn to do anything about security. Too fucking reckless."

"It's my fault," Kane said, kneeling down beside Toulla. "I led them here."

Kane's head dropped and his shoulders sagged. He exhaled, air escaping his lungs. Escaping his guilt was something Kane couldn't ever do.

"Sorry," was all he could manage and it wasn't enough and he knew it never would be.

A dense quietude filled the room. Kane stood and stepped away, leaning on a wall as Toulla reached over and stroked Jeremiah's beloved Alsatian, Fantome.

"Why are you really here?" Toulla asked over her shoulder without turning.

"You know why I'm here," Kane said, confused.

"No, I mean, really? You can't believe the treasure is in the Money Pit, not with what you've learned. So what is it? Are you being paid? Are you working for a collector?" She arced her neck and locked eyes on Kane. "Or is it something else, something more... personal?"

Kane was taken aback by the question. She seemed to know the answer already, although in truth it was a combination of all three.

Kane decided that, under the circumstances of what had just happened to her uncle, Toulla deserved to know the truth.

"I was approached by someone, a Frenchman, maybe French-Canadian. He essentially told me he believed the treasure was still here, and said that because he was no longer allowed in Canada—he didn't explain why—he wanted me to go in his place. He provided me with unlimited funds to search and said I was to do whatever it took. He also added that it was all more important than I could know, though he left that last bit vague."

Toulla nodded, clearly not surprised by anything Kane had yet said. She sensed he wasn't finished, and waited for him to divulge the rest.

He took the cue. "And yes, it is something more personal. As you've probably read—"

"I did," Toulla said flatly, a hint of sympathy in her eyes.

"Then you'll know the last couple of years have been difficult. Traumatic. Especially what happened in Egypt. I've lost everything... my career, my reputation, a good friend, my grandfather... my love. I almost lost my life. I needed to find purpose, something to pull me back from the brink and give me something to... well, to live for. I thought this might be it. I hoped it was, anyway. So... here I am."

Toulla Corti stood up and stepped away from her stricken Uncle Jerry and moved towards Kane. "And, here I am. I can help you in this thing, this quest you're on. We are in this together now," she told him.

"No way, Toulla. It's too dangerous. Look what... look what they did to your uncle. I won't take you with me. I can't."

"You don't have a choice, Hiram." She looked down at Jeremiah, cold and lifeless on the floor. Fantome, the dog, had come to stand by her legs. She'd need to find a home for the old Alsatian. Inhaling, Toulla held the breath in for a few seconds and closed her eyes. Finally, she let it out and opened her eyes again, settling them on Kane. In those eyes Kane saw a mix of emotions. Stoicism. Anger. Sadness. Most of all, determination.

"I've lost everything too. They've taken it all from me. But I know where it is, the treasure. I'm sure of it. Take me with you, Hiram. I need this now, too. Not just for me. For Jerry. My dad. For myself."

"I don't know, Toulla. You've seen what these people are capable of. They tried to kill me, twice. I'm certain they killed the professor down in New Orleans. They've murdered your uncle, Toulla, and it's obvious—"

"They also killed my father," Toulla stated quietly. "Ten years ago. I was only seventeen. Uncle Jerry took care of me."

"They killed your father? Shit, Toulla, I'm so sorry. But why? And who did? Who are these people? How do you know it's the same guys?"

"He got too close. My dad, he… he found something."

"What? What did he find? Where?"

The sound of a distant motorboat engine roaring nearer shattered a silence only punctuated by their voices. Both spun on their heels and raced to the wide window, which was just a foot above the ground level outside. Kane didn't see anything but felt sure it wasn't good news.

"Listen, if you let me join you, I'll tell you everything I know." The hint of a grin glinted in Toulla's eyes as she said, "I'll be your goddamned partner," evoking a scene from *Raiders of the Lost Ark*.

Kane exhaled through his nose. He got the reference, but it wasn't funny. None of this shit was funny. He'd think about what to do with Toulla later. Now they had to get out of there—

The window exploded as automatic machine gun fire destroyed the timber wall and obliterated the ceiling above their heads.

Chapter Forty-Three

They flung themselves to the floor, only to be showered with flying chunks of timber and jagged shards of glass from the devastated wall and window.

"What the fuck?" Toulla yelled, doing her best to cover Fantome with her arms. "Jesus!"

Kane kept his head down as the firing ceased. He ran a quick mental pain check and found he wasn't hit and somehow uninjured by cascading debris. That could only have been pure luck. It wouldn't last.

Fuck! How the hell do we get out of here?

"Toulla, do you have a car here?"

"Yeah. No… it's a couple blocks away. Too far to make it."

Shit! "Did you hear a boat? Is that what that engine was?"

"Yeah, I think so… there's a small dock on the lake. Jerry has a small boat here but I don't know if it's in service or even in the water."

Kane listened for the inevitable sound of approaching

bad guys. He heard nothing, which wasn't a good sign. It meant they'd upped their game. They'd let Kane slip away before. They wouldn't let it happen again.

He turned towards the log-built wall facing the lake, which was now shredded and barely worthy of the name. What it did provide was sufficient cover to take a look outside without being seen. He edged forwards and, narrowing his eyes, he scanned the vast rear garden that sloped down to the lake. Two large figures were striding with intent towards the cabin. The men—certainly the same bastards from New Orleans—split and spread out over the grassy, undulating ground, now a hundred yards away; a pincer movement, covering all escape from the rear. For all Kane knew they had more men blocking their escape from the front of the property too.

Kane believed their only hope was that the two men circled the property on either side to the front, allowing he and Toulla to flee from their spot in the rear centre of the cabin and make it away in the would-be killer's own boat. That would need these clowns to be alone, and stupid. Preferably both. Kane's experience of the men suggested that although they were killers, they weren't especially good at killing. He'd out-manoeuvred them twice already.

Yet, where they were hidden, at least for now, they remained sitting ducks. It was only a matter of time until they were discovered. They needed to do something. It had to be soon.

Kane felt Toulla slide in next to him against the wall.

"What's the plan?" she whispered.

"Don't know… hold on…"

One of the men continued on his steady trajectory towards the northern side of the cabin. Kane couldn't make out his face, but his head was moving slowly from left to right, clearly scanning the scene and searching.

The other guy also continued towards the south side of the structure. That suggested they were working alone; it gave him a surge of hope. "See the two men?"

"Yeah. Fucking murdering bastards."

"I think they're alone. I think we wait to see if they continue to the front. If they do, we sprint for their boat." Kane heard Toulla breathing deeply through her nostrils. He cast a glance sideways and saw her eyes were closed, as if fighting to regain control and not do something stupid... something that would get her killed. She'd just found her uncle, slain inside his own home. Kane couldn't imagine the levels of grief she was dealing with, and his heart ached for her.

He turned back to the garden and spotted something else which added more hope to his plan. Another boat, presumably Jerry's. It was far to the south, still on the property but with perhaps a hundred and fifty yards to cover across open ground to reach it. Risky. Even if they made the boat unseen, it might not be operational. There might not be keys. Maybe no engine. If they found it unusable, they would surely be spotted running for the gunmen's boat. Kane exhaled.

"Wait," Toulla said, a little louder than she'd meant. "Shit, sorry," she whispered.

"What is it?"

"Uncle Jerry's boat, its name."

"Its name? What about it?" Kane asked, unsure if this was the right time for reminiscing.

"It's genius... he was a genius."

"The name of the boat is Genius?"

"No… even better. *Houdini*. The boat's called *Houdini*, named after—"

"The world's most famous escape artist," Kane said, finishing the thread. "Perhaps the old man wasn't as unprepared as you thought… eh?"

Kane looked back through the hole and spotted the guy to their right disappear around the northwest corner of the cabin.

Good. Keep moving…

His eyes drifted south in time to see the other gunman edging closer to the southwest corner.

Come on, come on, Kane thought, willing the universe for just a fair chance of making it to the boat alive. *Almost there…*

"On three," Kane hissed. "Ready?"

"Ready," Toulla answered. "Ready, boy?" she muttered in Fantome's ear. "We're going for a run."

"Three… two…"

"Where the hell are they?" yelled one of the men from somewhere around the side of the cabin, perhaps thirty yards from Kane and Toulla.

"Keep heading to the front," came the shouted response, mercifully farther away.

"Right," yelled the first voice, also sounding farther away now.

Good… here's our chance.

"One," Kane said quietly. He leapt to his feet and hustled to the door, Toulla and Fantome right on his heels. He eased the door open silently, miraculously undamaged by the earlier onslaught. He poked his head out, scanning the lounge area and up the stairs, seeing or hearing no sign of the intruders. He figured they had about forty-five seconds. Sixty tops.

"Shit, what about keys?" Toulla muttered. "I don't recall what kind of boat it is."

"We'll take our chances, but unless I've missed my guess, the old man anticipated this moment and keys won't be a problem. Let's go. And Toulla?"

Toulla glanced at Kane, a mixture of fear and—was that excitement?—glinting in her wide green eyes.

Green eyes, just like Ridley's.

"Yeah?" she asked.

"Run fast."

Toulla nodded, and a second later Kane, Toulla and Fantome were outside the cabin and sprinting for their very lives across the vast patch of land beneath which old Jeremiah Ball had buried secrets he would never now get the chance to reveal.

Chapter Forty-Four

"Je ne comprends pas," Clement spat. *I don't understand.*

"Where the fuck are they?" Claude yelled.

The two brothers had searched the entire house in less than two minutes, and there was no sign of Kane. Each brother thought the other one was a stupid fuckwit, but this time they'd both outdone themselves.

"It's impossible we've missed them. They cannot have —" Clement paused as he heard the roar of a motorboat starting up. "Merde!"

The brothers raced through the house and burst onto the back deck. From there, they saw Kane and a woman gliding along the lake a few yards out from the shore... towards their own boat. Clement wasted no time raising his semi-automatic and firing in the general direction of the moving boat. His aim had never been good and he missed his target by a country mile.

Claude had guessed the Englishman's plan and barrelled hard down the slope to intervene. Sadly, he didn't know the terrain and mis-stepped over a small ditch and face-planted into the firm ground, crashing in a heap of flailing arms and legs.

Fifty yards behind him, Clement had abandoned his long-distance firing and was running to join him.

"Get up, you fucking clown... we have to stop them."

Claude growled as he rose to his feet, scraping mud and grit from his battered face. "Fucking clown, am I? Watch your mouth, brother, or I'll show you who the clown is."

Clement ignored the threat and the two thugs raced on, now just a hundred yards from their quarry.

"Quick," Toulla yelled as she steered the *Houdini* towards the other boat that bobbed, untethered, at the shore, "jump out and snag the cleat on the bow."

Kane waited a few more seconds until their boat was close enough, then he jumped out and raced to the front of the other boat, one eye on his target and the other on the two killers determined to kill him. He snagged the cleat on the bow and pulled it around, now standing waist deep in the lake. The boat swung around easily, and he pulled it towards the *Houdini*, where Toulla waited with a length of rope.

It was risky, but the *Houdini* could not outrun the killers' boat, so their only hope was to haul it far away up the lake. By the time the men reached it, they would be long gone.

Toulla had told Kane she knew the vast network of small streams and creeks that fed the lake like the back of her hand, and was certain they could make it into one of those and never be found by the killers.

In a game of risk versus reward, the reward was their very lives.

Kane figured they had thirty seconds before the men reached the shore. "Come on, Toulla, tie it on. Quick."

He jumped into *Houdini* as Toulla dextrously secured the two boats together with a swift yet unyielding cleat hitch knot.

"They're closing in," he yelled.

Five seconds later, Toulla said, "Don't wait for me... grab the wheel and go. Now," she shouted, and with a final glance her way, Kane did as he was instructed and pushed the throttle forward, easing the *Houdini* away from the shore just as Toulla's knot bit tight.

Semi-automatic rifle rounds sprayed the lake surface all around them and Kane and Toulla flung themselves into the bottom of the boat, Toulla dragging a barking Fantome down with her. Kane had to risk keeping one arm extended to keep pressure on the throttle.

Several audible thunks suggested the killer's aims were improving, but a glance around showed Kane no obvious damage to the *Houdini*. He grinned as he realised they were shooting up their own boat.

Fucking idiots.

"What the fuck are you doing? Have you got shit for brains?" Clement bellowed as Claude's latest flurry of shots tore into the back of their vessel. "You'll destroy our own boat."

"It is worth the risk, bâtard. If they get away, we may never find them again." Claude raised his weapon again but before he could pull the trigger, Clement slapped it down.

"No, stop!" he shouted. "Think about it. They will never get away."

Claude glared at his brother, spittle spraying from

between his gritted teeth. With more than a little reluctance, he lowered the weapon, inwardly conceding that for once, his brother was right.

"I think we're clear," Kane said after no further rounds had been fired for a couple of minutes. They were almost a mile up the lake now, and way out of range.

"That was a brilliant idea," Toulla told him.

"A lucky idea. I didn't have time to think," Kane said. "When I have time to think, that's when I mess things up. Where are we headed? You said you know this lake well."

"I do. Listen, I need to go back to the house. I saw something. I think it's—"

"Are you insane?" Kane cut in. "We can't go back. The authorities will be crawling all over the place by the time we get back there. Not to mention the two men with big guns. It's not possible, Toulla."

"It's highly unlikely the authorities will be there. It's an hour from the nearest police station and no one else lives within two miles of the place. It's the remoteness why Uncle Jerry lived there."

"And the psychos with big guns?" Kane was incredulous. She had balls, he'd give her that.

"We leave the boat a tempting distance away, in sight of the western shore. We'll also pull a few wires out, and the fuel line. They'll find a way to get to it… it'll take them about a half hour. They will find a useless boat. By then, we'll be back to the house, I'll grab the thing I saw, then we'll use my car to get away. It's a solid plan."

Didn't sound that solid of a plan to Kane, though he saw the logic. Toulla nodded to the shore over Kane's left shoulder and he turned to look. He didn't see anything of note.

"What about it?" he asked.

"Like I said, I know this place better than anyone, better even than Jerry." Toulla's shoulders slumped at the mention of her uncle's name.

"I'm so sorry about Jeremiah, Toulla. I truly am."

Toulla cuffed a solitary tear from one eye and stared at Kane. "I'm going back to the house. Through those trees is a small creek. We follow the creek a mile east and then it veers south half a mile to a dead end adjacent to a friend's cabin. We leave the *Houdini* there and we can leave Fantome there too. She'll be fine with old Billy. Then on foot we cut across the forest back to the cabin."

"What did you see at the cabin?" Kane asked, unwilling to commit to returning to the cabin unless they had good reason.

Toulla held his gaze for long seconds, before finally answering. "Rather than tell you, I'll show you. Believe me, you'll want to know."

"Come on, Toulla, what is it? It's so risky to go back there. What could possibly be worth dying for?"

Toulla inhaled, then let it out slowly. Kane noticed a twinkle in her eyes. "It's a simple file, with the letters S. T. R A. P. printed on the front. Below that it says, The Allegiance." Toulla's eyebrows rose, as if to say, *What do you think about that?*

S. T. R. A. P. Kane mused, spelling the letters out again in his mind. *The Allegiance? What the hell is The Allegiance? And, Strap? STRAP?*

S. T. R. A. P.
Holy shit!

Chapter Forty-Five

"What are they doing?" Claude said as the brothers stared north up the lake towards their boat.

Kane and the woman—the brothers agreed she was collateral damage and needed to be despatched, just like the old—had just set their boat adrift and had sped across the lake to the eastern side, where they'd disappeared from view.

They hustled along the shore to the west in search of a trail that would lead them to their boat. "This English bastard is really starting to piss me off," Clement hissed through clenched jaws. "When I get hold of him I'm going to rip his head off and shit—"

"Just like you did last time?" Claude teased. "The guy broke your fucking nose, brother. Best leave the beating up to me."

"Are you serious?" Clement growled as they trotted along the narrow trail. "I don't recall you doing much better as he slammed you into that door."

They fell silent as they jogged northwards, both secretly

wondering if they'd lost their edge, or if they'd underestimated the Englishman. They wouldn't make the same mistake again.

Kane undid the knot at the cleat hitch and set the boat loose, nudging it gently away.

Toulla had already detached the fuel line, as well as drowning the spark plugs and pulling out any other exposed wires she spotted. It would take the thugs at least twenty minutes to rewire the boat and dry off the plugs, but none of that mattered without any fuel. She felt confident now her plan was solid, and as she steered the *Houdini* across Vaughns Lake, she allowed herself a moment of grief as her mind settled on her beloved Uncle Jeremiah and the condition of his body as it lay crumpled on the ground, covered in blood from where his throat had been sliced wide open and he'd been left to rot.

Naturally, Toulla was devastated he was gone, and the grisly, callous manner of his death broke her heart. But she was also frustrated. With Jeremiah. With her father. Even with Kane, who she'd only just met but who she now feared might be facing the same horrific outcome as the other men in her life.

She was frustrated with the way her father and uncle had kept things from her. She had long suspected they weren't always honest with her when discussing the enigma surrounding Oak Island, the Money Pit and of course, the *Fantome*.

She had her own theories, and while they had humoured her, she'd never felt as if she were welcome in their inner circle. It had driven her mad at times, while on other occasions she sensed the gravitas of it all and backed down. Now though, she'd spotted the file labelled S.T.R.A.P. and was more certain than ever there was more to all this than even she knew. She'd seen the file after the first round of weapons fire had decimated the cabin wall. It had fallen to the ground amid the splintered wood and rubble from the ceiling, and had clearly been hidden in its spot for a long time, based on the dust coating its surface. She'd scooped it up, but then more incoming fire had caused them to take cover and it slipped from her arms. The next thing she knew they were running for the *Houdini*.

Going back was risky, even foolish. Toulla knew it. But she was so certain there was something revelatory in that file that she was determined to retrieve it before the authorities, or the killers, closed in.

She focused on steering the *Houdini* into the creek, so hidden by overgrowth that to anyone who didn't know it was there, they would never find it.

Kane sat facing backwards, keeping an eye on their tail though certain the killers wouldn't be able to follow.

S.T.R.A.P.

Kane had heard the acronym before, though he knew there was no official meaning to it. Some theorists believed it was an acronym for STRategic Action Plan, and reserved only for top-secret military documents. Others claimed it was actually a British military codeword, and not an acronym at all. If the former were true, and it was an acronym, what the hell was it doing buried in the walls of a remote cabin in Nova Scotia?

What about The Allegiance? That sounded like some kind of secret cult organisation out of a Dan Brown novel. To Kane that actually seemed more plausible, but the fact they were printed together on the same file was bewildering to him, and not for the first time in recent days he was facing more questions than answers.

"Here's the dead-end I mentioned," Toulla told him, snatching Kane from his thoughts.

Toulla hopped out of the *Houdini*, and Fantome jumped out after her, seemingly recognising where she was. Kane followed suit, and after securing the boat to the tiny dock at the end of the creek, and after Toulla had encouraged Fantome through the concealed gate amongst some bushes, she led Kane away from the creek and into a dense wooded area.

"How far back to the cabin?" he asked.

"Fifteen minutes if we trot," Toulla called over her shoulder from up ahead, already powering along the trail. Kane had to hustle to keep up, once again reminded how determined the young woman was, and how old he was feeling.

He wondered about her relationship with Jeremiah, and was curious how much she really knew. More important, how little she knew. Kane was getting the sense the old man's death had left too many unanswered questions for Toulla, and now that the best source of those answers had been eliminated, she was taking it upon herself to seek out the truth, whatever it might prove to be.

Kane didn't want to feel responsible for her. She was a young woman with her whole life ahead of her. He didn't need reminding that at least one person had been killed since this all began, and likely two if his fears about Anja Peerdeman were true. The way Toulla was rushing head-first back into potential danger filled Kane with an all too familiar dread. But he was powerless to stop her, especially in her own country. All he could do was try to help keep her safe, and to get this over with as fast as possible.

He lengthened his stride and caught up to Toulla, negotiating the winding, narrow trail as easily as if she'd navigated it a hundred times, which he supposed she probably had.

A few minutes later she slowed down and then as they approached a less dense section of woods, she stopped altogether.

"We're here. Just through these trees is the far eastern edge of Jerry's property. Listen… no sirens. No flashing lights. Nobody anywhere near here."

Kane edged forward. He wasn't worried about the authorities. They hadn't done anything wrong. He was more concerned with the psychotic brothers whose idiocy would only spare Kane a certain amount of times, and he didn't want to serve himself, nor Toulla, up on a plate.

They waited silently, listening, watching for movement. Kane sensed Toulla's reluctance for patience, but after a full five minutes, now certain the coast was clear, he said, "Okay, let's go."

They moved stealthily out of the treeline and darted across the clearing, and made it to the cabin in seconds.

Chapter Forty-Six

The mercenary brothers maintained a decent pace, considering their sizes, their long, strong legs powering them on. In truth, it was their target that inspired such commitment to reach their boat in quick order. Kane had eluded them too often now, and with that bitch alongside him, they would have double the fun when they finally despatched them.

"Buy one get one free," Clement had said halfway to the boat, and despite himself, Claude had chuckled. He wiped the smile off his face though and focused on the trail, which widened and narrowed at irregular intervals and made the going treacherous. Getting whipped across the face by low-hanging branches wasn't helping his mood either.

It's okay, he thought, *I'll take it out on Kane and make his whore watch before she and I enjoy a little private time.*

They were soon trotting up alongside the boat, which drifted thirty foot shore.

"In you go, little brother," Clement said without even trying to disguise his glee.

"You fucking get it," Claude retorted, though he knew this was one argument he couldn't win. Regardless of how he felt about it, for now his brother was still his boss. For now. Secretly, Claude had plans afoot to shake up that hierarchy in the not-too-distant future.

He decided against stripping off his jeans and waded into the water, which was deeper than he'd expected and he was soon in frigid water up to his neck. He ignored Clement guffawing on the bank and hauled their boat towards shore, before clambering out of the lake and helping secure it to a nearby tree trunk.

Clement tried the electric ignition. Somehow, he was surprised when it didn't start first time. He tried again, and when it didn't start on the third attempt he knew the boat had been sabotaged.

"Fils de pute!" he growled. *Son of a bitch.* "Get it fixed," he shouted at Claude, who was more mechanical and had already started checking things.

"No fuel," he stated matter-of-factly after a minute of checks. "Wet spark plugs. Wires yanked out. We're dead in the water."

"Putain de mère!" Clement bellowed, this time invoking Kane's mother and what he'd like to do to her.

Kane remained on the back deck to keep watch while Toulla went inside. She knew where to find the S.T.R.A.P. file, but she'd also asked for a moment alone with her uncle, Jeremiah.

Kane had reluctantly agreed, on the condition she wasn't too long. He didn't want to be insensitive, but at the same time, getting yourself killed by paying respects to the dead seemed a counter-intuitive compromise. Toulla had simply nodded and stepped inside, returning a moment later with the mysterious file, which she handed to Kane before stepping back inside the cabin.

"Five minutes," he called out to her. "Please."

Kane glanced at the cover of the file with something like awe. Of course, he had no idea what was inside, but the fact it had been hidden inside the structure of an ancient log cabin in a remote corner of Nova Scotia, at the end of Gold River and very close to Oak Island, not to mention in the home of an Oak Island and *Fantome* scholar, who just happened to be a direct descendent of none other than Samuel Ball... well, it couldn't just be nothing.

He wanted to open it now, find out what it contained, but decided to wait until they were safely away from the cabin. Kane knew he'd been sloppy lately and to let his guard down now might put them both in danger. He didn't care much for himself, but now he had Toulla Corti on his watch, and after being in part responsible for the death of her uncle, he wasn't going to let anything happen to the young archivist.

Is that all she is? He was starting to doubt it.

He tucked the file into his satchel and focused on the lake and the trails meandering away on either side, almost expecting to see the big thugs charging their way with weapons raised and ready to commit bloody murder.

Toulla knelt down beside her uncle, Jeremiah Ball. She inhaled and, tentatively, she reached out and placed her palms on his cheeks. They felt cold to the touch and an involuntary shiver made the hairs on her neck stand up.

"What were you hiding from me all these years, Jerry?"

she whispered, cognisant of the fact that he would forever be hiding it now, whatever it was. "What did you and Dad know that you wouldn't let me in on?"

Toulla didn't think it was because they didn't trust her. She knew that they did, and in fact, they told her often that she was the best of them all. In her heart of hearts, she knew it was because they were protecting her.

But from what? From whom?

It drove her mad realising she may never now learn their secrets. Would never know what they knew.

However, they hadn't raised her that way. Not her Uncle Jerry, nor her father until his death. They had taught her to be curious. They'd shown her to dig for answers. They had shared all their wisdom about all the secrets surrounding the greatest unsolved mystery of the last two hundred years, and which was right on their doorstep.

Well, obviously not all the secrets. Certainly not the most important of them all.

On their doorstep. Hmm…

Toulla's mind settled on the bizarre folder she'd found. She didn't know what it contained, but the fact it was here in Jerry's house was surely significant. They were descendants of Samuel Ball. They had lived their entire lives within an hour of Oak Island and the Money Pit, and a few miles from where the legendary *Fantome* had sunk. She had only moved to the city to work as an archivist at The Archives building downtown in hope of learning more about the enigma surrounding the area, otherwise she'd have been content pulling pints and serving food at the Salty Dog, happy to be close to the action on Oak Island.

Toulla leaned over and kissed her beloved uncle on both cheeks, and remained there for a full minute before easing herself away and standing up. She swiped at a couple of tears, though as she turned to leave, she paused.

She kneeled down again, and reached for her uncle's hand. Something had caught her eye there, and as she unfurled his fingers, already stiff from the onset of early rigor mortis, she gasped when she saw he was clutching a note.

Carefully, she removed the note and unfolded the paper. In her uncle's recognisable scrawl, the note read:

> *You were always the best of us.*
> *Be careful my darling.*
> *Never come back here.*
> *The Allegiance has the answers.*
> *Love,*
> *Uncle Jerry x*

Toulla inhaled and once again stood up. She looked down at her uncle and said, "I will find my answers," before turning and leaving her uncle's side for the very last time.

Kane turned upon hearing the back door of the cabin open. "Everything okay?" he asked, though of course it wasn't.

"Yeah," Toulla replied, calmer than she felt. "Come on, let's get out of here."

Just moments later they were cruising in Toulla's Jeep down the remote road away from Jeremiah Ball's lakeside cabin, just as a pair of police cars came roaring up the other way, their sirens wailing and their blue and red lights signalling the rush they were in, and which were closely followed by a series of local and national news vans.

"I called them," Toulla said, her eyes focused only on the road.

"What did you tell them?" Kane asked.

"I told them that the Oak Island enigma had been solved, and that the only person who knew the truth, local legend Jeremiah Ball, had been murdered for his secrets."

Chapter Forty-Seven

"We need to know exactly what's in the file," Toulla stated, leaving no room for compromise.

They had driven at speed away from Jeremiah's cabin and the media circus now gathering there, and had taken a couple of off-road trails that put them literally off the grid and somewhere they both felt confident they couldn't be tracked.

"We're safe here. So go ahead, open it," Kane said quietly. He was keen to look himself, but he wanted Toulla to have the first look. It did belong to her uncle, after all, or at least, it was under his guardianship.

Guardians? Hmm, Kane mused, the first flutterings of an idea forming in his mind.

A clap of thunder somewhere in the distance startled them both. Under the cover of the forest, they hadn't noticed the beginnings of a storm approaching.

They stepped out of the Jeep and moved around to the hood, where Toulla placed the file out before them. Somehow, the moment seemed tense. Toulla's chest rose and fell, as if she were nervous and reluctant to learn what secrets the file might or might not hold.

"Go ahead," Kane said, encouraging her to proceed. Although he felt safe, there was no point dilly-dallying now.

Toulla inhaled and rolled her shoulders, as if about to engage in a bout of sparring. Then she took a step back. "I can't. I don't know why, but I just can't. Sorry. Please, open it."

Kane nodded and placed a hand on Toulla's arm. "It's okay. I've got this."

A steady breeze had started up and cool gusts of air whistled through the trees above.

Kane moved closer and lifted the file. He was surprised to feel his hands were clammy, and a bead of sweat formed on his brow. He shook his head and lifted the front flap of the file.

His first reaction when he looked inside was one of disappointment. A single sheet of aged paper rested there. It was old, but not quite parchment-old. At first glance Kane dated it at around a hundred years old, maybe two hundred at a stretch.

At the top of the page was a diagram, faded, though Kane could still more or less make it out. He instantly recognised the Masonic compass and square. Above that was a version of the all-seeing eye, plus a sun and a moon, classic Masonic iconography. He also saw a few other less recognisable marks and couldn't guess at their meaning.

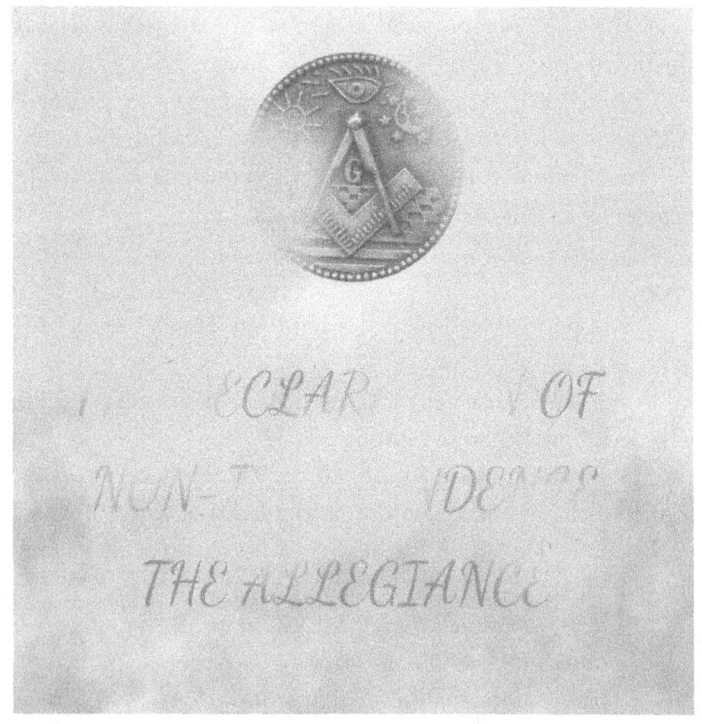

Below that was a series of words that formed the title of the document, though they were so worn Kane couldn't make them out.

Only two words were clear: THE ALLEGIANCE

"Who and what is The Allegiance?" Kane said.

Upon hearing Kane mention The Allegiance, Toulla stepped closer and leaned in to get a better look, her anxiety having receded somewhat. She also reached into her pocket to retrieve the note Jeremiah had clung to even after he'd been slain.

"I don't know," Toulla told him, "but Uncle Jeremiah obviously did."

She showed Kane the note, which he read aloud.

"You were always the best of us.
Be careful my darling.
Never come back here.
The Allegiance has the answers.
Love, Uncle Jerry x

"Have you ever heard of The Allegiance before?" he asked.

Toulla thought about it for a moment, her brow furrowed in concentration. Kane watched as her eyelids twitched, as if some memory or other was flashing somewhere in her mind.

"Maybe. I can't be sure. Sorry, not much help here, I know."

"It's fine. So, we need to find out who this Allegiance is as a priority. But first I need to… well, you're not going to like it…"

Toulla's eyes settled on Kane's. She saw a mix of determination and mischief there. It was a good look, and one she recognised in herself. "Go on," she encouraged, though she had an idea what he was about to propose.

Suddenly, another clap of thunder heralded the arrival of heavy rain. Kane scooped up the file and the pair of them hustled into the sanctuary of the Jeep. Huge raindrops drummed on the roof and glancing out, they realised how dark it had become, despite it only being midday.

Kane turned to face Toulla in the driver's seat. He waited, trying to assess her state of mind. *Bollocks to it*, he thought, then said, "Have you got access to any diving gear?" Kane shrugged, offering Toulla his best naughty schoolboy grin.

"Oh, hell no," she stated.

"I need to know. I have to be sure," Kane said.

"Know what?"

"I want to dive on the *Fantome*."

"It's a waste of time and too dangerous. I already told you there's nothing there to see."

"I don't care about the danger... I need to—"

As another bout of rumbling thunder echoed through the trees, the more slender of which now bucked and swayed under the strong winds, Toulla dug into her pocket for her mobile phone. She knew these parts as well as anyone. Knew the weather. After looking at her phone for a few seconds, she flashed the weather report before Kane's face. "No, it's impossible," she told him. "Huge swells. Season-high seas. It's not only suicide, but as I said, again, it's a total waste of time."

Deflated, Kane nodded. Then the hopeful boyish grin returned. "The Money Pit site then. At least let's go there. I need it. I need to look inside."

"Have you seen the show? On Netflix?" Toulla asked, tilting her head to one side as if to challenge him.

"No." Kane didn't even own a TV.

"The site itself is very secure... those brothers, the... Rick something... they've spent millions and torn up most of the island. There's nothing to see. Believe me, I've been."

"You've been?"

"Yes, I interviewed him once, for The Coast, a newspaper in Halifax. It was just before I graduated and got my job at the Archives."

"But you've been there? You've seen the Money Pit site with your own eyes?"

"Some of it, yes. There are many sites."

"Well, I'm going then, with or without you. I need to... I need to sense the place. It might trigger something."

Toulla's shoulders sagged, resigned. "Okay, we'll go

tonight. But you have to behave, and only go where I let you. It'll be treacherous at night. Fair?"

Another massive thunder clap reverberated around the Jeep and a series of wild lightning bolts lit up the sky. It was time to go.

"Fair," Kane said, though he didn't like it. "Let's get out of here."

Chapter Forty-Eight

Claude grunted and cuffed away the sweat dribbling into his eyeballs. The humidity was rising and he sensed a storm brewing. He had managed to repair the boat and was now just waiting for Clement to return with some gas. They figured the old man they'd killed likely had some fuel stored on the property. So Clement traipsed back there, and seeing the coast remained clear, undertook a quick search which revealed a few cans of fuel stored in a small wooden outhouse.

He was back in less than an hour, just as Claude had finalised the last repair.

"What took you?" Claude teased from his position perched on the edge of the boat. "I'd have been back in half the time."

Clement was too worn out to retort and instead dumped the hefty jerry can beside the boat and took a seat beneath a tree. The sky above was darkening and the imminent storm matched the thug's mood. "Just fill it up," he demanded.

Claude smirked and got to work refuelling the boat.

"What's the plan?" he called over. "Does Big Boss Man have a plan?"

For once Clement was at a loss. They didn't know the area. They didn't know much about the girl. All they really knew now was what Francois had told them about Kane, and what the Englishman had been tasked to do. That was, to explore Oak Island and the Money Pit, and search for some kind of important lost artefact. Their part in the original plan—which was long out the window—was to keep an eye on Kane during his days of searching, keep some pressure on him using a little violence where necessary, but also protect him from anyone who meant him real harm. And, not to let what, if anything, he found, into enemy hands. What the end game of all of that was meant to be, Clement neither knew nor cared. It was all redundant now that they'd taken matters into their own hands.

Based on that, Clement had to assume Kane would at some point turn up at Oak Island. The man obviously knew the brothers were hunting him down. But he'd seemed a tough bastard, a man driven to excel, and Clement believed he would still endeavour to go to Oak Island.

So that's what they'd do too.

"We're going after Kane again," he declared.

"Obviously," Claude stated back. "Where?"

"Oak Island. Let's finish this shit once and for all."

Kane and Toulla agreed they needed to lie low until dark, somewhere they couldn't be tracked. Toulla suggested a remote campground a few miles south that also offered humble cabins. Kane agreed. An hour later, they were hunkered down out of the burgeoning storm in a simple wooden cabin set back in the far corner of the RayPort Campground property.

"Tell me about Jeremiah," Kane said. "Seemed like a good man."

"A great man," Toulla corrected. "Though as you know, as stubborn as old boots." Despite the remark, Toulla smiled. "I guess he was into more than I knew, eh? My father, too."

Kane nodded. "Seems that way." Kane grabbed the file from the counter of the simple kitchenette and laid it open on a coffee table in the centre of the room. He recited the letters on the cover. "S.T.R.A.P. Do me a favour and Google this, could you? Might learn a little more."

Toulla did and in a couple of seconds had found an interesting document. She read out the highlights.

"S.T.R.A.P. is described as a set of nationally agreed principles and procedures," she explained, "designed to enhance the 'need-to-know' protection of sensitive intelligence, as well as related operational information. Apparently created by British intelligence agencies several centuries ago, it's thought to be the first of its kind anywhere in the world. This last bit is interesting," she added, glancing at Kane. "It's said to include military branches of government."

Kane's mind spun. "Why on earth would your uncle have this document hidden in his cabin? This seems to suggest British involvement, right? But your uncle's Canadian... ah yes, Canadian, but related to former slave and loyalist, Samuel Ball. Is that the link to the British then?" he asked, but it seemed to be clear.

Toulla shrugged. This was all so shocking to her. All these years she had believed her family were really just treasure hunters and men who knew more than most—almost anyone—about the enigmas surrounding Oak Island, the Money Pit and of course, the *Fantome*. The fact it seemed now as if it were much more than that was something she was struggling to comprehend.

"You know, privately, Uncle Jerry always believed the treasure was taken from The Money Pit decades ago. At least, that's what he let me believe. And what he told you. He always used to say that it had never been found by treasure hunters. Probably not even by Samuel Ball, our ancestor. He always claimed there was some government involvement, but not *our* government. It obviously wasn't the United States government. They were the ones who the treasure was taken from in the first place. A lot of this country is of French origin, of course, though he never hinted at French involvement. Guess that only really leaves the British then, doesn't it? Who, by all accounts, put the stolen treasure there in the first place." Toulla shook her head as the maelstrom of possibilities swarmed around her mind. "Perhaps he had been lying to me all along."

Lightning lit up the sky beyond the cabin windows, though the thunderclaps were becoming more spread out and further away. Kane figured that was not what Toulla wanted. If the storm held, she would try to convince him it was too dangerous to head to the island.

So, right on cue, he said, "I think the storm's clearing. Should be good to go tonight, eh?"

Toulla ignored him. "We always believed that our government did bury selected items in the ground on Oak Island, planted a range of average artefacts, so to speak, so when they were found occasionally, the legend would remain just about enticing enough to keep the treasure hunters coming back and keep the dollars for the expensive permits flooding into government coffers. Same for the *Fantome*, too, as I told you before."

Kane nodded. It did make a lot of sense, but as a purist when it came to exploring and finding long-lost treasure or, in his case in the past, a legendary lost city, he had trouble accepting that. In his gut, he believed Toulla's declaration that all the treasure was gone. Still, he had believed Francois' theory, that it was still there, even if the man's integrity was very much under scrutiny.

He glanced down at the open file again. Something was missing, he felt certain. He lifted the page with the emblem and largely unreadable words, and this time, with a sudden spike of adrenaline, he realised there was a second sheet of paper hidden beneath the first.

"Shit, come and look at this," he said, and Toulla joined him kneeling at the low table.

Kane laid the second sheet of faded paper on the surface. This time the words were more legible.

Captain Wordsworth Corti III

July 3, 1776

The accompanying document is to remain hidden at all times, and its contents are to remain known only to the one sworn Keeper of the vital secrets held within. That is I, Captain Wordsworth Corti III.

This document is one of only seven such documents in existence, and I am not privy to the identities of the possessors of the other six. It is my duty to employ a maximum of six other trusted accomplices to know the whereabouts of this document, and whom I have successfully engaged.

I understand that my failure to honour this pledge and to succeed in this solemn duty will be punishable by my death, but that it will also carry with it much graver consequences for all and future generations.

My selected accomplices are also aware that they undertake this duty upon pain of death.

Signed,
Captain Wordsworth Corti III

Kane turned to face Toulla. Her eyes were wide, as if in disbelief. He assumed they mirrored his own.

"Well I never," he said. "What have we here then?"

Chapter Forty-Nine

A few hours later, after darkness had fallen, Toulla steered her Jeep out of the campground and onto Shingle Mill Road, then left onto the Lighthouse Route highway towards Oak Island. It was only a few minutes' drive, so there wasn't much time for them to be spotted if the thugs chasing them earlier had gotten their shit together.

"I'm telling you it's a waste of time," Toulla told him yet again, though she understood Kane's burning need to find out for himself, or at the very least, to see it with his own eyes. That's how she had felt before her first visit. All those years her grandfather had insisted there was nothing there, and yet she hadn't been able to accept it, at least not then. In recent times she'd been on board with his beliefs.

So, she would humour Kane. For now. If they stayed too long though, she would have to put her foot down, and Toulla could be pretty forceful when it really mattered.

"Thanks for understanding," Kane muttered.

"Whatever," she replied, but added a wink for good measure. As she'd hoped wouldn't happen, the storm had cleared and although a light rain still fell, the weather was good enough. She'd suggested they approach the island by boat, as it would be more discreet and they wouldn't feel so cornered. There was only one narrow bridge onto the island, which could easily be blocked. Kane had agreed, and when he asked where they would get another boat from, she had simply said, "Trust me."

Toulla parked the Jeep at the end of the unpaved and little-used Alexander Drive, and when Kane offered her an upturned eyebrow, she said, "Have a little faith in local knowledge, will ya?"

Kane shrugged and followed Toulla as she led him along a winding dirt path towards the beach. A tiny jetty protruded out into the calm bay, and moored to one of the supporting pillars was a sleek-looking speedboat.

"You're not thinking of stealing it?" Kane asked, though he feared he already knew the answer.

"Friend of a friend's," Toulla said. "We're all friends around here. Just borrowing it. Bring it back later."

Kane somehow doubted that as a knot of uneasy tension began to tighten in his guts.

Apparently again surprising Kane with her knowledge of how to do almost anything, Toulla had hot-wired the craft and was motoring them slowly out along the small bay towards the dark, brooding mass that was Oak Island.

They moored the speedboat at another tiny service dock on the southernmost tip of the island, and beneath an almost full moon, now shining bright since the storm clouds had dissipated, Toulla led Kane onto the legendary Oak Island.

It had been a while since Toulla had stepped foot on the island herself, but she recalled enough to know not to take the main, official site road. She knew there were a series of subtle CCTV cameras situated along that road, so she led Kane off trail and into the woods that circled around the north of the main site and approached it from the Sellars Cove direction. She felt confident that even the TV brothers weren't paranoid enough to have installed cameras back there… especially since she felt certain they had all but given up on finding anything significant on the island.

Using only her memory and the moonlight to illuminate the way, Toulla led them into a clearing at the top of one of the low hills to the east of the original dig site, known as Borehole 10X. It was an evocative name, but that was as far as the excitement had gone. Nothing of value had been retrieved from the excavation, and it had cost them millions of dollars and most of one 'dig season' permit. Panting a little from the short climb, they paused to catch their collective breaths.

"See there," Toulla whispered. "That's the remains of the first hole sunk by the TV brothers. It's what all of their initial research had suggested was the most likely site to commence their dig all those years ago. All they found in that pit was some wooden beams, that suggested a previous dig site, and a few coins of little or no value."

Kane nodded. He knew all this, but was hoping for more.

Toulla shone the torch to the west of the original pit. "That's site two," she informed. "Again, they pulled up nothing but a few rotten timbers and some trace metals, but nothing they considered prolonging that dig for. A waste of three months, as far as I know."

Kane also knew this. He had known it, but he had felt an almost overwhelming urge to come and see for himself. Of course, it was a risky move. Those murderous fuckers weren't going to quit searching for him.

There's got to be more, though, he thought, desperation beginning to settle in. *There has to be.*

Two miles north, Clement steered the brothers' repaired speedboat carefully south towards Oak Island after sliding it off the trailer at Goose Creek. They couldn't know if it would be a wasted journey, but without any other information to go on, it was about all they could do. They couldn't let Kane and the chic get away. The bastards knew their faces and possibly their names. They had to be taken out. It had to be soon.

In the back seat, Claude was busy cleaning and checking their weapons. He was the more hands-on and practical of the brothers, and this was one chore he was happy to do.

Clement the dumb fuck wouldn't know which end was which anyway, he mused as he completed his tasks and stepped up to stand beside his brother. "What are the chances of this hunch of yours being correct?" he asked, doubting it could be higher than 30/70 against. "I'll bet you a beer you're wrong."

They were close to the island now, and Clement angled the speedboat around the gentle curve of the eastern coast and towards the south, where he'd learned there was a service jetty they could moor the boat.

What he saw caused his lips to curl into a wicked grin. "Brother Claude," he said, "I'd say you owe me a beer. In fact, make it a case of wine. Look." Clement pointed to the service dock a few hundred yards ahead.

Under a bright moon, bobbing on the gentle swell of the North Atlantic Ocean, was something to get both the brothers' murderous juices flowing.

Chapter Fifty

Kane glanced around at the landscape of what was one of the most heavily dug archaeological sites anywhere on the planet. Not only regarding recent activity, but for a prolonged period stretching back two centuries. He'd read many accounts of the first people to have chanced their arm here, and although he hadn't watched the TV series, popular in recent years, he had read of it. That series had firmly cemented the Oak Island enigma into popular culture, and while Kane thought that, overall, that was a good thing, it had also inspired a new wave of Indiana Jones wannabes. Since Kane had long ago claimed that fun little title for himself, that didn't sit well.

In truth, the mysteries surrounding Oak Island had inspired generation after generation of would-be treasure hunters to risk it all on a whim, and many had lost fortunes in pursuing their dreams of unimaginable fame and wealth. Many had paid the ultimate price, and if Kane were someone who believed in ghosts, he suspected there would be many stalking these low forested hills surrounding the infamous dig sites.

"Alright," he said, turning to face Toulla. "I suppose I'm ready, albeit unwillingly, to concede defeat. What say I let you buy me a beer or three to commiserate?"

Yet, Toulla didn't answer. She didn't even acknowledge his question. Kane followed the young archivist's line of sight, turning 180 degrees to face in the opposite direction, upon which he found himself staring down the barrels of not one but two semi-automatic rifles.

"Bonsoir, Monsieur Kane. If you're a praying man, I suggest you start now."

Claude pulled the trigger and the empty, hollow click that followed gave Kane the split second he needed. He launched off his powerful right foot and with a ferocious swing of his right arm, he clothes-lined Claude directly in the throat. The momentum of Kane's forward motion sent Claude and his weapon toppling backwards down the hill.

"Run!" Kane yelled. "Toulla, run!"

Clement was sluggish to react and, by the time he had turned to face them, Kane had slammed his right foot into the back of Clement's left knee. The entire leg buckled as the thug compressed the trigger on his weapon, but as he went down, so the gun flailed upwards and the rounds zinged harmlessly into the night sky.

Before Clement could recover, Kane followed up with a left knee to the chin, and though not out cold, he was down for the count.

"Get out of here Toulla!" Kane bellowed again and was relieved to see her fleeing down the hill towards the jetty.

Kane descended at pace towards Claude, who was scrambling to his feet. "Hey, big man," Kane called out as he approached, "haven't you taken the hint yet?" He closed in on Claude with such speed that he met the rising thug with a straight-armed, open-fisted tiger claw punch to the chin, and though he didn't pause to be certain, Kane thought he heard the sound of bones crunching.

"You can't beat me," Kane growled, feeling a little like his old self. Muscle memory was a powerful ally in a fight when you weren't at your physical best, and as adrenaline flooded his veins, he called out, "And I'm getting awfully weary of beating you. Back off, or I won't be held responsible for my actions." With that, Kane unleashed a flurry of right and left crosses that, one by one, sent the huge French-Canadian thug temporarily back into childhood.

Satisfied they were down, albeit not totally out, Kane set off at a clip after Toulla and caught up with her a minute later as she approached the pier.

"You didn't, you know, kill them?" she asked, although they had killed her uncle and she really didn't give a shit.

"No, I'm not like them. They're down, but not for long. We have to get out of here."

They sprinted the last hundred yards to the small service dock and just a couple of minutes later they were scrambling onto the 'borrowed' speedboat which Kane now doubted would ever be returned.

He glanced back towards the trees, and to his horror saw both the killers emerging from the moonlit woodland and making haste in their direction.

"Jesus... tough bastards," he muttered. "Let's go Toulla, we've got company."

Once aboard, Toulla fired up the electronic starter and the powerful boat roared to life just as the first volley of rounds slammed into the jetty and the surrounding water, once again missing their target.

There was no time to sabotage the killers' boat this time,

and Kane willed Toulla to get them away as fast as possible as he glanced back at the chasing thugs. This time he was surprised to see one of them pause on the brow of a small hill and take aim.

Now, Kane had learned these bastards were poor shots. They'd proven it time and again. Yet he also knew at some point either his luck would run out, or the universe had finally decided it was simply his time to die.

So, with nowhere to hide anyway, when Kane watched on almost distractedly as the big thug steadied himself on the hill, and taken careful aim, and first one round and then a second slammed into the back of the speedboat, missing the outboard motor by inches, he wasn't entirely surprised.

Oh, shit, Kane thought.

"Holy fucking shit!" Toulla yelled.

Chapter Fifty-One

"Go, Toulla, move it," Kane yelled, feeling the propellers kick in and churn through the water, powering them away from the threat of imminent death.

Kane dared a glance at the killers' boat. Unfamiliar with speedboats, to his untrained eye the two vessels looked a reasonable physical match. If it were to become a chase, he believed it would be a combination of the drivers' ability and luck that would prove decisive.

Kane clung tight as Toulla skilfully steered the boat away from the island. She hugged the coastline, and as they flew past it Kane recognised the small horseshoe bay from which they'd procured the boat. He craned his neck to look back and was dismayed to spot the brothers gaining on them.

Come on Toulla... come on...

Toulla then angled the craft away from the mainland and headed northeast towards a cluster of smaller islands. Kane assumed she knew the layout well and trusted her not to slam them into some submerged chunk of lethal rock.

Glancing back, he had momentarily lost sight of their pursuers, but still heard the roar of their powerful motor and knew now they couldn't outrun them.

Toulla darted left and right at speed through the smattering of small islands, and Kane was once more impressed by her range of skills. They emerged past the western end of one slightly elongated island, and Kane was horrified to see the killers' boat appear from the eastern flank at the exact same time. It was the younger brother driving, which meant the other brother was free to take shots at them as they closed in.

"You got a plan?" Kane yelled above the roar of the huge engine.

"Survive!" was all Toulla shouted back, and Kane thought it a noble idea. "Hold on tight," she added, as the speedboat thumped over the small waves.

Glancing forwards, Kane noticed they were heading towards a wide inlet, and hoped her local knowledge was about to pay off.

However, just as they entered the inlet, all bets were suddenly off as their large outboard engine erupted in an explosive ball of steel, fibreglass and diesel.

Kane and Toulla flung themselves to the deck of the boat as shrapnel exploded all around them. After a few seconds, everything had fallen still and Kane dared a glance up. He didn't know if it were a lucky shot or if his time on this mortal coil was up, but either way, as the boat juddered to a watersnail's pace and drifted painfully slowly to a stop at the narrow end of the cove, he knew it was goodnight Vienna. Claude powered down the chasing craft, letting it drift towards them, their weapons raised.

Kane inhaled a lungful of salty air and turned to Toulla, who had come to stand by him. It was obvious there was no escape. The water was shallow and they were still too far from shore to make a swim for it. They had no weapons of their own, and if they tried to make a dash for it in the sea they'd be no safer than large fish in a fairly small barrel.

"I'm... I'm sorry I got you into this," Kane told Toulla. "If I hadn't come here, if I hadn't been so sloppy and weak, none of this would've happened."

"You're wrong, Hiram," Toulla said calmly. "This has always been inevitable." She glanced over his shoulder at the two men now standing on the speedboat that had come to a stop just a dozen feet away. The men seemed prepared to wait, enjoying the moment before they extinguished two more of what she expected was a long list of expendable lives.

Yes, this was always going to happen.

Kane shook his head, but turned to face his killers. He had always thought that when death became inevitable—he'd been very close before, but there had always remained a sliver of hope—like in the movies, his life would flash before him.

That's what he thought might happen.

It was not even close.

"Well, Monsieur Kane," Clement called from the other boat, "you got lucky a few times, but now it's time to end to this bullshit. I wish I could say it's been fun," he added, touching a finger to several of the injuries Kane had inflicted upon his face. Then the glint went from his eyes, and his face turned hard and serious. "But it has not." Clement glanced at his brother Claude, who nodded. Both men raised their weapons and took careful aim.

Toulla grabbed Kane's hand and they looked at each other, taking comfort that, in the end, they had a good person standing by their side.

From out of nowhere a deafening roar filled the cove and made all four actors in the deadly tableau turn to face whatever Armageddon was coming their way. From the western end of the bay, a Bell CH-146 Griffon helicopter rose, a massive front-mounted spotlight illuminating the entire cove. It hovered above them just fifty yards away. Kane and Toulla clamped their hands over their ears in a futile attempt to block out the horrendous roar. They shared a terrified glance as the nose of the chopper angled towards them. That's when they first noticed the side-mounted missiles aiming directly at their speedboat.

On the other boat, Clement and Claude seemed equally shocked and had lowered their weapons. But as the chopper angled away from them and pointed its missiles at Kane and Toulla, Kane saw Clement grinning.

Kane dropped to his knees. Finally, thoughts of his family, Professor O'nians, and his friends all swirled in his mind. He was moments from death, and yet he felt a strange peace. Finally, Alex Ridley's beautiful smile filled his vision, and as he glanced up to take one last look at the world, the chopper angled back in the other direction, steadied itself facing the killers' boat, and unleashed two missiles that struck the boat dead-centre and sent the vessel and its two occupants to a fiery, explosive hell.

Chapter Fifty-Two

"What the fuck was that?" Kane yelled.

"Who the fuck was that?" Toulla screamed.

Kane stared, wide-eyed in shock as the chopper disappeared over the bay in the direction from which it had arrived. Kane and Toulla held still until the sound of the monster had dissipated and all that was left was the gentle lapping of the waves against their half-destroyed boat, and the clunk of debris from the killers' boat against what was left of their hull.

Kane turned to Toulla, and without saying anything, he motioned with his head towards the shore, now only forty or so feet away. Without a word, the two of them slipped into the chill water of the bay and let the current drift them calmly onto the beach.

"What now?" Toulla asked as they emerged from the ocean and shook themselves a little drier.

It was a simple question, but Kane found it impossible to answer. "I... well, I don't know. What... what just happened there, Toulla? We were seconds from death, and then our hunters were destroyed. By whom? Who were they?"

Toulla's head shook automatically, her eyes blinking, the shock now starting to wear off as the reality of their situation kicked in. They were miles from anywhere, cold and wet, and with no transport... and lucky to be alive. "I don't know... any of it," she replied simply.

"We have to get to the Jeep, then return to the cabin," Kane stated. "After that, well I don't know either. Come on, we need to move to stay warm."

After an hour of trudging along the fringes of the nearby highway, and then managing to thumb a ride the rest of the way, they made it back to the Jeep without interference. Fifteen minutes after that they pulled into the campground.

"Stop," Kane warned, and Toulla pulled up sharply as she too spotted what Kane had seen. Their cabin, in the far back corner of the campground, was ablaze, the flames twisting and swirling high into the night sky. There was just a shell of the former log cabin remaining.

"But who could have done that?" Toulla asked. "The bad guys are dead... aren't they?"

"There are always more bad guys," Kane conceded quietly and without humour. "Come on, let's get out of here. Who knows who these people are, but we aren't safe here."

"Where?"

Kane remained silent for many seconds as Toulla waited to turn east or west on the highway. Subconsciously, Kane rubbed his chin, his thoughts muddled, confusion about all that had happened wrinkling his brow. Finally, he glanced west, away from Oak Island and away from the city of Halifax. Then he nodded, and turned back to face east, though not before laying eyes on his bag that nestled on the back seat. He reached his arm back and slid a hand inside the bag, relieved to feel the smooth surface of the ancient file Toulla had found at Jeremiah's cabin on the lake.

He nodded gently, as if to himself, then said, "To the airport, Toulla. Take us to the airport. We're going to London."

Chapter Fifty-Three

"I tried to tell you," Toulla said as they relaxed into their first-class seats aboard the Air Canada flight out of Stanfield International Airport, Halifax, to Heathrow, London. "It's what my grandfather always believed. Me too."

Kane simply nodded. Exhaustion had gotten the better of him, and he'd surprised even himself when he'd turned down the complimentary champagne on offer. Toulla hadn't refused, and was now on her third flute while the aircraft was still boarding.

"Wake me when we get there," Kane muttered as he slipped a little deeper beneath the fluffy blanket, fairly sure he wouldn't sleep but determined to at least pretend for the next few hours out of the six it would take to cross the North Atlantic Ocean.

Before they'd boarded, Kane had tried multiple times to call John O'nians, but without success. That was a surprise. John had always been an early riser, and since it was two in the morning there in Nova Scotia, he felt sure John would have been perched behind his desk, even though it was barely six am. If anyone would know anything about the mysterious S.T.R.A.P. file in their possession, it was John. And if the great man himself didn't, he would definitely know someone who did.

Kane had decided that, if by the time they left Heathrow, and if he hadn't managed to get ahold of the professor, they would take the file directly to the U.G.L.E. building, the United Grand Lodge of England, in London. There were definitely some Masonic markings on the file's cover, so someone at the main Freemason's Hall could surely help them get to the bottom of what was becoming a real pain in Kane's—

Kane awoke with a jolt as the huge aircraft touched down into a predictably dreary London morning six hours after take-off. He sat up in his luxury seat and stretched, cuffing some dried dribble from his chin before glancing over at Toulla, embarrassed. Luckily she was still asleep, though her eyelids fluttered as if in the midst of a bad dream. He reached over and gently patted her shoulder.

Toulla pulled the eye shade from her face and squinted as the stark overhead lights seared her retinas. Yawning, she turned to Kane.

"Guess we're here," she said, though it was more of a croak. "Man am I thirsty... too many bubbles."

Kane chuckled. "Yes, we're here. London saw fit to greet us with a downpour... least surprising thing of the week."

With no luggage to collect, and a very welcome gallop through immigration, Kane and Toulla were soon through to the arrivals hall and making a beeline towards a taxi rank. There he placed a series of calls to John O'nians on

The Oak Island Enigma

Toulla's mobile, and when he received no reply, he left several voice messages that were all a version of the same thing: *I'm in London, John. I have a strange Masonic file. Does the acronym S.T.R.A.P. mean anything to you? Where are you? I'm going to the U.G.L.E. building. Please return this call.*

An hour later, their black cab dropped them off on the corner of Great Queen Street and Wild Street, right around the corner from the U.G.L.E. Masonic headquarters.

It was only then Kane realised just how close he was to The British Museum, a couple of blocks north in Holborn. Unbidden, a bout of anxiety brought on by shame caused him to duck into the doorway of The Prince of Wales pub.

Toulla noticed Kane's face had paled, and she hustled over to him. "What is it?" she asked, glancing about in case they'd been followed. "Is everything okay?"

Kane let his gaze settle on Toulla's, whose face showed how concerned she was. Kane offered a smile, and she stepped back, appraising him.

"I'm sorry," he said. "I'm fine. Just had a moment. It's a long story for another day, okay?" desperately hoping this was the last long story he'd ever be in.

"Okay."

Kane nodded. "Look, we're on our own. No Professor O'nians. No Anja Peerdeman. No Jeremiah. Just me and you, kid. Ready?"

"Yes, I'm ready," she said, and they stepped out into the almost perpetual drizzle of London at this time of year and headed to the main entrance of the U.G.L.E. building just around the corner on Great Queen Street.

Kane led them through the busy foyer and towards the rear of the bustling room, and approached the vast reception counter, behind which stood a dapperly dressed man with a wizened face and a large moustache. He was busy organising paperwork on the counter when Kane spoke, apparently startling him.

"I'm sorry, pardon me?" he said, straightening a little and seeming to force the smile onto his face.

"Oh, I'm sorry, I didn't mean to startle you." Kane cleared his throat. "I'd said, my friend and I would like to speak with someone about Oak Island and the *HMS Fantome*." He leaned in a little closer. "I think I might have some new information regarding the enigma. Could you help me?"

The man with the moustache blinked a couple of times, as if processing what was being said, and by whom. He glanced between Kane and Toulla, then checked his watch, as if it were important, then recovered his composure a little.

Kane looked at Toulla, whose raised eyebrows suggested she might be thinking what Kane was thinking; that the man had almost been expecting them.

The large moustache rose a little, suggesting a smile, then he said, "Excuse me just a moment." He took a couple of shuffling steps sideways, and leaned over to look at a computer monitor sitting somewhere below the counter. He glanced back at Kane, held his gaze for a few seconds, then looked back down at the screen. Nodding to himself, he returned to come and stand once again in front of Kane and Toulla.

"Please wait here a moment," he said quietly, then disappeared through a door behind the counter. A moment later, he returned and ushered the pair over to a quieter corner away from the growing hubbub in the reception. There he motioned to an in-house phone mounted on the wall. Kane and Toulla shared a curious glance. The phone then chimed, making Kane jump. He looked at the enigmatic receptionist, who nodded, as if to say, Go ahead, answer it. So, Kane did.

"Hello? Who is this?" he asked.

"The question is," came a male voice with a thick Glaswegian accent, "who are you?"

"My name is… it's, uh…." Kane had trouble saying his own name. *What the hell?* Had his confidence fallen so low? Was his perceived reputation so bad now that he didn't want anyone knowing who he was?

"I, uh…"

"It's okay, Mister Kane… we know who you are."

"We? You do?"

"We've been expecting you, though I'm sorry to tell you that you're in the wrong place. Very wrong. Some would argue the wrong country, but that distinction is down to the politicians, I'm afraid, not me."

"Wrong place?" Kane asked, confused. "Wrong country? How do you know that… since you don't know me, nor why I'm here?"

"We know more than you think," the Scotsman stated, not doing anything to lessen the mercurial, mysterious quality of the last two minutes. Just then the line fell silent. Kane glanced about, his gaze settling on Toulla's, whose expression spoke of her confusion. He briefly relayed what the man had said, and that confused expression morphed into one of trepidation and edginess.

More and more people began milling about the huge reception, and with its high vaulted ceiling, the noise levels rose. There could be dangerous men in that crowd, and they wouldn't know until it was too late.

"Okay, don't be alarmed," came the voice, "and stay

calm... but you two need to get away from here now. I can't say anymore, only this... do as the wise men did, and be wise yourselves. Go, now, and Godspeed."

The line went dead. So did the expression on Kane's face.

What the hell's going on?

Kane glanced at the man with the moustache, whose blank gaze offered nothing, at least until his eyes drifted to the satchel hanging over Kane's shoulder. He nodded at the bag, inhaled, then said, "Good luck, son," before turning back to his desk and welcoming the next visitor to his counter.

Chapter Fifty-Four

Kane's gaze settled on Toulla's once more. He saw what he'd expected; concern mixed with stubborn determination. Kane told her what the Scotsman had told him, and he watched as Toulla inhaled, as if to steel herself for what was to come. Then she exhaled and nodded.

"Right. Good," Kane said. He clutched Toulla's hand, gave it a good squeeze and said, "We'll be fine. Okay, let's go," then he led Toulla through the crowded reception and out into Great Queen Street beyond, where the light drizzle had worsened to a steady downpour.

Kane knew this part of London well, and in case they were being followed he led them at pace on a circuitous route southeast along Wild Street then rapidly on a slight northerly tangent along Keeley Street and across onto Sardinia St, at the end of which was the entrance to the Lincoln's Inn Fields public park, where he pulled Toulla into the shelter of a large oak tree.

"I can't see anyone, but I get the distinct impression we're being followed," he whispered into Toulla's ear after easing her in close for a clandestine hug. Don't worry though... we're safe here for a minute. Listen, the man on the phone said to 'Do as the wise men did, and be wise yourselves.' Do you take that to mean head north?"

Toulla leaned out of the hug a little so she could see Kane's face. "The wise men? They did follow the northern star, if you believe in all that stuff."

Kane grinned. Clearly Toulla didn't lean much into those fairytales either. "Yes, the northern star is what I thought too. So, we go north. But where? The man said we were in the wrong place, but not only that, but the wrong country."

"So, Scotland?"

Kane nodded as his eyes cast about the park, which, despite the morning hour, was becoming dark as the rain fell in heavy torrents. The tree's canopy was keeping them relatively dry for now.

"Pull out your phone. Google other masonic landmarks in Scotland, could you? That's probably where the guy on the phone meant for us to go. Why, I don't know."

Toulla nodded and slipped out of Kane's hug far enough to access her mobile. "So, the search is for a famous place in Scotland... other than Rosslyn Chapel, of course... to do with the masons?"

"Exactly!" Kane's eyes roamed about the park.

Within seconds, Toulla's dexterous fingers had received a hit. "Got it. Kilwinning Abbey," she whispered, "is the home of Scottish freemasonry. Near Glasgow. Scotland it is!"

From his position tucked up tight against the tree's large trunk, over Toulla's shoulder Kane saw dozens of people scurrying around beneath brollies being pummelled by five-pence-sized raindrops. Others without umbrellas weren't so fortunate—Kane wondered how anyone who knew London could be surprised by sudden rain. Kids splashed in puddles while being shouted at by frantic mums. Pigeons flapped up into the trees. An old hippy cycled past in shorts and a colourful t-shirt, whistling the theme tune from *Singing in the Rain* as he went.

Just then, however, Kane spotted something he wished he hadn't. Three men, walking with intent in their direction, oblivious to the rain. They weren't commuters. They definitely were not tourists. It was time to go.

"Toulla, stay calm but listen carefully." Kane felt Toulla's muscles tense as she squeezed in a little closer. "I think we're being followed. In a few seconds, we'll have to go. Quickly, delete all recent searches and make a new one, okay?"

"Okay. Where?"

"Actually, make two searches, and do it fast. Temple Church London and The Louvre Paris. Okay?"

"Got it." Toulla did as Kane suggested and watched as the Google app showed millions of search results in less than the time it took to type them. "Now what?"

"Drop your phone on the ground."

"Wait, what? Ah… red herring. Nice. You'll owe me a phone though," she said as she dropped the phone on the wet grass and nudged it against the trunk of the tree. "Done."

"Ready?"

"Where're we headed? Might help."

"Ha. Good point," Kane said. "Far corner of the park. Newman's Row Taxi rank. Go!"

And with that, they ran.

Chapter Fifty-Five

Kane hustled them out of the park, angling in a direct arc north towards Chancery Lane, choosing a few quieter back streets that took them on a circuitous route past Red Lion Square Gardens, then through Lamb's Conduit Passage onto Theobalds Road. There they paused to breathe and to check their tails. It appeared they weren't but Kane would not become blasé, and bustled them northwards towards their target destination: Kings Cross Station, via Great Ormond Street Hospital on one side and a lap of the Charles Dickens Museum two streets to the east.

Finally, after fifteen minutes of hard jogging, and taking one last detour around the full circumference of the British Library, they entered St Pancras Station, hot, sweaty and confident they had thrown off their pursuers, whoever the hell they were.

As usual, the crowds surrounding the Harry Potter store and adjacent monument in the north of the station were vast, and offered welcome cover in case they were in fact still being pursued, though it seemed they had thrown the men off their scent. For now.

Using cash, they swiftly bought two tickets to Canterbury in the southwest of the country, then two more to Glasgow. Kane only intended on taking the latter, but he couldn't be too careful… he knew it wasn't only in the movies that people behind counters could be bribed for information.

The train to Glasgow was due to depart in just fifteen minutes, but they spent the time waiting out in a quiet corner near the platform for the Canterbury train, which also afforded them a good view of the comings and goings of the vast concourse. When there were just a couple of minutes left before the departure to Glasgow, they made a late dash to that platform, scanned their tickets and boarded the first of two dozen carriages.

Kane suggested Toulla make her way to the last of the carriages whilst he stayed here at the doors of the first until the last moment, making sure the men following them didn't board the train. As the whistle blew for the doors to close, Kane slipped inside, confident they weren't followed. He then made his way internally through the carriages as the train pulled slowly out of the station on the 5-hour journey north and to who knew what dangers might lay ahead.

By the time he reached the final carriage, he found Toulla curled up across two seats and fast asleep.

Kane took a seat opposite and ruminated on who the new set of pursuers were. They'd given them the slip quite easily, which made him think that perhaps they weren't hired killers. If they were, they would surely have done a better job of sneaking up on them and killing them before they were even aware they existed. Something didn't quite add up, but then again, none of this made any sense to Kane at all.

Who was the mysterious Scotsman on the phone at the U.G.L.E. building? How had he known who Kane was, and that he was there at the United Grand Lodge of England? Unless someone had told him? Kane had sent those garbled messages to John O'nians, but they hadn't been returned and Kane felt sure John wasn't involved. Although…

Kane's mind drifted to the slain professor, Anja, back in New Orleans. O'nians had sent him there, so…

The gentle rocking of the train and the whoosh of the wheels over the steel tracks as the train peeled out of London into the rolling hills and into the heart of the English countryside lulled Kane into a drifting slumber. He felt safe and secure for perhaps the first time since he'd met the mercurial Frenchman, Francois, back in Cambodia. Who even was that man? Who were his people, who seemed to have gone rogue on their boss and had met with a horrific, fiery demise?

Again, more questions than answers as Kane slipped off to sleep, comfortable in the knowledge that for at least the next couple of hours, they were safe.

Toulla awoke slowly from a dreamless snooze, and for a moment she had forgotten where she was. Only when she spotted Kane dozing on the seats opposite did she remember. She stretched, and glanced out the window. *Ah yes… a train to Scotland.* Toulla was suddenly hungry and realised they hadn't eaten since the shitty meal on the flight from Nova Scotia, which seemed an age ago.

She patted her pocket to check she still had her wallet… her phone was gone, but that was okay. She made her way back along the train in search of sustenance and soon found the onboard cafe, where she bought some sandwiches, coffee and water, and made her way back to her seat. Kane was still snoozing, so she tucked into her sandwich and stared out at the rainy, windswept fields beyond the window.

Toulla hadn't visited the UK for many years and hadn't planned to do so again anytime soon. This surprising, literally last-minute visit was the last thing she'd expected when she had turned up at work a couple of days ago. That's when she'd seen Kane sitting at one of the public computer terminals. It had taken her a moment to get over the shock of seeing the world-famous explorer sitting there in her place of work, but one surreptitious glance over the man's shoulder confirmed her immediate suspicions... that the reason he was there in Nova Scotia was of course to do with Oak Island and the Money Pit.

The fact she was now with him here, in possession of some ancient, apparently important secret documents was hard to fathom, and yet in a way, something like this was always going to happen. Her family were integral to the history of the *HMS Fantome* and the Oak Island legends. Her ancestor, Samuel Ball, was one of the key figures in the entire story, although some part of Toulla had always remained sceptical about the truth of all that. Well, in a few hours from now, she might finally get the answers she had always craved, as her father and uncle had before her.

Or had they? Even that was in question now. If her uncle Jerry was knowingly in possession of this S.T.R.A.P. file, whatever that was, then it seemed obvious he was more involved than he'd ever let on. He had even said in his last note to her that The Allegiance had the answers. Those few clues had led them first to London, and now to Scotland.

Nova Scotia. New Scotland.

It couldn't be a fluke. Could it?

"Good afternoon." Kane's gravelly voice startled Toulla from her musings.

"Ah, it's alive," she teased as Kane sat up and stretched. "Sandwich?"

"My hero… I'm starved. Thanks."

As Kane tucked into his food, Toulla realised that once they got to Scotland, they didn't really know where they were going. They needed access to a phone. Toulla turned to look at her reflection in the train window, and after making a couple of adjustments to her hair, she said, "Be right back," and left Kane to his snack.

She returned a couple of minutes later and sat down opposite Kane, brandishing a shiny smartphone. "We need to research, and since you made me dump my phone, I had to improvise. Don't worry, it's on loan."

"On loan, like the speedboat?" Kane teased back, but he didn't really care. "Well done."

Toulla set about researching Kilwinning Abbey and soon learned that the former Templar building was now a ruin in a residential area near the coast thirty miles southeast of Glasgow. She read on. Apparently, the location of the former abbey wasn't random. Some theorised it was in fact the birthplace of Freemasonry, and where many Templar Knights first sought sanctuary after fleeing persecution from a jealous, zealous Pope Clement V in France in 1307.

"Whatcha reading?" Kane asked. Toulla caught him up on what she'd learned so far.

"Also, next to the Abbey is what's known as Mother Lodge Number Zero," she explained, "considered the oldest established Mason's lodge in the world. But get this… these buildings are near the ancient port of Ardrossan on the eastern shore of the Firth of Clyde."

Kane stared blankly at Toulla, who rolled her eyes.

Glancing back at the phone, she read, "It says here that many scholars argue the lost treasure of the *Fantome*, AKA, the Money Pit treasure, was smuggled into the remote, ancient port by the British." She looked at Kane, whose tired eyes registered intrigue. Toulla continued. "However, others argue that the port was just a decoy, and that the booty actually ended up farther north, at Mingary Castle."

Kane nodded. This was all speculative. Was there any real treasure? Was it all a hoax? If it was real, where the hell was it now? Did anyone even know anymore, hence the enigma? And what did the Masons have to do with it? And what the hell, or who, were The Allegiance?

Weary beyond belief, and now beginning to wonder if this was all just one big waste of time, Kane asked, "So, Toulla, miss Money Pit, descendent of Samuel Ball and owner of a bizarre ancient document that may or may not be important, where the hell are we going?"

Toulla's face scrunched up just a little then, as if Kane's joking words were not in fact very funny, as if the enormity of it all was suddenly just a little too much to bear. Then the hint of a smile crinkled her eyes, and finally, she grinned.

"I think no visit to this Kingdom is complete without a trip to an ancient castle… eh?"

Chapter Fifty-Six

Five hours after setting out from London, Kane and Toulla exited the train in Glasgow's Central Station, their eyes peeled for unwanted attention. Within minutes they'd left the station. Half an hour after that they were speeding north in a rented car on the M8 Motorway, across The Clyde and then east on the A82 before cruising north into the Highlands, skirting the western flank of Loch Lomond as the late afternoon sun glistened on the calm, dark surface of one of Scotland's most visited natural landmarks.

The rental's Sat Nav told them it would take around two hours to reach the tiny town of Corran, where they would spend the evening before taking the short ferry ride across Loch Linnhe in the morning for the last two-hour stretch west to Mingary Castle.

The drive to Corran passed by quickly and, more importantly, uneventfully. Neither Kane nor Toulla had much energy to chat, so Kane focused on the road, letting his mind drift between Ridley and O'nians and Francois. Toulla spent most of the drive gazing out at the mesmerising landscape of the Scottish Highlands and the bewildering natural beauty of Loch Lomond and The Trossachs National Park.

Kane often caught Toulla craning her neck to look out the back window. He couldn't blame her.

"It's fine," Kane would say, but to Toulla, he suspected it didn't feel fine. He remained focused on the road.

Toulla closed here eyes. What had started out as a bit of an adventure and a chance to learn more about the mysteries that had haunted her throughout her life, alongside none other than Hiram Kane, of all people, had somehow developed into a dangerous quest in which some people had already died and surely more deaths were inevitable, likely even her own.

It was these thoughts jumbling around her mind when Kane finally announced they had arrived at the Birchbrae Highland Lodges, nestled amidst a small pine forest a few hundred yards from the shores of Loch Linnhe.

They'd called ahead on Toulla's 'acquired' phone, and confirmed a reservation for one night only.

"Just in time for a late dinner," the owner had informed them as they checked in, "but I'm afraid you've missed the view."

Darkness had fallen, and not just the usual dark skies seen above most developed countries. Here in the depth of the Highlands, the darkness was all-encompassing, and other than their own voices, the next most notable thing to Kane was the pervasive silence. He imagined it was how it felt to be buried alive, and the thought sent an involuntary shiver creeping up to his shoulder blades.

After a quick dinner in the small restaurant, washed

down with a couple of glasses of red each, Kane and Toulla hustled to their cabin. Kane insisted they stay in the same cabin for security, and claimed the large couch while Toulla took the bed. Both were exhausted, and after Kane had checked and double-checked the windows and doors were locked and secured, both were asleep within minutes.

The phone alarm woke them at six. The first ferry was at seven and they wanted to get on the road early. After a coffee, breakfast was demolished in minutes and by 6:50 they were waiting at the tiny Nether Lochaber ferry dock, essentially a concrete slipway upon which they could drive onto the humble car ferry. It was barely dawn and the sky to the west remained near dark, lending an ominous feel to the cool, quiet morning.

Toulla had awoken rested but anxious. She hadn't quite shaken the feeling of being watched throughout the drive from Glasgow, but since she'd spotted no cars that seemed to be trailing them, she'd put it down to nerves brought on by extreme tiredness and the remarkable situation they had found themselves in as a whole.

At 6:55 the helmsman had docked the ferry and the row of a dozen vehicles, of which Kane's was first in line, slowly drove onto the waiting boat for the short passage across to the western side of the loch.

At the very last moment before the helmsman's mate pulled up the barrier, the motorcyclist eased his huge roadbike onto the boat and settled at the back of the line. The ferry pulled away no more than two seconds behind schedule.

By the time Kane had bumped the car off the ferry on the far side of Loch Linnhe the sun had risen enough to have cast an ambient golden glow on the distant mountains ahead, and if it wasn't such an important journey—that's how it felt now, anyway—it would have been a wondrous sight and one worth slowing down to enjoy. As it was, Kane put his foot down and accelerated away from the ferry dock, first south and then west on the narrow A861 road en route to Mingary Castle.

They'd been driving only half an hour, through the low hills and largely hugging the northern shore of the long, narrow Loch Sunart, when Toulla felt the hairs rise on the back of her neck. Her eyes flashed to the wing mirror, yet she saw nothing. The rearview mirror offered nothing more and she spun in her seat, staring out the back window expecting to see some huge SUV closing in, in an attempt to ram them off the road and into the icy waters of the loch below.

"There's no one there," Kane said, noticing Toulla's sudden concern. He'd been diligently checking the mirrors himself, which he'd been doing since they'd rented the car in Glasgow. "It's fine, Toulla, trust me."

That's the exact moment Toulla screamed.

Chapter Fifty-Seven

Kane slammed on the brakes but the surface, damp beneath the morning dew, didn't play ball and the car skidded, fishtailing left and right before straightening up and coming to a juddering halt in the middle of the road.

Just fifty yards ahead of them, blocking the narrow highway, were two men standing either side of a huge motorcycle. One of the men held what appeared to be a semi-automatic rifle to one shoulder, the barrel pointing directly at Kane's windscreen. Worse... much, much worse... the other man then crouched down and lifted what looked to Kane's uninitiated eye to be some kind of portable rocket launch—

Holyfuckingshit!

As Toulla's wails continued to rattle the car's windows, Kane shoved the car into reverse and accelerated backwards along the thankfully deserted road as the first missile screamed by just feet above the car's roof. Kane wasn't a fan of driving at the best of times, but hurtling backwards at fifty miles per hour on a narrow country road with a steep bank on one side and the rocky shore of an icy loch on the other, this was not his idea of fun.

Then things got worse.

Filling his rearview mirror, from out of nowhere emerged a black Transit van, blocking any chance of escape.

Is the van with the motorcycle?

It was so remote, the motorbike ahead and the transit van behind were the only two vehicles they'd seen on the road since they'd left the ferry. The chances of them not being in cahoots were slim.

Oh, bollocks.

"What are you going to do?" Toulla yelled as Kane once more shuddered the car to a stop. "There's no way past… and they have big fucking weapons."

Kane ignored her, his mind racing and his eyes scanning the road ahead and the terrain to his right, the opposite side from the loch. At first glance it appeared they were indeed trapped. The rocky beach was unnavigable in their regular car and he cursed not renting an SUV instead. To the right a steep yet relatively low bank prevented them fleeing up into the woods beyond. The van was blocking the exit to the rear. It seemed there was only one thing for it.

"Hold on tight," Kane stated.

"Wait… no, you can't… it's suicide," Toulla near screamed.

"Just hold on," Kane repeated, "it's our only chance." He inhaled, glancing at the rearview mirror and noticing the van had come to a stop just thirty feet back, blocking them in. Up ahead, the man with the semi-automatic waited, poised to unleash hell the moment Kane's vehicle lurched forwards. The bastard with the missile launcher remained in his crouched position, waiting, patient, ready to kill.

Kane let out his breath through pursed lips, eyes narrowed, focused on the road ahead. There was going to be an impact, that was unavoidable. Whether that was with the stationary motorcycle or the men with deadly weapons… or both… only time would tell.

"Get your head down," Kane yelled as he flexed his fingers around the steering wheel and repositioned his foot above the accelerator pedal.

3…

2…

The first rounds from the semi-automatic zinged into the front of the car too low to penetrate the window.

Now!

Kane stomped on the pedal and the car surged forwards, the Transit accelerating behind them. To his left, Toulla screamed from the footwell of the passenger seat. In the rearview, the van was closing. Up ahead, a killer took deadly aim.

More rounds thunked into the metalwork of the car and one pierced clean through the top of the windscreen, slamming into the rear window and obliterating the glass into a million tiny sherds.

Just thirty feet remained between Kane's car and the waiting death squad.

Twenty…

More rounds zinged into the car's body and once again Kane abstractedly thought about miracles and how he might have to rethink his notion that they didn't exist.

Ten feet… closing in fast.

He heard rather than saw the missile launch. A kind of buzzing, whistling noise as a puff of smoke indicated the next rocket had indeed been fired. Kane closed his eyes as every muscle in his body tensed for impact.

He was right. There was impact. The front of the car slammed into the rear wheel of the huge motorcycle, parked directly across the road. The impact thrust Kane hard against his seatbelt, but the forward momentum kept them moving. The motorcycle toppled over several times before coming to rest against the low bank. Kane didn't know if the killers had dived for safety before he reached them.

Somehow, the rocket skimmed a fraction of an inch above the roof of their car and instead slammed into the chasing Transit van, which erupted in a devastating ball of raging fire, strewing ripped fragments of metal and upholstery and human flesh and bone a hundred yards into the air.

Kane opened his eyes in time to see the loch directly ahead of him, and as the car's left-side wheels skittered and bumped over the cobbled edge of the road, Kane righted his course just in time to avoid veering straight off the side and plunging into the loch.

His eyes shot to the driver's wingmirror. He saw the fireball that was once the transit van. He also saw the two men hauling the motorcycle upright and clambering aboard.

Oh no, Kane mused, wishing this was all just a bad dream.

Oh, no, no NOOO!

Chapter Fifty-Eight

Kane punched the accelerator pedal hard to the floor. The narrow road closed in around them and if anything came from the other direction, the inevitable collision would be fatal to all involved.

The road twisted and turned, weaving along the northern shoreline of the loch, dipping and rising as an ocean swell might. But this was no vast ocean, and Kane felt the pinch on all sides as the motorcycle closed in from behind and he braced himself for the inevitable incoming rounds.

"Stay down," he demanded as Toulla tentatively lifted her head.

Toulla obviously couldn't help herself and risked a glance up, stretching her neck as the first of a hail of rounds clanged into the rear of the car, zinging off tarmac and steel, and showering the road in a light show of sparks.

Kane reached over and with a strong left arm—and with zero ceremony—shoved Toulla deeper into the stairwell. He didn't need to yell at her. She'd learned the hard way.

The road continued clinging to the very edges of the shoreline and one false move would see Kane's car tumble over onto the rocky shore, causing almost certain death to both occupants.

He would not let that happen.

He could not let that happen.

From the corner of his eye he saw the S.T.R.A.P. file still nestled in his satchel on the back seat, although now covered in a layer of shattered glass.

Is it all worth it? he wondered as he saw the motorcycle looming larger in his mirrors.

There wasn't much more he could do. He wasn't a racing driver. He wasn't even an especially good driver, he assumed. He hadn't driven much at all in recent years and always preferred to take the train whenever he could. Or walk. He was good at walking.

Suddenly a tree up ahead of the vehicle exploded as a missile from the hand-held launcher slammed into its trunk, skittling branches and foliage across the road and leaving Kane no choice but to take his chances and smash through it. Through gritted teeth he cursed and wondered how much longer he had left to live, and all for a piece of fucking paper.

Why do these people want me so dead? Do they actually want the file? If so, they were going a funny way about it because if the next missile hit its true target, the file, along with Kane and Toulla, would be obliterated.

Still, he had to assume they didn't want the file and that their only intention was to kill. Didn't make him feel all warm and mushy inside, it had to be said.

More rounds from the semi-automatic pinged off the

car's metalwork and the road on either side, and Kane knew it was only a matter of time until one found its mark.

Something caught his eye up ahead. Something large, organic, and... moving?

For fuck's sake!

Of all the times for a herd of sheep to be blocking the road, this was not it. It meant only one thing. Kane and Toulla had seconds to live. He had no choice but to slow the car and as he looked in his rearview mirror, he watched as the driver of the motorcycle eased down through the gears and pulled it to a stop a dozen feet behind the car.

Everything fell silent then. All Kane could hear was the beating of his own heart, Toulla's heavy breathing down to his left and the idle ticking of the over-worked car engine. Oh, and a few muted bleats from within the vast herd of sheep blocking their escape. Then he spotted a lone human figure moving slowly behind the herd.

No, please, go back... get the hell out of here!

The figure paused, and Kane watched as he calmly stepped out of view behind a tree.

What...?

"What the hell's going on?" Toulla asked from the footwell.

Kane didn't see any point in lying to Toulla now and told her. "Sheep blocking the road. Bad guys closing in."

Toulla closed her eyes as she inhaled, then, exhaling, she eased herself back up onto the seat. Once settled, she clasped Kane's hand and squeezed. "What a fucking mess."

Kane was well aware of his penchant for understatements. Jesus, Toulla had just smashed his very best. He almost chuckled. Almost. A glance in the wingmirror prevented that. The passenger of the bike, who now somehow wielded both weapons, was now approaching from the rear left of the car, semi-automatic weapon raised as he moved cautiously closer. In the left-hand wingmirror, Kane saw the other man approaching, a revolver raised in front of him.

At least the rocket launcher was gone.

"Out of the car!" one of the men yelled. He also had a French accent.

What is it with the French these days? Kane thought but didn't say.

"No, we can't," Toulla said. "They'll shoot us."

Kane nodded. "I do believe you're right." Kane's eyes drifted towards the tree behind which the shepherd guy had stepped. No sign of him. No movement.

Good, he's scarpered.

"Listen, Toulla, if I'm right, they're going to kill us anyway. We have to make a run for it. Why make it easy for these bastards, eh?"

Toulla sucked in a series of rapid breaths, in, out, in, out, as if settling her nerves. "Okay," she said quietly. "What's the play?"

Kane let his gaze drift right, towards where the sheep were heading. There, a farm gate sat nestled into the low stone wall, laying open as the sheep drifted towards it.

"See the gate?"

After a moment's pause, Toulla said, "Yeah, I see it."

"On three, we swing open the car doors and charge straight into the herd and bundle with them through the gates. The trees beyond, you see them?"

"Yeah, but we'll never make it."

"Stick low behind the wall. The sheep will hold them up, and we'll have a slim chance to get far enough away, but we have to run, and run hard. Are you ready?"

"Yeah, ready," Toulla said, and Kane didn't miss the lie.

"Okay. On three…" He risked a quick glance in both wingmirrors. The men had come to a standstill just half a dozen yards behind the car. For trained killers, it was almost point-blank range and Kane knew they were already as good as dead. He reached in the back and grabbed his bag with the file, and wrapped it around his shoulder.

"Three," he muttered. "Two… One."

Kane and Toulla flung open their car doors and as they scrambled around to the front of the car, instead of hearing the inevitable barrage of automatic gunfire, they heard two single shots, just a second between each.

They froze on the spot, each expecting to see a bloodstain blossoming on the other's chests. The sheep continued their shuffling march into the field through the gate. When Kane realised he wasn't dead, or at the very least dying, he turned to face his killers. Yet his killers were no longer visible. Standing calmly behind the rental car, twenty feet back, was the shepherd. Or at least, a man dressed like a shepherd.

Instead of a crook, however, this man held some kind of a rifle, which he now lowered as Kane and Toulla looked on. Without a word, the man nodded at Kane, and as if it were the most normal thing in the world, he slung the weapon over his shoulder and strode past Kane and Toulla without so much as a sideways glance in their direction. Then, he hustled the last of the sheep through the gate into the field, and Kane watched on in disbelief as the man followed the sheep up and over the small hill and eventually out of view beyond the tree line.

Chapter Fifty-Nine

After staring on dumbfounded as the mysterious shepherd became their second unlikely saviour in as many days, Kane and Toulla wordlessly climbed back into the half-destroyed rental car. Though the road was super remote, another vehicle could still come along at any moment. And surely the authorities had already become aware of the fireball a few miles back down the road. They had to get out of there. Now.

It was many miles until Toulla at last broke the silence as Kane steered them west.

"Who... who're these people, Hiram?"

Kane remained silent for long moments, trying to piece together all the fragments of what had happened to them over the last however many days it had been since they'd met.

Finally, he said, "Honestly, Toulla, I don't know. The shepherd guy obviously wasn't just some random dude. Someone knows we're heading to the castle, and they're doing everything in their power to ensure we get there in one piece."

"One piece. Ha." Toulla chuckled but the mirth never reached her eyes.

Kane glanced over to her. Her face was pale and the sparkle had long-since vanished from her eyes. She was worn out, mentally and physically, and the strain showed in her features.

"It's only another half hour to the castle. Listen, something bigger is happening here, and I don't know about you, but after the chopper in Halifax, and now this... well, someone wants what we have so badly they're willing to kill others to make sure we deliver it. I think we're going to be okay, Toulla. I really do."

Kane had spoken with sincerity. At least, he had tried to. Did he really feel safe? No. Not even close. What's to say that whoever was there at the castle weren't the real bad guys, and would kill them as soon as they arrived? Or, somehow the bad guys were in fact the good guys, and it was all some big fucking cover up for the greater good. Whatever. It was all madness, of that he was sure. He had another thought and this he shared with Toulla. "Anyway, isn't the castle actually some fancy hotel nowadays?"

Toulla nodded. "It is, at least according to Google."

"So if it's a hotel, it's probably safe, right?" Kane said, ignoring the fact the French thug brothers had shot at him in New Orleans... in a hotel. *Right.*

Toulla didn't answer but her shoulders did sag a little and Kane took that as a sign she'd agreed with him. "Listen, why don't you get some shut-eye for the next few miles. I'll wake you when we get there, okay?"

Again, she didn't answer, but she did reach out and

place a hand on Kane's forearm before snuggling back into her seat and closing her eyes.

It was a further forty minutes before the sat nav told Kane he'd almost reached his destination, the Mingary Castle Hotel. Dusk had fallen quickly and by the time Kane had pulled the battered rental car into the near-deserted hotel car park, it was almost completely dark. That didn't do his nerves any good. He noticed that the few cars dotted around were all top-end machines. For a fleeting moment he thought he recognised one, a Bentley, but he was too tired to read the license plate and soon forgot about it. He reached over and gently nudged Toulla awake, and as he stepped out of the car and went around to open the door for her, he couldn't help but keep his senses alert for any unwelcome attention.

Keeping the satchel close to his chest, Kane and Toulla left the car and bustled across the carpark towards the hotel entrance.

If there had been any doubt as to whether this was actually a hotel or not, the moment they stepped inside the foyer, all those doubts dissipated. The entire place oozed luxury. Flamboyant chandeliers hung from high, vaulted ceilings. A grand piano stood in one corner, close to a small yet tastefully lit bar, at which sat several well-dressed patrons. Several portraits hung on the walls, which Kane recognised as works by Renaissance artist Titian. *Wow!* he mused. If those were originals, they'd be worth many millions.

"Good evening, sir, madame," said the clerk behind the reception counter. "Do you have reservations?"

"Uh, hello," Kane said. "Um, no, unfortunately not. I was hoping you had a couple of rooms?"

"Certainly sir, we have two very nice rooms available for you."

"My name is Kane—"

The clerk glanced up from his monitor and fixed Kane with a knowing look. "We're so glad you could make it."

Kane turned to Toulla and with his eyes, motioned to her pocket as if to say, *Please can you get out your credit card.*

The clerk cleared his throat. "Yes, Mr Kane, I have you on the list. We've been expecting you."

Kane and Toulla glanced back at each other, their already bewildered expressions becoming even more comical. Just then, a porter approached. Kane had to double-take as a wardrobe of a man with shoulders the size of a stuffed headboard came and stood quietly off to one side. He was literally the biggest human Kane had ever seen.

The clerk said, "William here will show you to your rooms. Your friends will be awaiting you both at—"

"Wait, friends?" Kane said, cutting him off. "I don't have any friends here. No one knew I was coming."

"That's right," the clerk said. "No one knows." He smiled. "As I was saying, your friends will be waiting for you at ten o'clock in The Fantome Suite."

The Fantome Suite? WTF?

Kane glanced at his watch. It was already 9:30.

"William will be at your door five minutes before ten to accompany you to the meeting." The clerk nodded at Kane's bag. "You'll want to take that with you. I hope the rooms are to your satisfaction. Mr Kane, Miss Corti, I bid you a good evening," he added, and with that the clerk stepped away from the desk, and with a subtle bow, he went about his business.

Toulla stared at Kane, and mouthed *How does he know my name?* Kane simply shrugged.

"This way, Mr Kane, Miss Corti," the massive usher said as he led them off towards a double bank of elevators.

A couple of moments later, and what felt about two floors up in the lift, the usher led them along a well-appointed corridor and paused outside two adjacent doors. "These are your rooms. I trust you'll find them acceptable." He handed them each an electronic key card.

The usher glanced at his watch. "I will be back to collect you in fifteen minutes. Please be ready."

Kane turned to Toulla. "For now, just come in my room with me, okay?"

Apparently relieved, Toulla simply nodded as Kane presented the keycard to the pad next to the door. After a gentle beep, the door clicked open, but just before Kane closed it behind him, the usher said:

"Mr Kane?"

"Yes?"

"Good work, Mr Kane."

Chapter Sixty

Kane and Toulla had barely had time to splash their faces in the bathroom and try to make sense of what was happening before there was a gentle knock at the door.

Kane checked his watch. Exactly 9:55 pm. He almost grinned. Yet, he didn't know whether to be nervous or excited. This was an upmarket hotel. Wasn't it?

Mingary Castle was built in the 12th century by one of the leading clans of the time. Over the centuries it had served as the stronghold for various warring families, as well as myriad orders of monks, and even a legion of Templar Knights. Perhaps most notably it had unofficially served as the first Grand Lodge of the Combined British Freemasons. At least that's what Toulla had told Kane early on their drive from Glasgow.

So, as they stepped out into the corridor, where the man-mountain porter, William, stood guard as if he hadn't moved an inch in the last fifteen minutes, Kane had no idea what to expect when he met his so-called friends.

Yet somehow, for the first time in many days, he didn't

feel afraid. There was a familiar feeling about the place, and although he had definitely never been here before, something about the profile of the huge structure as they'd approached in the car, silhouetted as it was against the last fading light of the day, had given Kane an unnerving sense of déjà vu.

William led them back along the corridor towards the lift, and they were surprised when the usher walked straight past it and on around a corner, where they were faced with a dead end.

Out of the corner of his eye, Kane sensed Toulla tense, and he grabbed her hand, giving it a squeeze.

William turned to a simple, nondescript door that blended into the wall on their left, so seamlessly incorporated into the wall in fact that they hadn't noticed it until he swiped a key card against a barely visible panel set into its form. The door slid back, revealing a secret lift within.

"Please," William said, showing them inside with a waft of one massive hand.

Somewhat reluctantly, yet also intrigued, Kane stepped in. He had to nod encouragement at Toulla for her to follow suit.

Once they were all inside, William said, "Fantome Suite."

Silently, the lift began to descend, and Kane mentally counted how far down they were going. Once they'd passed what he speculated was first one floor, then another, Kane knew they were lower than the ground floor lobby into which they'd entered the castle. A few seconds later, the elevator came to a gentle stop and the door slid open, unprompted.

"After you," said William, and Kane and Toulla duly obliged. Rather than follow them out, however, William remained inside the lift. As the lift doors slid closed, he nodded respectfully at Kane.

A momentary tug of anxiety pulled at Kane's guts and instinctively he stepped in front of Toulla, reaching his arms back and enclosing her in a protective embrace.

Gazing ahead, Kane noticed the exposed stone walls of the castle's internal structure. The space before them was dimly yet tastefully lit, with just a few strategically placed lamps creating an ethereal and welcoming glow. A warm breeze fluttered their way, and gentle classical music drifted to them from an unseen source. Kane felt his shoulders relax and Toulla came and stepped beside him.

"What the hell is this place?" she asked. "I'm guessing The Fantome Suite isn't in the brochure."

Kane smiled inwardly, but didn't speak. He remained wary, but found himself stepping slowly forwards into the room. Toulla remained at his side. They had made it a dozen steps into the vast space, when a voice came from somewhere out of sight and it froze Kane where he stood.

"My boy, Hiram, I am so very, very sorry."

Chapter Sixty-One

From a shadowy recess, Professor John O'nions stepped out into the light. Kane's first instinct was to rush over and embrace his mentor, then shake the great man's hand as he always did. But something rooted him where he stood.

Kane fixed his gaze on the professor's eyes, and saw in them a mixture of sadness and regret. *Is that also pride?* Kane wondered, and thought it was. John O'nians looked older than Kane remembered, as if he'd been suffering great stress lately, perhaps even an illness. But when they'd spoken on the phone recently John hadn't mentioned anything, and he rarely kept anything back from his star protégé, Hiram Kane, the son he'd never had.

John took a couple of tentative steps towards Kane and Toulla, and when he was close enough, he extended his hand. Kane took it almost automatically, and it felt good.

John's eyes remained on Kane's, and finally, they glinted. It was in that single moment, right there, right then, when Kane knew everything was going to be alright.

"You have no idea how happy it makes me to see you,"

John said. "To see both of you," he added, turning to look at Toulla. "Truly, truly happy. Please, would you both follow me?"

Without waiting for an answer, John turned on his heels and with a little more energy than before, he led Kane and Toulla through the space into a wide, circular room, whose single encompassing wall was constructed from the same ancient stones as the previous ante-chamber. Kane's eyes darted about the cylindrical room, and he had to admit it was mightily impressive.

"Wow," he heard Toulla mutter beside him, and he found himself nodding in agreement. *Those understatements keep on coming!.*

Ahead of them Kane saw a wide, floor-to-ceiling window, though the sky beyond was jet black and only a few sporadic stars twinkled to confirm it was indeed the sky outside the castle.

John stopped and motioned Kane and Toulla to take a seat on a plush couch, across from which he sat on a matching armchair. "You're going to want some answers." It was not even close to being a question. Kane simply nodded.

John inhaled, and appraised his former student. It was time to come clean. "First of all, let me offer my deepest apologies to you both for all that you've been through in these last frantic days. It was never supposed to have been this way. Please, forgive me."

"Forgive you? Who are you, John? What is all this? What even is this place?" Kane stood up. He suddenly felt anger rising and had to stop himself from taking a step towards his mentor. But something in John's eyes made him stop. There was genuine sympathy there. Genuine regret.

"You're quite right to be angry, Hiram. What you've

been through... what almost happened..." John paused, his lip trembling, and for a moment Kane thought the old professor was going to cry. But then he inhaled, and said, "But, if you'd honour me with ten more minutes of your time, and after I've explained what all this is about, I think you'll understand. That is my greatest hope, my boy, that you, and dear Toulla here, will understand. Beyond that, I pray you'll also both forgive us."

"Us?" Toulla asked, speaking for the first time. "Who is 'us'?"

"Well, my dear, that's a very good question. Hiram, may I?" John asked, holding his hands out for Kane's satchel, which was still hanging around his neck.

Kane turned and faced Toulla. He didn't say anything, but when Toulla saw he was waiting for permission to grant John both their time, and hand over the S.T.R.A.P. file, she nodded. That was enough for Kane, so he turned to John and handed him the satchel, then took his seat next to Toulla.

"Do you know what you have here in this bag?" John asked.

Kane shrugged. "No, not really," he admitted.

The professor looked at Toulla. "And is it right, Miss Corti, that you found this hidden in the walls of your Uncle Jeremiah Ball's cabin?"

Toulla turned to Kane. Both shrugged. "Yes, that's right."

"In just a moment I'll explain why, and how, but may I first inform you both that together, you have performed for your respective countries a service so great that it might just have secured trans-Atlantic peace for another hundred years."

"Trans-Atlantic peace?" Kane was incredulous.

"I know it sounds dramatic. Please, let me explain why." John carefully slid the S.T.R.A.P. file from Kane's satchel. With even more caution, he opened the file and removed the first two sheets of ancient paper. Then, and in a move that surprised both Kane and Toulla, he removed a third piece, which they had somehow missed.

"Secret compartment," John said without any trace of humour. He held the ancient sheath of parchment between delicate fingers and gazed upon it with awe. He remained silent for long seconds, and they watched on as he silently shook his head in wonder. "Finally," he muttered, so quietly they could barely hear it. "Finally."

"Finally what?" Toulla asked.

John looked over at Kane and Toulla with something like hero worship in his eyes.

"Go on, John," Kane encouraged. "Tell us what it is that almost got us both killed."

Chapter Sixty-Two

"Almost two hundred and fifty years ago, a group of men in England came together and made a brave, bold and decisive decision. They were joined in this pact by several high-ranking French politicians."

"The Allegiance," Kane said. It wasn't a question.

John nodded. "Yes, The Allegiance. The reasons they came to this allegiance, and the subsequent agreement, were simple: these men didn't agree with what was about to happen in the New World."

"Independence?" Kane asked, though that too wasn't really a question.

John nodded. "That's right. As you both know, the United States' original Declaration of Independence was first published on July fourth, 1776. It is widely agreed that, although first signed and overseen by John Hancock, Thomas Jefferson, Benjamin Franklin and John Adams, many other men were crucial and active members of congress on the day of the signing…"

Kane noticed John had let his words trail off, waiting for their reaction. When they offered none, he continued.

"Well, Hiram, as you know, history is only ever written by the victors. History tells us what we know of the past, and it has never been truly questioned that the then fledgling United States both wanted, and won, independence from Great Britain. Well…"

Again, another somewhat dramatic pause, a tactic the world-renowned professor was famed for back in his scholarly days, lecturing both in the U.K., and various Ivy League schools in the U.S.

"Are you saying the truth surrounding the Declaration isn't exactly what the world has come to believe?" Toulla asked, and to this John smiled, though he quickly straightened his face. It wasn't a laughing matter.

"Well, yes, you could say that. Let's just put it this way," he added. "Of the fifty six official original signers of the Declaration, almost two-thirds of them remained loyal to the crown. Which means…"

Kane stood and walked over to the professor. "May I see the file cover?"

"Handle it gently, my boy," John said as he handed the ancient document to Kane.

"Toulla, come and check this out," Kane said, beckoning Toulla over to him. He led her over to a lamp that stuck out from the stone wall, before gently lifting the document towards the light.

They both leaned in close, tracing the faded letters with their eyes. Suddenly, they saw what they had failed to notice before. Kane whistled.

"No way," Toulla said.

"The Declaration of Non-Independence," they both whispered, almost in stereo.

"The Declaration of Non-Independence," John repeated as he came to stand beside them. "Put simply, the Declaration of Independence, the Constitution, and the Bill of Rights were not written by, and for, the benefit of the United States, but in fact, they were written by, and for, the benefit of Britain, Canada and France, who, two centuries ago, secretly joined forces, determined that together, they would control the new, New World. It's the single greatest cover-up in the last two hundred years."

John had led Kane and Toulla back to the couch and duly took his seat opposite them.

"But why me, John? Why put me through all that?"

"My dear boy, you don't need me to answer that, do you?"

"Actually, yes, I do." Kane's tone had hardened. He wasn't the man he once was, not since Egypt. Did that make him expendable if he'd failed? Worth John risking Kane's life for?

"Despite what I know you believe, Hiram, that you have lost your edge, none of the rest of us believed that. It was only you, son, only you that had lost faith in yourself and in your brilliance."

Kane shook his head. He was having a hard time believing John's words. It was the first time ever.

"But… well, we were lucky," he said.

"You think that was luck, Hiram? I know you don't really believe that."

Kane closed his eyes, fighting back a tear that threatened to spill.

"The only luck was when young Toulla here turned out to be the perfect ally. Miss Corti, I'm so sorry about what happened to Jeremiah. He was a good man. One of the best."

"Wait, you know my uncle? You knew Jerry?"

John nodded. "Of course I knew him. He was one of us."

Chapter Sixty-Three

"One of who?" Kane asked.

"The Allegiance."

"You're one of The Allegiance? What are you, some kind of secret society? This is insane."

"I admit the name is a little dramatic, and these days it does sound a touch Hollywood. But when those men formed The Allegiance, as I said, almost two hundred and fifty years ago, that's exactly what it was. Of course, now, it would never happen. However, the countries involved, Great Britain, France and latterly, the United States were, and are, great allies. We've fought wars together, and we will always have each other's backs, so to speak. Unless…"

"Unless this document fell into the wrong hands," Toulla stated.

"Exactly."

"So who owns those wrong hands?" Kane asked. This time it was a solid question.

John smiled. "There are those in France, and of course

the French half of Canada, who would love to see this conspiracy exposed. Let's call them French separatists, loyal to no one but themselves."

"Francois?" Kane asked, another solid query.

John chuckled. "No, not Francois. I'll explain more about our French friend shortly. But imagine this scenario, Hiram, Toulla. Imagine if these true declarations became public knowledge. It would undermine almost two hundred years of peace between the British and the United States, since the war between our two great nations in 1812. We can't allow that to happen. It can never happen. The way the world is going, with more and more right-leaning parties gaining power in nations across the globe, imagine if that happened in the U.S., and these ancient documents became common knowledge.

There would be anarchy on the streets, and the U.S. government would be pressured to act. Think about it. If the wrong president was in power at the wrong time, and wanted to make a political statement that would cement his legacy—even fame—forever, it wouldn't be unreasonable to consider these, albeit ancient documents, as an act of war, despite being written a quarter of a millennium in the past."

Kane shook his head. If he thought things had been crazy until now, the fact John was suggesting trans-Atlantic peace might be on the line was a whole new level of bat shit.

After a few seconds of silence as each of them sitting in the circular room contemplated what they now knew, finally it was Toulla who addressed the remaining elephant tucked in the shadows.

"That's all very well, John. I suppose it makes sense. But what the hell has this all got to do with Oak Island?"

John smiled, and this time he allowed it. "Hiram, I know you've done plenty of research on this. Our watchers were quite diligent in their efforts in reporting back, until they went rogue. A very unfortunate turn of events."

"The thug brothers? They worked for you?"

"Yes. They were part of our team, although it was a hastily put together outfit and well, sometimes we get it wrong. Sorry," John added quietly, and Kane knew it was sincere. "It sounds callous to call it collateral damage when so many people have died. But as an organisation, we feel it remains of the utmost importance, right up to high-levels of government. Of course, certain sections of the military are aware of our operation, and if need be, would be called in."

"And the professor, Anja?" Kane asked. "She was one of The Allegiance?"

John inhaled. "Anja was a good friend and a proud member of our cause. Her death was a very, very sad day for our group, but rest assured she would have died immensely proud of playing her part to the last."

"I'm sorry," Kane said, recalling how he had left her at the mercy of the thugs. Of course, he had no idea what he was dealing with then.

John continued. "Toulla, we have known of you for many years through our dealings with Jeremiah and your father, and their fathers and grandfathers before them. They were part of our organisation, it is true. Fully committed members of The Allegiance. Thus, we knew you were somewhat of an expert on all this stuff. Of course, we never expected to have to act so quickly, and it was never our intention to put you in harm's way."

Toulla shrugged. "It's fine, John. Please, get on with it," she said, a little impatiently.

John exhaled. "As you both know, on the twenty-fourth of August, 1814, as the war between the United States and the British raged on, British troops swarmed into Washington and unleashed fiery devastation on the U.S. Capitol building, other significant landmarks and of course, the White House. During this raid, the troops stole unimaginable treasures from the White House, which were then secretly stowed onto the *HMS Fantome* and other sloops that formed a British flotilla in Chesapeake Bay during the war. This convoy, believed to contain one of the greatest single hauls of treasure ever stolen, made its way north to Nova Scotia, taking shelter in the bay off Halifax. There had long been a plan in place for this mission, and the night a huge storm arrived from the North Atlantic provided the perfect cover to pull off the plan. By all accounts, it went off without a hitch.

"The treasure, vast quantities of gold, silver and jewels, as well as paintings and other priceless artefacts, were carefully removed from the sloops and by way of a series of smaller boats, were taken onto the mainland. Then, the entire flotilla was scuttled, leaving a very convenient red herring, and sparking the mystery that has endured ever since. So, as I said, the treasure was transported away, first to the mainland—"

"But not to Oak Island, and certainly not to the Money Pit." Toulla had declared it with such clarity, it was as if after all these years of uncertainty, she had finally put all the pieces together. "It was never in the Money Pit, was it?"

John nodded. "That's right. The whole Oak Island/Money Pit scenario was always just an elaborate hoax. No one then believed it would still have to be continued to this day. Our friends in Canada were very keen to join The Allegiance, and to retain autonomy from the United States, even if it meant remaining loyal to the British crown. One man in particular was crucial in the successful plan…" John let his gaze settle on Toulla's.

"Samuel Ball," she said, and the last of the missing jigsaw pieces slotted in like a charm.

"Yes, Samuel Ball," John said. "Miss Corti, your ancestor Samuel was in fact the man who presented the idea to The Allegiance in the first place. It was a wild idea, and a brave and dangerous thing to have done, but he pulled it off with such diligence, none of it may have been successful without him. It could be argued there was never a more loyal loyalist."

"So Samuel was a British operative, essentially, like many of the so-called Founding Fathers then? Which ones?" Kane asked.

John shrugged. "Sorry, I'm afraid that's going to have to remain confidential. For now."

"So what happened to the real treasure, the physical, tangible stuff that people still look for today in the Money Pit?" Toulla probed.

"Another good question. Some small items, as well as a smattering of gold and silver coins, were scattered into a pit we ourselves labelled the Money Pit. More still were deposited in various locations around Oak Island."

"Don't tell me the brothers from the TV show are in on it?" Toulla asked.

John's face remained deadpan, but a single wink of the left eye told Toulla and Kane everything.

"Jesus H," Toulla muttered. "Those boys are good actors."

John shrugged, then continued. "The bulk of the treasure was sailed across the North Atlantic to this very castle, where it was sold off, bit by bit, to fund the cover-up. The greatest benefactors were of course—"

"The Masons," Kane finished.

"Yes, The Masons were our main guardians of the secret. In fact, one of our key men on this latest attempt to retrieve the last missing official document of the original seven that were created, was, and still is, a leading Mason."

"Francois?" Kane asked, though he already knew.

"Yes, Monsieur Dumas was tasked with recruiting you, Hiram, to the mission. I was reticent to allow it to begin with. I know how much you've been through lately, how much you've sacrificed. But when it came to it, there really was no better person for the job. You can blame me for everything. It was I who signed off on Francois recruiting you."

Kane nodded. "Are you saying you're in charge of this... cover-up, as you called it? You're the head of The Allegiance?" Again, incredulity was Kane's overriding emotion.

Professor O'nians stood up from his seat. Kane stood too. O'nians inhaled, then let it out slowly, as if feeling a great release of tension. Finally, he smiled. "Yes, I suppose you could say that our respective governments... the French, our allies the Canadians, our own British government, and of course, the Americans, who have been on board ever since Jimmy Carter, have put their faith in me for the last four decades to maintain this vital secret and finally, to retrieve the last, lost Declaration of Non-Independence, which,"—John cast his gaze towards Toulla—"for almost two centuries, has been in the capable hands of Toulla's family, the Cortis, and her ancestors, the Ball family."

John told them he was going to fetch some refreshments and let them have a moment to digest all they'd learned, then turned left the circle room.

As bombshells went, that was as explosive as Kane had ever experienced, and the power of it sent him slumping back down onto the couch.

Epilogue

After several minutes of quiet contemplation, Kane rose from the couch and went to stand in front of the large bay window that, if it were daylight outside, would have afforded spectacular views out over the Sound of Mull to Tobermory, nestled in the northeast corner of the island of Mull, where a distant lighthouse occasionally flashed a warning.

His mind drifted to how this had all started, how the events of Egypt had led him to hide away for several months in Cambodia. He wondered if he should feel angry with his mentor, John. Essentially, via Francois, the professor had used him, lured him in with a chance of redemption, played on his weaknesses for adventure, all while knowing it would likely be dangerous, and potentially fatal.

But as he mulled this over, Kane found that he wasn't angry. Not at all. He had been on a downward spiral anyway since Egypt. He had been so down, so lost after that episode that he had even contemplated if it was worth carrying on. The way he was slowly drinking himself into the ground was evidence enough to Kane that he had almost given up, almost quit on life and was essentially hell-bent on nothing more than a slow demise towards only one ultimate end.

His death.

Then, out of the blue Francois had appeared, and before he knew it, Kane had seized the opportunity, despite never really being convinced of the man's integrity. This in itself was evidence to Kane that he had believed there was indeed reason to carry on. That there was good to be done. That there was value to his life, and that he, despite everything, was still useful to someone. To a cause.

"Madness, eh?" Toulla had come to stand beside Kane, her right hand entwining his left. "Total madness."

"I thought I was good at understatements," Kane said, and they both chuckled.

"What do you see out there?" Toulla asked. It was closing in on midnight. More stars had shown themselves and the pitch-black sky was a veritable blanket of shimmering twinkles.

Kane didn't answer for many minutes. Toulla didn't push him. Kane assumed she was asking herself the same question, enjoying the safety of the castle and the recent resolutions of so many long-held questions.

He continued to stare out at the vast void. He let his mind wander. He spared a thought for Professor Peerdeman, and how she had paid the ultimate sacrifice for a cause she'd invested her life in. Ultimately, she had given Kane a chance of survival, and success, by that sacrifice. He had barely known the woman, but he would never forget her. A true hero.

He thought of his mentor, Professor O'nians. Kane thought he had known the man. They had enjoyed a student/teacher/mentor relationship for over two decades, and since leaving university, the two men had become the closest of friends. Their mutual respect knew no bounds, and despite recent events, Kane bore the man no ill will. Would he have used John if the roles would have been reversed, for the greater good? Yes, of course he would. It made Kane wonder, though, what other secrets the great man held. He smiled inwardly. In that moment, Kane made it his mission to find out.

Finally, despite his best efforts, Kane's mind swarmed with thoughts of his lost love, Alexandria Ridley. Life just wasn't the same without her in it. He had no idea where Alex was, or what she had been doing since he'd last seen her at the Kane family estate all those months months ago. He believed now that it was a massive mistake to have even considered mentioning marriage. The actual words hadn't been uttered, but Ridley was too smart for Kane, and somehow, she had just known. It had been enough for her to run a mile, and Kane silently cursed himself for even thinking he was worthy of such a woman. Alex Ridley was not one for permanence, and Kane would rather have her as his friend than to have lost her forever.

As he looked out at the stars, he said, "Hope," startling Toulla out of her reverie.

"I'm sorry? Hope what?" she said.

"Your question. You asked, what do I see out there?"

"Ah yes, sorry."

Kane gazed out across the vast emptiness and made a series of decisions. He would never again allow himself to slump into darkness. He would never again go on any kind of wild mission, unless the cause was noble and unless it were for an official, charitable organisation. He would retire from this crazy, selfish lifestyle once and for all and do something more productive with his life. And finally, he would track Alex down, tell her he was sorry for frightening her off, and offer his hand in friendship, and nothing more.

Kane inhaled, cuffed away a stray tear and exhaled slowly.

Something had changed. He felt lighter, somehow. More at peace.

Alive.

"Hope," he muttered. "I see hope."

Next in The Hiram Kane Archaeological Thriller Series

vinci-books.com/killing-koreana

A spiritual retreat turns into a battleground for justice and revenge.

In a South Korean mountain retreat, Hiram Kane's search for inner peace is shattered when an old foe resurfaces, threatening his life and the very essence of Korea's cultural heritage. As a priceless treasure vanishes and the life of his mentor's cherished son hangs in the balance, Kane must tread carefully in a world of organised crime and ruthless killers. With time running out, Kane blurs the lines between justice and revenge.

Turn the page for a free preview…

Killing Koreana: Prologue

Sejong the Great, a humble Korean fishing boat named after the legendary Joseon dynasty's King Sejong, chugged beneath Busan Harbour Bridge into the dark, passive waters of Busan Port. Several hundred yards to the west lay a vast series of fishing docks, spread out over half a mile and where most fishing boats unloaded their catch before it was sold off and transported overland to various fish markets in the southern regions of South Korea. Most of it, though, ended up at the nearby Jagalchi Fish Market.

Rather than veer west to those docks, however, the modest fishing boat steamed onwards north, heading instead towards the international ferry port still five hundred yards ahead. Just a hundred yards in front of the small vessel was a huge passenger ferry inbound from Fukuoka, Japan, slowing as it approached the port exactly on schedule.

Several hours earlier, and far out in the Sea of Japan, the man now in control of the *Sejong* had gone to his humble bunk and retrieved from his backpack a small object wrapped in a leather cloth. He'd gone to the wheelhouse and engaged in small talk with the captain, discussing the weather and sea conditions as they made their way to port. The other three crew were busy at their tasks, two below decks managing the catch and repairing nets, and the third on deck tidying and scrubbing and pretending to be busy like all good deckhands should.

The captain stood calmly at the wheel, and equally as calmly, the man now in charge had removed his recently sharpened filleting knife and, stepping close up behind the captain and saying nothing, he swiftly reached his knife arm around the man's head and drew the blade hard across his throat. Blood sprayed out onto the window, the wheel and the controls in the bridge house and, almost too quietly it seemed to the killer's amusement, the captain succumbed, the new man in control easing the slain chief to the floorboards with his strong arms. He then took his pistol from its leather case, a silencer already fitted, and just to make sure, fired two rounds into the back of the already dead man's head.

Without any discernible difference in his heart rate, the new captain stepped out of the wheelhouse and went to the back of the boat, concealing his weapons on the way.

"Tae-won," he called out to the deckhand. "Tae-won, come here," he said in English, smiling at the young man.

Dutifully, Tae-won dropped the mop he'd been leaning on and hustled up the stairs to the upper level, where he turned the corner and ran straight into the new captain's deadly blade, which he thrust to its hilt in Tae-won's gut. As he had with the former captain, the new man in charge spun Tae-won around and fired two slugs into his skull.

He dragged Tae-won's body to the top of the stairs that led below decks and called out, "Help. Help!"

Kyung, the boatswain, immediately dropped his crate of fish and bounded up the stairs, his long legs making light work of the dozen or so steps. Before he had reached the top, however, the first of two precisely placed bullets entered his skull, the second of which exited from the front, taking with it most of the boatswain's face and scalp.

Not waiting a second, the new captain deftly reloaded the gun and scrambled down over Kyung's sprawled body and leapt into the cargo hold. First Mate Il-sung found himself facing the business end of the man's gun and cowered back against the wall, unsure what was happening but clearly fearing for his life. He didn't have to fear for long as the new chief surged forwards and smashed Il-sung's head with the butt of the pistol and as he slumped unconscious to the ground, the new captain flipped him over, and like the others, he fired two rounds into the back of his head from point blank range.

Ten minutes later, all three of the crew were face down atop their impressive oceanic haul, blood streaming from their wounds and, mixing with the stench of dead fish and squid, the new chief hustled back above decks to breathe of the crisp night air. The entire crew, including the captain, had been dispatched in less than fifteen minutes, and with the first half of his mission complete, the new chief glanced down at the slain captain and sneered.

No hard feelings, he thought and grinned as he continued on his course towards the ferry terminal now less than a couple of hours away.

A flash of blue light caught his eye and he looked right. A boat from the National Coast Guard was approaching fast from the east. He had expected this. It was part of the plan and so far, everything was proceeding like clockwork. He pushed forward on the throttle and accelerated, now angling the boat around the side of the slow-moving passenger ferry and directly towards the port.

As expected, the coast guard boat accelerated too and cut across the bow of the fishing boat, which was now cruising at its full speed, a little shy of fifteen knots. The coast guard boat stayed a safe distance from the now charging fishing boat, trying to ascertain what the hell was going on and attempting to guide it away from the ferry and prevent it getting to the terminal.

The pseudo captain grinned and kept his eyes fixed ahead.

It is almost time, he mused, mentally preparing himself for what was soon to transpire.

"This is the Korean Coast Guard," came a voice through a loudspeaker from the coast guard vessel, the words spoken in the official's native Korean. "We demand you cease your progress and cut your engines now. Failure to do so might result in the destruction of your vessel."

The Japanese man steering the fishing boat didn't understand the Korean words but wouldn't have paid any heed if he could. He was on a course that he would not falter from under any circumstances. Even if they destroyed the boat, it wouldn't change the desired result, and in fact would only speed up the process already set in motion.

"Cut your engines now or we will fire upon your vessel."

Again, the Japanese man ignored the words and narrowed his focus on the easternmost dock of the official ferry terminal. As he pulled alongside the huge ferry, he glanced up. His boat was just a blip in the harbour compared to the towering behemoth that was about to enter the terminal; a baby duck next to a blue whale.

Just then a second coast guard boat roared up on the inside, now between the ferry and the fishing boat. The pilot glanced out of his left window and saw several men clad in military-style clothes bracing themselves along the rails, each with a rifle of some kind aimed at him in the wheelhouse.

"Kanzen," he said in his native tongue. *Perfect.*

He glanced at his watch, and then ducked down below the level of the wheelhouse's windows and knelt at the device that had sat at his feet for the last hour, since he'd dispatched the crew. He had stowed it aboard the vessel in secret before it had set out from the docks at Jagalchi three days earlier. He had served under the slain captain on this fishing crew for the last month and had gained his and the rest of the crew's trust as a hard-working deckhand.

He pressed a series of small switches and nodded in satisfaction as one after the other, a row of green lights flickered in the darkness.

Two minutes.

He stood up again and, with the boat's steering column now locked in place, on course for the terminal, he stepped out of the wheelhouse and edged to the railings. He raised his arms and waved in a frantic manner.

One minute.

"Mian mian," he yelled in Korean. *Sorry, sorry.* It was one of a few select words he'd memorised. "Bot-uh mun-je," he added. *Problem with boat.*

"Stop your engines immediately!" demanded the coast guard through the loudspeaker. "You have thirty seconds or we will destroy your vessel."

The Japanese man glanced from one coast guard boat to the other, then glanced at his watch and couldn't help but smile.

Fifteen seconds.

At the railing on the starboard side of the boat, he waved his arm now towards the first coastguard boat for a few seconds, then, with one final glance at his watch, without preamble he inhaled a deep breath and dived over the railings and disappeared beneath the dark surface of the frigid harbour waters. He kicked as hard as his powerful legs would allow and made it thirty yards from the fishing boat, where he surfaced, surely unseen by any coast guards as an enormous *boom!* shook the fishing vessel from within, splitting huge planks of wood as easily as if they were lolly sticks. The glass of the wheelhouse shattered outwards and a fireball the size of a double-decker bus exploded upwards into the night sky, casting an ethereal glow across the water.

In less than twenty seconds the hull of the boat had split in two and the two separate sections of the stricken vessel now bobbed gently in the slight swell of the harbour waters as the two coast guard boats closed in, their water cannon operators trying desperately to douse the flames with their powerful jets.

It was all to no avail, and less than a minute later, both sections of the fishing boat, complete with the dead crew members and their captain, were sinking slowly to the bottom of the harbour, the surface water settling back to its previous calm.

Now a hundred and fifty yards away, the Japanese man was closing in on the craggy shoreline to the eastern edge of the harbour. The gelid water had numbed his extremities but he was still strong enough to scramble up the small but jagged stone cliff and into the copse of trees that lined the deserted harbour edge. A moment later, a nondescript family car cruised to a stop beside him and the door swung open. He ripped off his sodden clothes and dressed fast in the dry clothing provided on the passenger seat, and with a last glance back towards the harbour he spotted the two coast guard boats, their blue lights flashing, now drifting, aimless, their occupants no doubt bewildered and in shock about what they'd just witnessed.

He then shifted his gaze to the ferry terminal a little further north and inhaled a satisfied breath as the passenger ferry from Fukuoka docked safely and right on time. He couldn't stifle the chuckle that escaped from his numbed lips as he climbed into the car and closed the door.

"Oku yatta, kyōdai," said the driver as he pulled away. *Well done, brother.*

Killing Koreana: Chapter One

A rapidly disappearing sun from a pastel-hued sky meant it was almost dusk when they boarded the ferry from Japan to Korea.

A biting chill had settled around the busy port of Fukuoka, but Kenji Omaru ignored it. Cold was for wimps. He led his team of three—himself and two scientists—to a quiet area of the ferry, away from nosy do-gooders and returning South Koreans, heading home from shopping or business trips to Fukuoka and beyond.

Fucking Koreans, he thought dispassionately.

He'd never liked them, and was only heading to their country himself for business. The faintest hint of a smile curved his lips.

Special business indeed.

"It's three hours until we reach Busan, Kenji-san," one of his team members informed him in their native Japanese.

Kenji merely nodded. He wasn't one for small talk. There was nothing to say anyway. They all knew the drill. Everything for their 'business trip' was in place. He just needed to secure the team *in country* and set to it. He pulled out his phone and checked a few messages, nodding subconsciously to himself as he scanned his inbox. His own boss had been planning this endeavour for a while now, and it was finally 'go time'.

Kenji felt that same barely perceptible shiver of anticipation he always felt on the eve of a big operation such as this, and as he mentally ran through the procedure in his mind—as he had a dozen times already this day—he knew it would go off without so much as a hitch. They always did. That's why his boss hired him, and why he was paid so well. Kenji Omaru was the very best at what he did.

He glanced over at his two colleagues. His brother, Nanmi, and his sister, Kyota, looked back, expressions void of any discernible emotion . They were the two people he trusted most in the world, and he knew he could rely on them. Comfortable in the knowledge he had the best possible people around him, Kenji allowed himself the luxury of closing his eyes for a few minutes. It was going to be a long night ahead, and a busy few days beyond that.

A couple of hours later, after crossing the Sea of Japan, Kenji headed to the outside walkway on the starboard side of the ferry. He looked down at the dark waters, scanning the surface for any sign of a boat where a small boat shouldn't be. It took him a few moments, but at last he spotted the faint twinkling of lights from the bridge of a small boat that was gradually catching up to the ferry. It was still ten minutes until they were scheduled to reach the terminal.

Kenji checked the time on his mobile phone. He nodded to himself and sent a two-word text message:

: *Everything ready?*

He received an immediate one word reply.

: *Yes!*

Kenji inhaled, keeping his eyes on the small vessel far below that was now pulling up alongside the ferry. He glanced up and saw a set of blue flashing lights approaching, and smirked.

Right on cue.

A couple of minutes later, with the ferry terminal fast approaching as the huge ship lumbered slowly towards it, a second coast guard boat circled in, this time darting between the ferry and the fishing vessel. Kenji heard the coast guards making demands of the fishing vessel's pilot, though Kenji knew the pilot wouldn't respond.

At least not how they want, he mused and grinned without mirth.

Far below, he watched on as the boat's captain stepped out onto the decks and waved his arms in the air.

Nanmi and Kyota had joined Kenji on the starboard walkway and all three looked on with wide eyes as a huge fireball erupted from the fishing boat below, huge sections of the boat cartwheeling into the air as the massive ball of flame lit up the sky above the waters of the harbour.

Ten minutes later, having docked safely, Kenji led his small team of 'scientists' off the ferry. As expected, they passed through immigration with the minimum of fuss. The border patrol section had descended into chaos amid rumours of a bomb blast that had spread like wildfire, the result of which had sent many of the security staff scrambling. Kenji and his team remained calm and polite as they made their way out through the various checks, and his small team was soon greeted at the exit of the ferry terminal building by the other half of their group.

The driver of the SUV, a Japanese colleague stationed in Korea, greeted them without speaking and ushered them into the sleek black vehicle. The driver manoeuvred them out of the terminal and into the heavy early-evening traffic, where they were soon cutting through the colourful streets of west Busan, past the gaudy, neon-rife areas of Daechang-dong and Jung-gu, and headed towards the world famous Jagalchi Fish Market nestled between the thriving districts of Nampo and Jagalchi itself.

Some forty minutes after disembarking the ferry, the SUV carried the team away from the main streets criss-crossing Busan, and entered a more industrial part of the city. Lights flickered on the horizons of infamous Hae-un-dae and Gwan-galli beaches as night settled over the vibrant city. Kenji recognised the area, having been there twice before in recent months in preparation of this trip. This is what mattered most. This is when the real 'business' could begin, and again he felt that hint of adrenaline start coursing through his veins.

The driver steered them between two large warehouses right on the docks in the southernmost quadrant of Busan. Moments later, just as they approached a large unmarked building, two men stepped out of the shadows caused by the high, sodium vapour floodlights lining the vast yet deserted dock, and pulled open the double doors. The SUV came to a halt beside a shipping container marked with the innocuous words:

The Oak Island Enigma

Japanese Cultural Mission #4478

Once again, Kenji felt himself smile, though he quickly forced ambiguity into his face. He couldn't let the others see his calmness. They had to remain focused. Had to keep them on point and *mission ready*.

"Welcome, sir," said one of the men, also Japanese.

"Everything is ready?" Kenji asked, though it wasn't really a question. His voice was devoid of any trace of... well, anything. He knew the answer—everything had been ready a long time—asking was a mere formality.

"Yes sir, everything is prepared and ready to engage."

Kenji nodded. He knew this, but still, he wanted to check one last time. "Open the doors."

The man nodded and did as he was commanded. Moving to the shipping container, he first unlatched and then swung open the hefty steel doors, which offered the merest of protests by way of a gentle creaking whine. Kenji stepped inside the large container and approached a single wooden pallet, secured with straps in the centre of the temperature-controlled space. He pulled back a large sheet of cloth covering the contents of the pallet, then took a small step back.

Kenji stared for a long moment at what had lain hidden beneath the cover, imagining the job ahead, his mind drifting beyond the confines of the shipping container and indeed the warehouse, transporting him north of Busan into the mountains in the heart of South Korea. He inhaled deeply, savouring the salty tang of the nearby sea, and the fission of anticipation of the action ahead. He nodded, almost as if to himself, then turned and stepped with purpose out of the container. The man closed the doors behind him.

Kenji looked first to his brother, then to his sister. Neither smiled nor spoke, and instead they merely nodded. Kenji returned their nods, then stepped away.

The leader of the Japanese Cultural Mission then took out his phone and placed a call.

Grab your copy...
vinci-books.com/killing-koreana

About the Author

Englishman Steven Moore grew up by the seaside, thus his first true joy was the great outdoors. His innate love of travel and a degree in anthropology, archaeology, and art history, help inform his fiction writing. Steven also loves painting, photography, and both playing and watching sport.

The travel bug bit the now perpetual nomad early, and to date Steven has lived and worked on five continents, and visited almost seventy countries. Steven combines an age-old writing adage; Write what you know, with his own mantra; Write where you know, and sets most of his novels in places in which he has either lived or spent an extended period of time.

When not on the road, Steven divides his time between Norwich, UK, and San Miguel de Allende, Mexico, which he shares with his rescue cats Ernest Hemingway and F Scott Fitzgerald (Ernie and Fitz), and his rescue puppy, Charles Dickens. Oh yes, and his beautiful travel writer wife, Leslie.

A lifelong love of food, wine, and beer, have demanded a new-found love of yoga and hiking in order to fend off the imminent arrival of middle age.

Acknowledgments

I don't know of any author who can finish a book of any kind without a lot of help and support, and I'm certainly no different. The assistance I've received for this novel and all my books has been both necessary and invaluable.

So, a quick shout out to these lovely folks—I couldn't have done it without you.

My gratitude to Anja Peerdeman, Michael Rhew and Tim Birmingham, my crucial BETA readers. Any remaining mistakes are my own. Thanks, guys.

I also want to thank the incredible team at Vinci Books for believing in me and supporting me on my journey. I appreciate you all.

And as always, to the one and only Leslie, my unstintingly supportive wife, I say thank you.

May you always be you!

Thank you! Merci!

Steven